UNCIVIL WAR

TRANSPORT BOOK THREE

UNCIVIL WAR

TRANSPORT BOOK THREE

Peter Welmerink

SEVENTH STAR PRESS

Cover art: Jason C. Conley
Cover art in this book copyright © 2015 Jason C. Conley & Seventh Star
Press, LLC.

Interior Illustrations Tim Holtrop
Interior illustrations © 2014 Tim Holtrop
www.timholtrop.com

Editor: Scot Sandridge

Published by Seventh Star Press, LLC.

ISBN Number: 978-1-941706-26-8

Seventh Star Press
www.seventhstarpress.com
info@seventhstarpress.com

Publisher's Note:
Uncivil War is a work of fiction. All names, characters, and places are
the product of the author's imagination, used in fictitious manner. Any
resemblances to actual persons, places, locales, events, etc. are purely
coincidental.

Printed in the United States of America

First Edition

ACKNOWLEDGMENTS

I would like to acknowledge again my family and friends, those interested, in giving me the opportunity to do what I do, even if sometimes the question is raised: Why, and what the hell? Thanks for being there.

Super special thanks to the incomparable Ken Campbell for insight and ideas throughout the unfolding of the book series. Thank you. Thank you.

Special thanks to Stephen Zimmer, Jason Conley, Tim Holtrop, Tyson Mauermann, Steven Shrewsbury, Tim Marquitz, Julie Bonner Williams, Rodney Carlstrom and Uncivil War's editor extraordinaire, Scott Sandridge. You all rock!

Dedication

This is dedicated to all those who fight the good fight, or make the effort, knowing if there is failure, it wasn't due to lack of trying.

Keep pushing on.

Also to my new friend, retired veteran, John Rainwater.

Chapter One

"You might be the first undead soldier ever to wander unhindered on city streets. On this side of the river."

Captain Jake Billet looks at the man walking beside him. "I am very much alive, Lettner. I'm certain the same can't be said for you."

The street lights flicker, each pulse a bright strobe going off before Billet's eyes. He curses through raw vocal cords, raises an arm to shield himself from the annoyance. With one final electrical throb, the lights along Ionia Avenue flare to life. Glare like miniature suns. Though a curiosity to his newly awakened senses, he avoids looking at them. He can feel the heat, minimal as it is, from the lights. It irritates the eyes, but it chases the chill he felt within himself.

"Little sensitive to light, Captain? You know what that indicates," William Lettner says. The heels of his shoes touch the sidewalk but make no sound. The man wears casual attire versus the garb he'd worn at the recent hospital visitation. A white buttondown dress shirt with top three buttons undone; his neck encircled with red, raw rope burns. A tweed jacket covers the shirt; blue jeans and a pair of brown polished dress shoes cover him beyond. He looks to be heading out to spend a night on the town.

Happy to see neither the ghostly, ghastly image of Rebecca

Regan nor his dead wife hanging upon the late NSC Commissioner's arms, Jake cares little how the man is dressed.

"What does it say when *you* aren't?" Jake replies to his companion who appears oblivious to the irritating gleam. On the other hand, if Jake peers straight at Lettner, the man wavers like an image upon rippling water.

He has to admit, he felt a bit out of sorts since leaving the hospital. He had glanced at the medical documentation hanging bedside as he pulled his clothes on. The small emergency exit light—which also had been too bright—illuminated his surroundings enough for him to read bold, black print on the chart: Coma, system shutting down.

Then Lettner, then escape, now down on the street.

Jake passes by the boarded-up doors of what was once a downtown church: the Christian Information Center. Scheduled for renovation into small apartments, the two story building consisted of a small chapel and fellowship rooms. Billet had gone there in his much younger days.

"Mem'ries, light the corners of my mind..." Lettner starts to sing, off key, sounds like two cats killing each other.

Jake glances back to the doors of the old church, finds them board-less; the church alive with lights aglow within.

Stopping, he steps to the glass double doors which, if entered, led to the small vestibule: a meeting place for the congregation before and after church services. Inside and down a carpeted hall, several people stand, chatting happily. They sip coffee from Styrofoam cups. Children play in the tight corridor, squeezing through and running between the adults, big chocolate chip cookies in hand, pieces crumble and pepper the floor.

"Father Marks," Billet mouths with his nose nearly to the glass. He recognizes the facility's priest by the rats' nest hairdo and black and white clerical collar. A tall thin man with a slight bow to his back, Marks stands in the center of the crowd shaking hands and conversing with parishioners.

The priest had died in a car accident a year after he had wed Jake and Jenna.

"Times are a'changin'," Lettner says in Billet's ear.

Still looking upon the interior scene, Jake whimpers and presses his hands to the glass pane. "Jenna. Joey," he rasps as his wife and child mingle amidst the throng. His young son runs about his mother's legs, playing with the other small children. The boy is not the 19-year-old young man he'd been when he horrifically died by his mother's side.

Jenna stands talking with another woman. Never a big coffee drinker herself, her friend holds a large Styrofoam cup of the steaming liquid. Jake notices the bottom of the cup start to drip like melting candle wax. The foam slinks down the woman's hand and forearm, the white, runny polystyrene material turns a reddish-brown as her flesh drools away like the foam cup.

"A sign of things to come, Captain," Lettner says with a slight chuckle.

Billet wants to turn his head and snarl at the man, but his gaze is frozen. Locked on the scene within the church, he watches in horror as the people in the hallway start to liquefy.

"No no no," he shouts, pounds his fists against the glass. The panes shake against his drumming blows.

Standing as if nothing is happening, Jenna keeps talking, her jaw moving even as layers of flesh and muscle slough away, drop to the floor, pool at her feet. Clothing falls apart like shredded paper. The naked bodies collapse into lumpy puddles where their skeletal frames curl into a fetal position or fall splayed and a-swim in the driveling ichor.

"Oh, and the real leaders of your local congregation," Lettner hisses in Jake's ear.

Billet stops his frantic beating upon the church doors as two new people enter the hallway from one of the connected side rooms.

"Now I *know* I'm seeing things," Jake says under his breath.

Stepping daintily through the pool of gore, Rebecca Regan walks with her right arm looped through the arm of Grand Rapids City Treasurer Rupert Largo. She wears the dark blue coverall outfit she'd worn the last time Jake had seen her, during the Lettner mission. With her sleeves rolled up to elbow, her twig-like forearms are wrapped in white gauze pale as her skin. Large spots of red seep through bandages. A bit shorter than Jake, the City Treasurer's five-foot-ten frame is beefier than his; years of good living as a city official. The overhead lights glint off Largo's bald head as the couple casually walks through the crimson, bone-laden slop at their feet.

"Largo's well known for his puritan anti-zombie stance," Jake says as he watches Largo and Rebecca stop midstride and midstream amidst the red goo. He blanches as they turn to each other, faces moving closer. The City Treasurer opens his mouth, wags his tongue like a snake before the pale woman's lips. She purses her lips, and kisses it before opening her mouth to accept it. "He might be an asshole, but he wouldn't be caught dead doing...*that*."

"Who you callin' asshole, asshole?"

Lettner's voice changes.

Jake glances over his shoulder, sees three young men walking his way. The late Muskegon regent is gone, ghost or otherwise.

"Little late to be saved," the cleanly-combed blonde one says of the trio. His friends laugh as he nods at Jake's hands.

Looking to his hands, they no longer touch glass but wood planks again which cover the church entry.

"What the fucks wrong with me?" Jake says under his breath. His heart thumps dully in his chest, slow, too long between heavy beats. He flexes the stiffness from his fingers as he moves his hands down to his sides.

"Hey, he's a soldier, Jonny," the guy to the blonde's right says. He wears his short sleeved shirt unbuttoned and open, a loop of several gold chains hang about his neck.

Jake touches his chest, feels the smooth unrumpled fabric of his Class-A uniform.

"You're kind of far away from the action, ain'tcha, buddy?" Blonde Jon says as the three stop before Billet.

In his gut, Jake senses something amiss within him. His heartbeat: much too slow. His joints: unusually taut. His fingers want to stiffen and curl. He doesn't know how long he'd been bedridden nor felt quite this stiff even on typical days. Yet his senses seem fully intact, if not a bit amplified as he can smell the booze each man exudes.

Gold Chain: been drinking bourbon and cola.

Their unspoken friend: "Shouldn't you be helping to keep the West Side Horde from strolling in and chewing on us?" he speaks, laughs like a hyena, elbowing Blonde Jon as if he had said the funniest line in the world. His friend doesn't react in the slightest.

Jake sniffs the air emitted from the laughing boy's breath. Green crème de menthe. White crème de cacao. Light cream. His grandma used to drink that concoction.

"Shouldn't you be drinking something more manly?" Billet rasps. "Grasshopper."

Grasshopper loses his laughter, balls his fists and starts to step forward. Blonde Jon walks in front of him, stops him.

"Tough talk without your buddies, old man," Blonde Jon says, deep inside Jake's personal space.

Tequila, Jake sniffs. Yeah, that always made him ballsy too. And hurting hard in the morning.

"I've got no beef with you, fellas," Jake says, tries to cool the increasingly warm moods of the drunken young men.

A red tide rises within him, a fiery fury stronger than he's ever felt, even in the heat of battle. It taunts him to let go of all rationale, give in to tearing into these pups who obviously have no respect for the military or their peers.

Jake continues, taking a step back: "I just got out of the

hospital." *Popped right out a coma, I did. How's that for fucking miracles?* "And heading back to HQ. I'm sure the local authorities and the GRCC are handling whatever's going on."

"What's going on," Blonde Jon says, moving nose to nose, "Shits blowing up. Shits coming down. You military fucks ain't helping nothing. Mayor Honeyfuck ain't doin' shit but ride around on his trains and suck up to those shitbags in Muskegon…"

"I'll get you a shovel. Now calm down," Jake snarls, anger percolating to boiling point. "You're crossing lines you aren't going to enjoy siding on."

"Fuck you, greenie. What's lone ranger going to do?" the agitated man says, pounds his index finger into Jake's chest.

Gold Chain and Grasshopper move up behind their lead man.

"Hey. *Billet.* Isn't that the name of that guy who…" Grasshopper says, points at the plastic name plate above Jake's right chest pocket.

Blonde Jon yelps. The yelp turns to a croaking sound as he tries to suck air through his constricted windpipe.

"You boys…better…get the fuck…out of here," Jake growls, grips Blonde Jon's throat with his left hand, fingers making divots in the other man's flesh. He holds the hand with the pointed index finger by its adjoining wrist, wrist bent at a painful ninety degree angle; painful for the surprised and gurgling Blonde Jon.

The red rage boils over, bubbles up into Jake's eyesight. He feels the other man's pulse pounding in his wrist, hears the strong heart thumping like cannon fire. He smells the salt-tinged fear-sweat. He always liked a bit of salt on his meat.

What the hell, he thought. He isn't going to eat these punks.

With a shove, Blonde Jon reels backwards.

Jake takes two steps back. He glances at the boarded doors to the Christian Information Center. The boards waver. Familiar glass doors appear.

The City Treasurer and Rebecca Regan suck at each other's

face.

Bodies bob in blood. Church floor awash in the pooling red liquid.

A field. A house.

The red skeleton of his wife curled over the red skeleton of his son; bones starting to bubble, boil, drool.

"Not…well. Go…away." Jake breathes, tries at least, lungs fight it. He returns his gaze to the three before him.

"Gonna put you back in the hospital," Blonde Jon says coughing. He springs forward with balled fists.

Tequila.

Suddenly sluggish, Jake tries to lift his arms to defend.

Blonde Jon's fist connects, solid, snaps Jake's head sideways.

Jake staggers.

Gold Chain curls Jake over with a roundhouse, up clip fist to the stomach.

Driving a fist into Jake's cheek, Blonde Jon snaps Jake's head again.

Jake goes down on his knees, scuffing his Class A slacks against the dirty sidewalk. He tastes blood where Blonde Jon's fist slammed his cheek to his teeth. He dabs his tongue against the area, swirls the blood and spittle around as he probes at a loose tooth.

"You're paying for dry cleaning," he growls. The red haze fills his vision, and his heart hammers in his chest. It hurts, like someone repeatedly thumbing at a bad bruise. But, it makes him feel… alive.

"What's that, soldier bo—" Blonde Jon says, leans over him. His words end as Jake spits the contents of his mouth into the other man's face.

Blonde Jon reels back coughing and spitting, wiping at his face.

"Gone too far now," the young man snarls, wipes his face with his arm. He grits his teeth and rears his right leg back, aims to hard punt his target.

"Exactly," Jake replies as Blonde Jon's foot swings in. He catches it, goal denied, and savagely twists the captured limb.

Blonde Jon yells as his foot is turned inboard at a forty-five degree angle. A sound like dry twigs crunched under foot follow the surprised exclamation. He screams over the pop and snap of bones breaking as his appendage is twisted a full ninety. He falls backwards, hits the sidewalk, grabbing his leg.

Jake leaps upon him the second the man hits the ground.

"Holey shit," Gold Chain huffs as both he and Grasshopper step back, too stunned to react.

Driving his fists into Blonde Jon's face, Jake only sees red. Red blood. Red hatred. Red kill. Kill him, kill the Meat. Kill it. Kill it. The skin of his knuckles breaks and weeps their own crimson, mingling with the life soup in the destroyed visage of the man beneath him.

"Stop it. Stop it, man!" Grasshopper shouts. "You…you're killing him."

"Exactly why we don't need the military, the fucking rotters across the river…" Gold Chain growls, grows his balls back, and steps into the fray. "We can forge ahead without you just like Councilman Largo says."

A fist connects solidly against the back of Billet's skull. He goes forward on hands and knees, straddles the mid-section of Blonde Jon; the tequila drinker's face a blob of pounded hamburger.

"We need our city back…"

Another hard fist stroke, Jake's arms buckle and his head falls towards the pavement. He stops himself, nose inches from the ground.

Punk must have some boxer in him, Jake thinks as blood drips from nose and mouth. The droplets on the concrete look black in his red gaze.

"We need it all back…"

Gold Chain punctuates each statement with a blow upon

Jake by fist or foot.

"We need the undead dead."

"We need our neighborhoods back."

"We need to be free, and not confined within these city walls."

The last statement brings another kick to Billet's side, rolls him against Grasshopper who had been standing backed up to the old church building. Jake grabs the man's belt, dragging himself to his feet. He climbs up Grasshopper's shirt until he stands upright. His legs wobble. He grips the man's shirt with both hands, looks into the other's horror-stricken eyes. For a flicker, Jake looks at Lettner's grinning face until it blinks back to Grasshopper.

"It's time for a change," Gold Chain says, swings a fist: an easy knockout now that his target stood at his level.

Jake punches him in the throat, the sensation like sinking knuckles into a soft bread loaf. "You'll make a great politician," he growls.

Gold Chain staggers, one hand clutching his caved throat, one grasps at Billet's shirt. He emits a croaking gasp and drops to the ground nearly pulling Jake down with him.

Something tears from Jake's vestment. He turns to Grasshopper with one steely fist gripping the young man's shirt. Still fear in his eyes, the man looks at his downed friends: one lying dead-still with his face bloody and unrecognizable, and the other splayed out on his back, gulping like a dying fish out of water.

Sirens wail from atop Spectrum Hill.

Jake notices a cellphone in Grasshopper's trembling hand. "Grown enough balls to call the police?" he says, more statement than a question. He grit his teeth, fury full, and cocks back his bloody fist.

Grasshopper's eyes drop to the Class A uniform.

"Captain Jacob Billet. You're responsible for takin' that murderous Muskegon leader out of commission," the man stutters, looking back up into Jake's eyes. "And now you really have murder on your hands."

Jake grasps Lettner. He grasps Stokes, Mulholland, and Loutonia. He holds the Huron's recent navigator, Colter Campau, by a wad of shirt. The image changes to Nate Parsons, the Huron's prior navigator, several years deceased. Each person faces him, rotten of flesh, eyeless sockets black as pitch.

"Father, what have you become?" the 19-year-old Joey Billet says as the image changes to his son. It didn't exactly look like the boy, a glistening yellow-boned skeleton donned in a Union Red Hawk's football jersey, but Jake knows it is him.

Jake jerks his hands away, peers at the blood-soaked appendages. The heel of his shoe bumps against the foot of the pulp-faced Blonde Jon. He looks down at the dead young man, and Gold Chain who he can't tell if the young man still breathes.

The red rage flees, replaced with cold blue dread.

The sirens bawling down the hill draw closer.

"I'm sorry. I'm… not myself," Jake says glancing up to where Grasshopper stood.

It is no longer crème de menthe smelling man, but Lettner standing in a black dress suit, funeral attire, arms folded across his chest, grinning and nodding.

Jake blinks and finds himself alone before the old, boarded up church building, except the silent bodies of the men he has fell.

"Oh God." He shivers, mind reeling. "I'm in trouble, in more ways than one."

Gonna have a hell of a time getting to headquarters and explaining myself in my current bloody ensemble. He's been in ruts before, sure, but he has never killed civilians outright and can only imagine the repercussions. Blasting the undead populace is a steep crime of citations and fines; killing the living upon their own streets, in his own town…

Jake doesn't have to *see* a ghost image of Lettner and the red raw ring around the dead man's neck to understand the consequences his actions will assuredly bring.

Across the west side of the street, the shadows of a bank building loom; beyond it, Ottawa Avenue, Calder Plaza and the city administration office and residences, Monroe Avenue and then the Grand River. Beyond the river, the UCRA enclosure and a smattering of safe houses lie where, besides clothing and weapons, one can get their shit together in times of trouble.

Across the river, he thinks as he hurries to the other side of the street, eyes on Michigan Street, watching for the emergency vehicle to come down around the corner. He trots to an unlit corner of the bank building, keeps moving, keeps moving as he knows his life surely depends on it.

Gold Chain jerks in his death throes. His fists relax, fall open. In his left hand, a name plate reads, in white letters: BILLET.

Chapter Two

The southwest edge of the city pulses red. Even with the inferno being several blocks away, the fiery color reflects in the glass panes of every building along Monroe Avenue. The sky above, limned with low cloud cover, boils an angry crimson.

A Spectrum Hill ambulance howls through the intersection at Michigan and Monroe, turns south, and speeds down the street towards the Fulton Outpost fire.

"Looks like Hell's come to town," Rupert Largo, the Grand Rapids City Treasurer, says standing at the large picture window on the tenth floor of the city administration building.

The floor houses himself and the city manager, though that man died of a sudden heart attack a few years ago. It left the floor, and position, vacant, giving Largo the entire level for a separate living space and office, and left him second-in-command when Mayor Honeywell is out.

Above him held the mayor's office and unused condo. Honeywell preferred to live "street level" with all the commoners. The mayor claimed he didn't need a plush place to reside, he wanted to be close to his people, and didn't like living so high above the streets. His parents died in the attack and collapse of the Forslund Waters Place across the river some years ago. Speculation was the latter reason was why Honeywell steered clear of utilizing that highest floor.

"Such a shame, such a shame." Largo tsks, shaking his head slowly back and forth. "I'm not afraid of attaining such lofty heights," he says to himself.

A thin wisp of Sandalwood-scented smoke curls about his bald pate, an incense burner on his desk. Arms folded across his broad chest, Largo mock-sighs and turns away from the window. "What is the latest, Mr. Tomes?"

Lieutenant Cedric Tomes stands in GRCC MultiCam military garb at the head of Largo's polished mahogany desk. The rank is real. The GRCC uniform: borrowed. Michigan citizenship: not quite. He stands a few inches taller than the City Treasurer. His rolled up sleeves reveal strong, ebon arms. His lack of belly paunch hints at a trim and fit body underneath the service uniform.

Tomes touches a finger to his right ear, listens to the reports coming through his earbud. "Fire department's got the blaze under control. They brought in an additional pumper truck, and got the line going to the hydrant down the street."

"I'll have to look into why our main water lines are so underpressured and dysfunctional," Largo says rubbing at his chin, grinning, more mock-concern. A twitch under the eye patch over his right eye sends his fingers to gently rub at the area. "In this heat and dry summer season, we can't have our waterworks failing."

Tomes looks at his present client, makes sure the man is done gloating before he continues. He sniffs, coughs, and wrinkles his nose at a darkened corner of the Treasurer's office.

Turning his gaze back upon Largo, the dark skinned lieutenant continues. "East end of the Fulton Street Bridge is in shambles. A bridge section crumbled and in the river. Military and city details from Pearl and Bridge Street outposts have gone to the UCRA enclosure across the river to shore things up. My men were able to slip into the enclosure as planned."

"Very good," Largo replies. *Another step to attaining the upper floor.*

"If you don't mind me saying, I think the gasoline truck was overkill. My men didn't get out and far enough away before you detonated it, and it took out a few power generators at the nearby plant also," Tomes says, eyes on the dancing red lights outside.

Largo growls, slides the remote control still sitting on his desk into a trash basket marked INCINERATOR. "I'm not paying you for commentary or concerns, Mr. Tomes, only action. As do my own loyal men, your men know the risk. I'll send out condolence cards if that makes you happy," he says, irritated, "but it'll come out of *your* pay."

Tomes growls deep in his throat, and thinks, *"You arrogant piece of…"*

In the darkened corner, the creature stirs that he smelled earlier.

Stiffly walking, Largo's zombie assassin steps towards him. The undead heading in one's direction is never a calming event. Though Largo's "pet" has always been there, Tomes has never seen the thing in action—once a living young man favored by the Treasurer and on his payroll. But he's heard many a story from Largo's other lackeys about how the undead killer treats his assigned targets.

Largo keeps the dead man near his person like a pet dog. And the feral look the creature casts at the lieutenant as it heads his way makes him surmise the thing is rabid and ready to bite.

"What gives?" Tomes says, hand on his sidearm as the zombie moves closer.

It sniffs the air, growls deep in its throat.

The creature wears black military fatigues like Tomes' men who had slipped into the cities' west side under cover of the night recently.

Largo looks as surprised as his mercenary friend.

Before Tomes can say anything, the creature hesitates against the glare of Largo's desk lamp. From atop its head, where a patch of black hair and peel of loose scalp precariously hangs, the rotting gunman pulls a pair of green-tinted goggles over its smoky eyes. Pivoting on heel, it turns towards the large window Largo's been peering, and looks down towards the street. The thing stands rigid, focused on something below.

Tomes clears his throat and moves his hand from his pistol.

Largo shrugs, returns to the conversation. "I'm contacting Reganshire tomorrow to make sure all is set, and will need an update from your men regarding the aircraft."

The lieutenant eyes the zombie warily. "The plane will be in the air tomorrow as a matter of fact. Sir." The last word lent a sour taste to his lips, but he masked it. "It's scheduled to land at the Weller Air Field just after dark," Tomes finishes.

The phone on Largo's desk rings. He checks his watch. Ten-oh-five. Punctual as ever. Like a good husband calling home to his wife while he's on the road. He picks up the receiver. "Hello, Mister Mayor. How are you this evening? How're things in Muskegon?"

Largo raises an index finger, gestures to his visitor to remain silent.

"Good to hear, sir. Are you still planning on returning Thursday? Yes? Excellent. Is the plan to keep the same schedule?" Largo waves at Tomes, pointing at the top of his desk. A notepad lay next to a small gold-framed picture. He gestures at it and a pen beside it.

Tomes leans over the desk, takes up the pen, and readies to write. A lone picture frame sits upon the City Treasurer's desk: an attractive black haired woman and three like-wise girls. He suspects the girls in the picture range somewhere between seven and fourteen. The Treasurer hasn't told him outright any back history on himself, but some of his underlings working alongside Tome's men had said the man lost his youngest and his wife to the blight a few years after the bird shit hit the fan. The other two were lost during a foray across the state with their father: attacked by a small town of people barely surviving. Word had it, they held Largo and his daughters hostage, waiting on Grand Rapids to pay the toll. Out in the sticks, without proper defenses, Ferals overran the place like a hungry wolf pack. He survived, the small town and his daughters didn't.

Largo snaps his fingers and gives Tomes an angry stare. Tomes nods and presses the pen to paper.

"Oh. Yes. *That* is getting under control as we speak. I was just about to go down there myself and assess the situation." Largo says as Tomes lifts the pen from paper. "Yes, we're planning on sending you a full report before tonight's news broadcast. I'm sure the citizens will take great comfort in your words while out of town."

Largo's straight face turns to an annoyed frown. "No. No sarcasm there, Dennis."

Tomes can tell the man is lying to his boss. Not really knowing much about the mayor of Grand Rapids other than what *his* boss tells him, he wonders if Mayor Honeywell likes being addressed by his common name from an under-councilman. He isn't surprised at the fire suddenly erupting between the men.

"We have shit hitting the fan hard over here. Initial reports point towards Reganshire operatives on *this* side of the river, within our own city, who've done this heinous thing. The people are asking questions, getting antsy, and you're off trying to say 'come out of your holes, rail service is fine.'"

Largo pulls the phone away from his ear, smiling like a mischievous child, lets the lieutenant hear: "Goddamnit, Rupert. If you don't start seeing the forest for the trees…"

Largo brings the phone back to his ear. He smiles triumphantly. "We'll get you the latest reports before the newscast and go from there," he says. "And in light of all this, I still need to know your exact schedule. Colonel Jackson is arranging GRCC units at all major waypoints between Lamont and Grand Rapids."

The Treasurer's eye widens and he bangs his finger on the desk, motioning it is time to take notes.

"Leaving 2 pm. Musketawa to Coopersville-Marne, to the

Lamont-Tallmadge rail line. Got it," Largo says pounding his index finger on his desk even as the lieutenant writes furiously. "Air support? Yes. I've arranged air support. Helicopter's down, but I have something coming up from Chicago."

Largo looks at Tomes. Tomes nods once.

"Coopersville 2:50. Got it. Lamont Station 3:15. Pull into Grand Rapids Union Station at 3:50." Covering the phone quickly, he boastfully adds, "And I'll be the top floor office penthouse occupant before dinner time."

Tomes completes jotting down the time schedule but his eyes go to Largo's killer dog. The creature has its palms to the window. Wrapped in bandages like it was ready to go a few rounds with a heavy bag, its ruddy fingers flex and claw at the glass. Its focus still lies on something on the street.

"Okay then. I'll get an update and report to you right away, and we'll see you in a few days," Largo says, nodding. "Yes. I'll continue to reiterate that to the citizens. Yes. Have a good evening. Good bye, Mister Mayor." He subtly emphasizes the last four words, gritting his teeth, half smile, half sneer, and hangs up the phone.

"He wants me to continue informing people the rail service is open and safe." He says, his tone in disbelief in his own words. "We'll have greater trade opportunities with towns, villages and connected big cities along the main lines, and be able to leave the city for other vistas."

Tomes turns the notepad so it can be read by Largo.

The City Treasurer scans the location and times. A broad smile spreads across his face. "The people will see how safe the rail lines are when our good mayor returns," scratching at the scar-wrinkled flesh below his eye patch.

Largo's undead pet gunman suddenly pounds his fists against the picture window. The creature makes a sharp grunting-barking noise from its rotted vocal cords, gnashing its teeth as it looks down towards the plaza below.

Tomes half expects the man-creature to bust through the glass and leap to its death.

That would be fine with him.

"What is it, Mr. Baddage?" Largo addresses the black haired Zee. "Are you anxious to get back out there?"

The assassin scratches at the window, leaves faint bloody smears and small pieces of skin on the glass. He moans, pointing with his right index finger at the plaza. "Tarr-gattt," Black Hair moans.

Tomes noticed the index finger of the zomb, the trigger finger. It is the only "new" looking part of the thing's hand. He can see faint stitch marks where the finger had been attached anew.

Largo steps closer to the window, and peers down. The lights shining above the plaza reveal a single person moving below: a man in a black military beret. Appears injured, moving quickly but with a slight limp. A lone GRCC soldier? *Strange*, Largo thought, *most are deployed to Fulton and the river front.*

The undead gunman, Mr. Baddage—Black Hair—appears to be choking. His head bobs. His upper body convulses. He gurgles deep in his throat.

"Go ahead. Speak," Largo says to the thing.

"Berrr… Brriil…"

Tomes thinks the thing is going to cough up a lung while Largo leans in closer.

"Buh… Billrt… Bill-ett," the rotting gunman finally spits out. "Bill-ett," he groans, still with index finger pointing downward.

Largo presses his face to the glass. The military figure moving across the plaza is almost to the Monroe Street pedestrian bridge, avoiding the low-hanging walkway lights.

"It-it couldn't be," he says incredulously. "That man was in a coma with no chance to pull through from what I was told. Mr. Baddage missed his opportunity last time, but…"

The zombie assassin abruptly moves from the window, walks

back to the shadowy corner he'd been positioned within when Tomes had entered. There is a flurry of activity, some clunking and clanging as something drops and hits the floor, and a series of grumbled words Tomes thinks he deciphers as curse words. The creature stumbles out of the corner with a Barrett M107 Caliber .50 Long Range Sniper Rifle slung across his back, and a black rucksack. A sheathed 16-inch bayonet and a 9mm pistol hang from his belt.

Tomes moves aside as the Zee heads towards the office doors; the gunman appears he'd walk right into the mercenary if the other didn't move.

Both living men watch the zomb leave.

"If Billet's still up and about, he won't be for long," Largo says, trying to spy the man down on the street but finds he's slipped deeper into the shadows of the buildings.

Tomes puts the notepad down, memorizing the times and locations of the Grand Rapids mayor's return trip waypoints.

"Billet?" he asks, not recognizing the name from any of his conversations with the City Treasurer.

"Another thorn in my side I've been trying to pluck. A GRCC soldier. 'Hero of Grand Rapids.' Did the bidding of Honeywell. Gave the populace a little peace of mind," Largo answers, staring towards the river to the west. "I'm a candle snuffer right now. I have to crush hope to rebuild hope, and the man is just another flame I need to extinguish for the greater good of our kind."

Tomes has an idea of what his employer means, but asks anyway. "Our kind?"

Largo glances over his shoulder and says with a sneer: "The living, Mr. Tomes. We have the means to cleanse the land of the undead, and take back our entire city and countryside."

The Treasurer's gaze returns to the window, his large frame heaving with rapid, excited breaths.

Tomes silently agrees with the man, and is paid well to remain on one side of the battle. He still can't help inwardly shivering a bit at the man's fervor. He glances towards the office doors, makes sure the dead gunman is gone.

"I've a hard time grasping you letting that thing wander about with a high caliber weapon and such," Tomes says, turning back to Largo who still faces the window. "You aren't worried it might take out some innocents, or you?"

Without turning, the City Treasurer replies: "Mr. Baddage was a superb marksman in life, a part of my underground loyalist group, and a loyal soldier and bodyguard in his unlife. He finishes tasks he's started. He's probably better adjusted than the re-assembled troopers at the test facility." He turns to Tomes. "And speaking of which…"

"As I said," Cedric Tomes nods, "My men have infiltrated the UCRA. All plans are underway."

Largo smiles and turns back to the window, eye cast to the chaos at Fulton Street, and then to the west side of town across the river. Blanketed in darkness, he envisions the entire UCRA in flame as Fulton is.

"It is time," he nods to his reflection in the glass, "It's time to bring Grand Rapids back from the dead."

Chapter Three

"...Back from the dead," Stokes says, the inferno across the river paints his face an angry red-orange. "The captain wouldn't go for that. I could tell he wasn't keen walking around the BTF when we stopped a few months ago."

Stokes stands in the front gunner's cupola, chewing the end of an unlit cigar. The commander's open stand: empty. He misses the man who typically resides there, but it doesn't bother him. Concerned as he and the rest of the Huron crew are for their captain, he likes his current position.

"Check that section over there," the gunner shouts at a pair of soldiers standing near the Fulton Street gate. They snap to attention upon his words. It makes him smile. "I think I see a sag over there. Make sure it's shored up."

"Yessir, Sergeant, sir," one of the men salute as he and his fellow trot off to where Stokes pointed.

Stokes grins, content.

"The captain also won't like when he gets the report you're flaunting your second-in-command-dom," Lance Corporal Loutonia Phelps emerges from the commander's hatch, checking the tarped .50 cal machine gun mounted on the hatch ring. Her fingers roam the hatch absently, her thoughts on the man who typically stood within the armored ring.

Stokes chews the cigar stump vigorously, then spits it over

the side of the transport. The wet blob splatters near the boots of a soldier standing on the roadway beside the huge M213 HTV, the Huron, named after one of the state's five great lakes. Stokes doesn't see the annoyed look and the grunt's middle finger salute.

"Baby," Stokes says, turning towards Loutonia, "you just have an issue with guys in command."

An explosion across the river, on the city side of the decimated Fulton Street Bridge, blows a fresh roll of red flame and black smoke into the air.

The dark skinned driver grows darker as an angry scowl draws across her face. "What the fuck is that supposed to mean?" She starts to climb from the commander's cupola in Stokes' direction.

Lance Corporal Eddie Mulholland pops up from the open rooftop cargo bay. The tallest crew member, his shoulders come in line with the roof frame. He bobs, trying to see around the 25mm cannon turret, not sure which of his crew members he should address. Yes, Stokes is in command of the Huron while their captain is out of commission, but Loutonia drives the rig, babies the rig, and claims it as her own. And, he hates to think this way, his momma down south taught him better, but…

…Stokes can be a dumbass hick.

"Forrester's callin' in. Wants a SITREP," Mulholland says, hoping to interrupt the imminent smackdown between his crew mates. Since their captain's become indisposed, Phelps seems on the verge of going nuclear, her emotional gun fit with a hair trigger, and Eddie knew better than to butt heads with the woman. Stokes had simply let his blind ego inflate more with assuming command of their big rig.

"I'll take it," Stokes says turning his back on Loutonia, focuses across the river. The CO of Huron's sister, the Ontario, stands over there with other troops while the GRFD fights the blaze.

Mulholland expects Lou to launch herself at the squat gunner. It doesn't happen. She looks at Stokes, and then at him, brow knit, and slides down the front of the vehicle, holding her holstered .45's at her waist until she hits the ground below.

"Huron here," Stokes says into the microphone hanging from his helmet. "Go ahead, Ontario."

Mulholland ducks back down into the bowels of the transport but listens in through his own helmet headset.

"Sergeant, how're things going over there?" the voice of Captain Frank Forrester asks.

"Nothing to report," Stokes answers. They had come across at the Pearl Street Bridge gate, hit the bridge, and headed to the opposite side of Fulton, south of Pearl. The explosion at the downtown outpost had occurred between shifts. It reduced casualties but disrupted the city's power plant building barely a block away. The GRCC scrambled men and vehicles from the Bridge Street OP and Pearl, dividing themselves between the east and west side of the river.

Concerns for the west side of Fulton related to the UCRA enclosure.

Explosion blew out and rattled windows all the way over here, Stokes views the remnants of the Eberhardt Science building at the foot of the bridge. No one wants the UCRA fence down and the city's undead waltzing into the metropolis.

"I have Banes and Ferretti going up and down the perimeter making sure everything is intact," Stokes says looking at the taillights of one of the BRV-O's as it follows the curve of the 131 Expressway overhead, heading south-southeast. The other "Bulldog," as Stokes likes to call them—the light tactical vehicle thick of body and squat, with a snub front end—heads towards the Huron coming along the fence line from the north.

Other patrol units rolled this side of the line between Bridge and Pearl, but didn't reporting to Stokes.

"Other than the citizens come to watch the fireworks," Stokes looks to the several dozen undead pressing their rotted faces against the fencing. They flinch every time a gush of flame glares, but press back in as it subsides, enticed by the sounds of chaos. "All is relatively calm at our location. Over."

The north patrolling Bulldog pulls up alongside the Huron which sits with her starboard side facing the enclosure. Ferretti, the vehicle's lead and manning the 12.7mm machine gun top-hatting the rig, gives Stokes a thumbs-up as they pull in front of the transport.

"Get your helmet back on," Stokes yells at the blond-haired soldier. His words lost under another loud blast from across the river.

Ferretti nods, gestures again with thumb up.

"What's going on over there?" Stokes asks, eyes cast across the river which reflects the boiling inferno on its east side. "Things don't look much under control," he says rather flippantly.

In the bowels of the Huron, Mulholland shakes his head. Billet would've kicked the gunner's ass if he spoke to a superior officer like that.

A heavy breath fuzzes the comm line, and Ontario's commander says: "Fire Department's been trying to cool down the line of vehicles someone was asinine to park here. They're getting a drizzle of water pressure from the hydrants and trying to get ahold of Waterworks to up the pressure. Like the conveniently positioned and detonated fuel truck, the cars left here appear as if they were all full up with gasoline. The boys manning the outpost earlier are going to have a lot of explaining to do. They know better than to let whoever park their vehicles this close to a military outpost."

"Someone mentioned insurgents from Reganshire. Any truth to that, ya think?" Stokes asks.

"Lots of reports. Lots of conjectures. I got a few crisped bodies, one with a Reganshire ID. Seems a bit convenient, yet..." There was a moment of hesitation. "I've a hard time understanding it completely, but it appears to be true."

"Should've capped that crazy bitch and her old man when we had the chance," Stokes mumbles into the mike.

Forrester must have not heard it, but Mulholland did. Other than concern for his old friend, Lucius LaFleur, living in Reganshire, he can't say he doesn't agree with his crew mate's statement. It is no secret the budding village, formerly known as Standale, holds hostilities against the big city regarding trade and industry disputes. Overseen by Silas Regan and his demented daughter Rebecca, the enclosed and well-armed village made it plain they wanted independence from Grand Rapids who held all major supplies and industry—and survival sources as it were—over the surrounding countryside. So bad was it that the Regans were taking in defectors and captured equipment, and even semi-undead Gurks, Zombie Troopers, into their midst.

Mulholland can still see Major Pike and his big Abrams, the Devastator, wheeling away in the village's direction while his captain clung to life: a supposed heart attack in the field, though Eddie had other, more disturbing ideas of what put Billet down for the count.

"If those sons of bitches got anyone still squirreling around the area, they won't be getting by me," Stokes says, pulling a fresh stogie from his vest pocket. Digging out a Zippo emblazoned with red skull and crossbones on its silver body, he rests an elbow on the handle of his quad .30's as he flips the lighter open. He raises the lighter to the cigar's tip, thumb ready to roll the flint wheel.

A single pop of gun fire.

Parked alongside the Huron, still with unprotected lid, Corporal Matt Ferretti's head snaps back, then falls forward. He slumps sideways against the Bulldog's gun turret, the back of his skull blown out.

Full on machine gun fire pours into the soldiers and vehicles like a sudden vertical hail storm from the other side of the UCRA enclosure.

Stokes ducks below the hatch crown, bangs his helmeted head

on the way down.

"What's going on over there?" Forrester says in the front gunner's ear. Stokes rights the helmet as he squats, listening to the barrage of bullets pinging off the Huron's hull.

"The civilians are attacking us!" Stokes yells into the commlink.

Mulholland pops up and grabs at one of the cargo door handles. He swears as a bullet tears across his right shoulder. Grasping the metal handle, he yanks the half door up, leaving it vertical.

"Say again?" Forrester responds.

"The West Side Horde is attacking us!"

Stokes grits his teeth and stands up in the open, grabs the grips of his quad .30 cluster of death. His thumbs start to depress the trigger button. He glances to the other end of the Huron, seeing Mulholland manning his single. His eyes move quickly to the enclosure. The milling undead on the other side jerk and thrash against the tall fence, stumbling, falling, chunks of their flesh winging into the air and ground. Muzzle flashes flare from the dark square orifices of the old Stow Davis factory building on the south side of Fulton Street within the enclosure. The same deadly star-shaped flares light the night from the lower levels of the old VSU downtown west side campus pile of rubble.

Unless the "domesticated" UCRA undead have found an GRCC arms cache and gained enough coordination to fire assault rifles, someone else has gotten into the enclosure and decided to wage war from the inside.

Behind one of the massive concrete overpass supports, Loutonia hunkers with a handful of soldiers behind her. Stokes makes eye contact with her.

A bright flare and bang snaps his attention back to the Stow Davis building across the fence line. A boiling smoke trail and snarling, growing hiss drives straight towards his position as Mulholland yells, "RPG!"

Stokes makes eye contact one final time with his driver and

then a deafening explosion snaps him back against the hatch coaming.

Human screams of pain, both living and unliving, cry over the rolling flame and smoke. Tortured steel fencing twangs and rattles from its mooring, peeling aside like the hide of a freshly ruptured balloon. Something large and wet hits Stokes in the chest, then drops into the hatch hole at his feet. He looks down, tries to bring his rattled senses back online, and finds a black blood-dripping forearm at his boots.

"Gawddaminit, gawddamit." He grabs onto his guns and swings them round. Feeling lopsided and as if drunk, he fires into the shattered fence line, haphazardly spraying the pile of undead, the street, and the factory building.

The rounds harmlessly bounce off their targets.

"Switch to live rounds," Stokes yells as he fumbles with the ammo canister hanging off his gun nest. He tears the orange-tipped cartridge from its cradle, cares little as it clangs off the Huron's rooftop and falls to the street below. He squats down in his stand. A bullet zips face level where he'd just stood. With brain still trying to right itself, he grabs for the box of live ammo located at his knees.

"Report, Sergeant. What's happening over there," Forrester yells in Stoke's headset.

"Hostiles in the enclosure," Mulholland says before Stokes can open his mouth. "Fulton Street gate and fence line are down. Gurk and UCRA casualties. We've gone live." His single barrel .30-Cal machine gun fires, the tracer round follows every third live round, shows him where his shots hit. The attackers in the old Stow Davis factory building return fire only when the angry bullets from his gun don't pound into walls and windows.

"Reinforcements are oscar mike, Huron," Forrester replies.

Stokes fiddles with the live ammo box, finally gets it in place. He feeds his gun cluster. He tastes blood in his mouth mixed with tobacco. His stogie gone except for the nub clenched tight in his teeth. Scanning the ground around the transport, a twenty foot section of the UCRA gate and fence lay in a jumble against Huron's face and starboard side.

Stokes has visions of their April storms and flooding experience. He growls like a bear.

The Bulldog parked in front of the Huron also has part of the gate lying against its hood. A few shredded bodies of the local undead ooze and drip, part of the mesh of the fence now, like bologna through a meat grinder. Ferretti has been taken aside and one of the other three men in vehicle assumes the dead soldier's position, firing live rounds into the enclosure. Soldiers on foot who've been caught in the blast and gun fire sprawl, unmoving, upon the street. Some of their comrades crouch over them, tending to them as others fire their weapons towards the factory and university.

"Phelps!" Stokes bellows, sees Loutonia sprawled upon the sidewalk slightly behind the concrete overpass column. He breathes a sigh of relief as she slowly gets to hands and knees, fingers still entwined about her pistol grips. Her face is chalk-white from the debris, cheeks bleed from several abrasions.

Staggering to a crouch against the concrete pillar, she taps the side of her helmet with the barrel of one of her .45's. "Thanks, Jamie. I didn't know you cared." She smiles, her teeth red with blood and grime.

Stokes opens his mouth to remind her, his name is James. It dies on his lips as the woman turns her gaze towards the destroyed enclosure, stands and runs suddenly full into the barrage of lead bees. She goes over a section of crumpled fence and torn bodies, onto the UCRA grounds.

Stokes casts his focus ahead of her, in the direction she runs. "What the fuck?" he gasps.

A local zomb in blue mechanic coveralls stands unfazed by the gun battle chaos around him. He waves in their direction, his arm looking ready to fall from its grimy and tattered shirt sleeve.

Bob the undead gas station attendant, one of the "satellite" Zees the GRCC uses to learn of goings-on within and outside the city and UCRA grounds, continues to wave as bullets pepper the ground around him. Phelps dives, arms wrap about the dead man's waist, and drives them both to the ground behind a rubble pile. Small geysers of dust and concrete spray in the path they just stood.

Stoke's comm crackles. "This is Big Bear. I'll be at your location in a minute."

He turns north, seeing "Big Bear"—one of the GRCC's two M60 Patton tanks—as it churns down the roadway from Pearl Street.

With that proclamation, as if on cue, the gun fire ceases from the buildings and rubble within the enclosure. Stokes sees dark figures disperse—far faster than the west side shamblers—from window, rubble and building.

Grabbing assault rifles, Stokes and Mulholland drop from the Huron.

"Uh. Umm." Stokes spins on heel, tries to determine where to go, what command to give first. Troopers lay, stand, sit all around, attending to their wounded or dead. A few of the local undead, now free to walk about outside their usual confines, move towards the blaze across the river, attracted to the light like prostitutes to a red light district.

Stokes wipes the blood from the corner of his mouth as an undead woman who'd been caught in the blast walks straight into him, her eyes pale, blank. Her clothing had been blown and burned from her body, as was one side of her head and face, and the left side of her chest and abdomen. Her right arm: gone from some earlier injury. It looks like some huge beast had taken a bite out of her. Her crisped ribs stand out as an unappetizing dinner entrée; part of her intestines drag behind her like a string of poorly filled sausage casings.

Stokes gingerly touches her by her bloody shoulder stumps.

"Not this way, ma'am." He turns her so she'd not head towards the river or the city. "Thank you," he says as she sniffs at the spot of blood on his hand, and then continues walking as if nothing has happened, now heading back into the UCRA area.

He glances at her naked, pock-marked buttocks as she shambles away. He hiccups and swallows the burning bile in his throat. "*That* does not interest me."

He sees Mulholland run to Phelps who still lies atop their undead service station friend.

"Hey, the captain ain't gonna like hearing you're doin' another man," Stokes calls out, chuckling.

Mulholland shoulders his M4, and helps Loutonia to her feet. A wicked gash runs across her right thigh.

"The roadway bit me," she winces as she rises with her lanky teammate's assistance.

"Thought you were hit, and…" Eddie starts to say.

Loutonia raises an index finger and shushes him.

Lower jawbone exposed. Both cheeks red, raw and eaten through in several places; Bob speaks. Mulholland and Phelps listen. To the rear gunner, not versed in anything zomb other than keeping himself from being overly chewed on, he can't understand a lick of what the undead mechanic says. From all their times rolling through the west side neighborhood, stopping to drop off the doped meat that keeps the UCRA crowd "docile and domesticated" (Mayor Honeywell's words, not his), and getting intel from Bob, the man's phlegmy grunts and pitchy moans are indecipherable to everyone except their driver. From her translations, the man seems memory-trapped in the 1950's.

"Mayor Goebel's puts on a hell of a parade and fireworks display," Loutonia says, wincing as she kneels back down. She removes her helmet and cocks an ear towards the jabbering gas station attendant. "Yes, yes. Eisenhower *is* a great president."

She grunts, moans and gargles, even spits a little, speaking the

Zee's broken language.

Bob responds in turn.

Mulholland shivers, thinking it's always damn weird with Phelps conversing with the dead. Weirder still them speaking back. He's never felt the calling during his military training to study zombie speak.

"What're you asking him?" the gunner asks as the guttural conversation continues between the two.

After checking to see the man isn't too damaged to be moved, Loutonia helps the Zee sit up, careful not to yank on his loose arm.

"I asked him if he knew anything about our attackers who've infiltrated the UCRA," she replies to Mulholland.

Loutonia emits three short grunts, a series of low, long moans, and two sharp coughs as if she's working up to spit. With foggy eyes, Bob looks at the woman, sniffs the air through the two nose-less nostril holes in his head. He responds in the same series of guttural utterances but what appears in backwards order to Mulholland.

Phelps gasps, eyes wide, mouth agape. Surprise, then anger, and her response seems short, severe, to the undead mechanic. He responds in kind, lifts his arms though the gestures don't make sense in their slow, jerky manner. Mulholland thinks the loose arm at any moment might simply slip from sleeve. Bob chatters, gnashes his black, broken teeth at Phelps though doesn't act as if he'll lunge at her.

"Are… Are you arguing with him?" Eddie says, watching the living woman and unliving man bounce heated grunts, snarls and moans at the other.

"What the hell?" She watches Bob continue to speak and wave. She places a hand on his shoulder to stop the gesturing of his loose arm. He doesn't seem to notice the touch but keeps on talking. "I don't get it. I'm not sure what he's saying. He's not making any sense, unless…"

"Um, you're talking to a dead guy," Eddie reminds her.

Loutonia listens to Bob ramble for a few more seconds, her awe-struck then exasperated expression doesn't diminish.

"What're you two love birds talking about?" Stokes walks up to them, smirking.

Phelps rises to her feet, fists clenched, and turns to her crew mates. Bob chitters and moans, oblivious to Loutonia moving from the conversation.

"Bob says," Her fists unclench. "Jake…er…the captain is heading over to see him tomorrow."

Stokes loses his smirk.

Bob tilts his raggedy face up at them and gurgles.

"He can slip the keys to the Buick in the mail slot if he drops off the Invicta before the garage opens," Loutonia translates. "Ten dollar oil change and tune up for his special friend."

Stokes guffaws. "Is that all?"

Bob growls, and then grunts twice, punctuating his statement with a phlegm-filled hiss.

Loutonia looks from Bob and then back at Stokes and Mulholland.

"He says we can get the Reds out of the neighborhood anytime," she says, one last glance at the undead mechanic. "And the hunter with the big gun isn't hunting animals," Loutonia's eyes wide with concern as she looks at her two crew members, "The hunter is hunting the captain."

Stokes looks dumbfounded.

Mulholland appears the same, and then: "Um, dang awesome." He scratches at his chin. "What's an Invicta?"

Chapter Four

Jake waits under a stand of short, thick foliaged trees lining the river. Eyes wide, he cannot believe what he sees.

Donned in buckskin vests and stitched pants, the Native Americans, the Obijwe people, if Jake's local history stands correct, walk a well-worn dirt path along the west side of the river. One fellow with black hair tied in a long braid wades along the shore of the rushing, shallow river's edge. Dripping wet from head to toe, he carries a hardwood spear in hand. His fellows carry corded hemp nets. Two of the American Indians step gingerly through the tall shoreline grasses with a thick branch resting upon their shoulders, the branch sags under the weight of a dozen salmon.

Dripping from his wade across the river himself, Jake watches in silent amazement at the spectacle. He glances across river, where he'd just ventured from, to the river's east bank. Grand Rapids stands with tall concrete and barbed wire walls containing her tall buildings and living, modern day denizens. He stands astonished, breathless, amazed because this authentic Obijwe tribe hasn't traversed the Grand River valley shoreline for over a century and a half when the area had only been a span of sparsely populated wilderness. Home to a handful of settlers and a missionary, and the simple but beautiful natives of the region; it was no more.

"You see crazy when your brains turning to mush," Lettner says in Jake's ear, standing over him as Billet squats amongst the trees. The late Muskegon High Commissioner speaks too loudly.

"Quiet, they're going to hear you," Jake shushes the man. He notices Lettner now wears a pair of dark swim trunks and muscle shirt—something Jake would've worn way back as a teen on a summer expedition to Lake Michigan. The regent looks comical, but at the moment Jake finds nothing to lift his spirits, finds nothing to distill the niggling feeling in his gut it is he who is a joke now.

"They? They who?" Lettner questions, nods back towards where Jake had been looking.

Nothing is there.

No Obijwe or Ottawa tribesmen comb the river's edge, fishing, hunting, gathering. Back to the quiet west bank of the Grand River and the sprawling grounds of the overgrown Ah-Nab-Awen Park. On the same grounds, closer to the abandoned expressway, sits the huge triangle-shaped museum immortalizing the 38th President of the United States, Gerald Ford. Just beyond the museum, below the highway, a tall concertina wire-lined fence lines Scribner Avenue, the "doorway" to the Urban Civilian Retention Area.

Jake shakes his head, tries to re-align the cogs which are obviously out of sync. He rises from his hiding spot, starts across the park lawn, the tall grass brushing against the knees of his wet dress slacks. The fires from the Fulton Outpost paint their redness against the face of the old presidential museum. He stops before the black wrought-iron fencing surrounding the bunker-shaped grave sites where the late president and his wife were interred decades ago. He can't help but wonder if his crew and the Huron crawl amidst the maelstrom of heat and flame.

The trip out of the barricaded city had gone fairly easy. The military and law enforcement personnel kept eyes on every inch of the concrete walls lining the river's east side. The chaos at Fulton drew a vast majority of them from overwatch duties. There were other means to getting around the protective barricade if one didn't mind slogging through the storm water drains and underground steam line tunnels that snaked throughout city proper. Off limits to regular civilians, military personnel and police who'd gotten on the wrong side of their commanders found their patrol duty down in the musty and malodorous pipes and tunnelways.

Billet recalled a few miserable patrols in the city's intestines.

Through an unguarded manhole cover, down into the crawlspace wide and tall enough to walk hunchback, he had made his way under the city wall. The summer heat did little to improve the overall dreariness found traversing the storm water pipe. Insanely humid and reeking of wet, rotting… who knows what, Jake was happy to reach the barred exit which hung over the river. His eyes still burned, and his throat felt painfully raw even after dropping into the dark fast-moving waterway. But the air, a little cooler than the stuff trapped inside the drain line, was more desirable as he struggled across the roughly one-hundred and sixty yards of river pushing against him and soaking him from head to toe.

He had discarded his coat and long sleeve shirt as he'd hit the river. Scuffed, torn and filthy as it was from the drain pipe excursion; his superiors could take it out of his pay, *if* he would wear such a uniform again. The two drunk young men wavered in and out of his mind's eye lying broken and dead upon the sidewalk.

"Smooth move, Captain," he says to himself as he creeps around the Ford's memorial.

More sirens, howling within the forest of buildings across the river, coax him onward.

Along the periphery of the Scribner Avenue fence line; emergency exits and entrances, chain link doorways if one couldn't make the actual larger gatehouses at Bridge Street, Pearl or Fulton. Moving up slowly, his cautious steps were rewarded by not walking into the path of a patrol puttering up the street in a military-accessorized ATV. He could hear three men talking even before he saw their faces. He had no time to run across the street to the door-shaped gate, his entrance into the UCRA.

For a moment he thinks of turning himself over to his fellow soldiers. He wants to change his clothes, get back into his real gear. He wants to get back to his crew and rig. After three months of being out of commission, it would be nice to know what the hell was going on. The last thing he recalls is Loutonia standing atop the turret of an Abrams tank, her pistols down its throat hatch as he has a heart attack, or whatever it was that laid him low. Had they brought back Pike and his tank, or had the man defected and taken one of the GRCC's last modern ass-kicking vehicles with him?

Of course, his rig kicked ass too. With his crew, a couple of rough and tumble gunners; one who could shoot the literal hair off a gnats ass, and the other turning to rubble everything around the gnat; and a driver who could spin easy circles around the insect maneuvering 72 tons of American steel like she was driving a sports car. That is his crew. They'd taken on a new navigator also, Pfc. Colter Campau, supposedly a very distant relation to Louis Campau, the founder of the downtown area of Grand Rapids almost two hundred years ago.

Wouldn't Grandpa Louis be surprised to see Grand Rapids now, Jake muses, wrapped in a concrete and chain link, barbed wire security blanket, packed with soldiers armed to the teeth, bordered by an equally fenced off west side neighborhood filled with the city's walking dead.

The thought of a 200-year old corpse rising from the city's oldest cemetery kills further ponderings.

Jake steps out onto the darkened Scribner Avenue, not far from the UCRA fence line. A pair of headlights glare a short distance down the street, coming his way. He hears the gurgle of a four-stroke engine; one of the GRCC's scout vehicles, a suped-up ATV.

"You gonna go or not?" Lettner asks, crouching directly behind Jake. "They're going to take one look at you and know there's something wrong," the regent snickers. "I doubt they'll take you back to the hospital. Well, probably the *hospital* at the Butterworth Test Facility. You know… to confirm things."

"Shut. Up," Jake growls.

"What's that over there?" someone shouts from the four seat All-Terrain Vehicle as it rolls closer.

"Shit," Jake says not sure whether to run or throw his hands in the air.

"Think over your options. You're never going to get back to your wife and kid to say good-bye if you turn yourself in. When one heads down that road of the unliving; memory goes, the soul is gone. No one really knows what's on the other side," Lettner snickers in his ear.

The off-road vehicle's spot light sweeps towards them.

"You can take them, just like you did those drunkards. The hunger is rising, isn't it? Hunger to kill, to eat. Hunger for blood."

Jake crumples to the edge of the roadway, within the tall grasses, as the bright light flashes over him. His eyes feel like two hot embers burning in his skull until he snaps them closed.

"What is that?" another Gurk says as the spot light sweeps up in an arc, the ATV revs slightly as it picks up speed and passes by.

Face to the cool ground, Jake gasps for breath. His heart should be pounding with more horse power than the military vehicle, yet it drives against his chest like a rubber mallet worked by an infant's hand. He turns his head, peers through the tall grass at what caught the soldier trio's attention.

"What the—? Shit. How'd that thing get up there?" the ATV driver says stopping the vehicle. He slides out of his seat, adjusts his combat helmet. The sleeve of his arm boasts three chevrons: a sergeant.

The front passenger and his buddy behind him step from the vehicle, M4's in hand.

Though the ATV's lights shine further down the street, and the area all around dark beyond that, the soldiers appear outlined with a faint white aura. More a subtle fog two fingers thick, it limns each man, curling and tumbling about each like mist from dry ice.

Jake looks to where the soldiers peer. Atop the fifteen foot fence, tangled in the circles of concertina wire, a ragtag human body hangs; front end droops down towards their side of the street, bent at the waist. Male, it wears the tattered remnants of pants and shirt, no shoes. Snagged by the sharp barbs, the body doesn't move, and Jake cannot see any ethereal aura about the dead thing unlike the soldiers.

"An UCRAer? Must've entered the expressway somehow, then fell over the guard rail up there," the sergeant says, nods towards the section of Interstate 131 above. The dead man appears to have fallen from the overpass another fifteen feet above the fence line.

"Is it still alive?" the grunt says who had been in the front passenger seat.

"Why don't you climb up there, Hammond, and give it a kiss to find out," the soldier who had climbed from the rear seat says, chuckling, giving his partner a nudge with the butt of his assault rifle.

"Fuck you, Roberts," Hammond replies as all three stand near the fence looking at the hung-up figure.

Time to go, Jake thinks.

He rises. Joints pop. He looks to the three soldiers, then at the gate directly across the street from his position. He steps out into the dark street.

Eyes snap open; the dead thing curled over the top of the fence comes to life. It turns its head. Jake can see its glassy eyes as if it were right up in his face staring at him.

The creature hisses.

"Jeezuz, it's alive!" Hammond jumps back, bumps into his two companions, nearly bowling them over.

Roberts gently shoves Hammond. "Isn't like it's gonna jump down and eat your face."

"Cripes. I'm calling this in," the young sergeant says, turning his back and putting a hand to the headset on his helmet.

"I'm not touching it, and it ain't touching me," Hammond says bringing up his M4.

"Don't shoot it, man. If I get one more citation, I'm gonna end up in the brigg and lose a months pay," Roberts says to Hammond as the other man aims at the struggling and moaning zombie.

"The wife and I are trying to have a baby. I'm not going to get another scratch by any of these things, and end up like Ferris or Carmichael," Hammond says, gun aimed at the undead creature.

"Put the gun down, Hamm. I'm calling a clean-up crew to take care of this one," the sergeant says.

"You ain't gonna Turn, you nimrod," Roberts raises his weapon also as the Zee continues to squirm. "Ferris and Carm's vaccine wore out. Everyone's system is different. You'd know if you're Turning without having that thing nibble on ya."

Jake walks slowly across the street, keeps his eyes on the patrol. He reaches the gate. A square pad, about the size of a shoebox, sits chest level and to the side of the chain link doorway. A thick bolt runs through it into a mating steel box on the door itself. The electronic lock has a finger print scanner and a nine-number button pad.

His hands shake as he places his thumb to the small square scan pad. It is the first time he notices the aura he himself exudes. The consistency of dirty smoke, tiny grey and brown wisps play along his exposed flesh interrupted by small lines of white almost in time with the dull thump of his heart.

The thumb scan turns from red to green, and he punches in 19-644-02, the last code he recalls they'd been given to access the emergency gates.

"Shit, it's coming over," Hammond yells at the same time the door lock beeps and bolt retracts.

The undead man wriggles, rattling the bail of razor wire. The balance of its weight over the street side of the fence causes the concertina to flex enough to let it slip forward. It hisses and snarls at the soldiers, arms out, fingers clawing the air.

Hammond jumps as Roberts snaps his rifle upright and, in full auto, sprays the zombie with hot lead. Like an over-ripe, pulverized melon, the thing's head and chest explode. The chunky red and rotten rain spills down. As if to further kill the already beyond-dead-thing, Hammond raises his weapon and, eyes closed, fires, screaming, as the awful body wash dowses both him, Roberts and the side of the ATV.

"Dammit, guys. I just had this thing washed," the sergeant shakes his fist as the gun fire ceases, looking at his vehicle.

"Fuck fuck fuck. I'm gonna do time in the brigg again," Roberts stammers, gun drooping in hand as he carefully backsteps from the bullet-churned front half of the body at his feet.

Hammond's rifle clatters to the ground as he hunches over with hands on his gore-splattered pants. "Oh god. I got some in my mouth. I think I swallowed it. Oh god," the grunt says, body shuddering. His chest heaves, then his neck, and then he vomits upon his already vile-stained boots.

The gate rattles loudly and squeals on dry hinges as Jake pushes it open. He takes one step through the portal when the sergeant yells at him.

"Hey, you. What do you think you're… Stop right there!"

The sergeant leaps from the vehicle.

Jake hesitates.

"Daddy, come on."

"Joey?" Jake whimpers.

His son, Joseph, all of 7 years, just as he remembers him, stands peeking out from behind a concrete support, smiles at him, waves at him to come on in to the UCRA to play.

"Come with me, daddy. You're going to love the old neighborhood," the boy says, trots up and takes Jake's trembling hand. "You're going to love it, daddy. This is where you belong."

"Halt! Stop! Wait!" the sergeant shouts, boots clatter against the asphalt as he runs towards the gate.

The gate clangs shut behind Jake.

"I'm coming, son," he says, tears stream down his face.

"I said, stop! Soldier, who are you?" the sergeant commands, pulls against the chain link fence, pointing a handheld flashlight in Jake's direction.

Jake growls. He throws his right arm up to block the annoying and painful glare of the flashlight, still feels the cool, small hand of his son in his left. "Captain Jacob Ethan Billet," he replies, wipes his wet eyes, stiffens his chin and resolve. "I'm going home."

With the tittering laughter only he can hear, he and his son run off into the heart of the UCRA.

"What the hell? Dammit," the sergeant swears under his breath, pissed at letting the obvious deranged soldier through the enclosure. *Billet.* Should he know the name? He doesn't know a lot of the men's names he works with, being only a few weeks new in town. He is surely going to get balled out by his GRCC superiors. He doesn't really give a fuck.

He looks at the two idiots, Hammond and Roberts, down the road, bantering back and forth at each other. There is a lot of shit going on in this town. The Illinois and the Chicago area isn't this messed up. Of course, there hadn't been many money-making covert excursions to be had there, so he was glad when Tomes and his Red Guard Security Consulting called him.

Automatic rifle fire and a small explosion a few blocks south shake him from his thoughts. He smiles as the planned chaos erupts on this side of the river along the enclosure. He hopes his companions who had made it into the enclosure keep their heads down. Though their mercenary team has the stealth, the city's military has the big guns to cut one's career short.

Thinking the time is right, the sergeant brings a hand to his helmet mike.

"Central, this is River Side Three-One, reporting a situation at…"

Something punches him in the back. Pressure, and then pain as a long knife blade sprouts through the front of his ACU just below his name patch.

"Bay-bayonet?" he stammers, lung speared, hard to breath, blood bubbling up in throat and mouth.

"Bill-ett," the words hiss in his ear as the long knife is yanked out and the sergeant topples.

"River Side Three-One say again?" the radio receiver calls back.

The sergeant rolls onto his back. His flashlight glares into the face of a man standing over him wearing green-tinted goggles. Dressed in black military fatigues, a sniper rifle and rucksack hang over his back. The hand which holds the long knife is encased in a tactical half finger glove.

The sergeant shrieks in pain as his attacker squats, kneels on his chest upon the fresh chest wound.

Hammond and Roberts turn.

The black-garbed man twists his head slowly towards the other men.

The sergeant's eyes widen upon sight of his assailants exposed neck as it consists of a torn hole revealing raw muscle and part of lower jaw.

A suppressed 9mm pistol comes up from the dark-clad man's hip. A trigger finger, looking fresher than its blackened and bony brethren digits, squeezes off two rounds.

Hammond and Roberts drop, a third eye hole dead center in forehead.

"River Side Three-One, report," the radio crackles.

"You… should have stayed… home," the shooter hisses, smiles with black-limned teeth and dark red gums. He holsters his pistol, still holding the knife in his other hand, and bends down closer to the sergeant's face. "Bill-ett," the man says again as he scribes the words in the soldier's blood spreading out beneath his back.

The dripping knife comes down again, slashes the sergeant's shirt open.

The man bends close to the sergeant's face, sniffs, smiles with that awful mouth. "I will need… rations for my journey. Thank… you."

The sergeant screams a bloody froth as the long knife digs in and peels away a large strip of his abdomen.

Chapter Five

Already the morning heat drives the mercury to 80 degrees Fahrenheit, promising another hot, hot West Michigan July day. The heat raging inside the City Administration Building swirls even hotter.

"There are civilians coming across the river. When will the enclosure be back up and secure?" a blond haired woman in the back row asks, concern in her voice. She stands in the small meeting room on the third floor of the City Building.

The meeting room has two dozen chairs facing a raised podium, every chair occupied by a concerned Grand Rapidian. At the podium stands the City Treasurer and a senior council member, Leon Sutter. On either side of them, sitting at long rectangular tables, are the other city council men and women and the head of the GRCC, Colonel Lee Jackson. Several soldiers stand lined along the walls, including Captain Frank Forrester and his crew: Stokes, Loutonia and Mulholland. Lt. Tomes stands next to Mulholland.

Never having met but knowing where the young man was stationed, Tomes wonders how the tall fellow didn't have a head full of lumpy knots from ringing his cranium against the transport vehicle when in the field.

"A temporary fence line has been erected and is being rigidly manned by your GRCC," Leon Sutter says. "I'm making sure, since this is the second time since the April floods the river side enclosure has been compromised. I am in council with the mayor and my constituents on designing a better, stronger perimeter to protect the city."

"My husband was shot crossing the river," the same woman pipes up. "I thought live rounds were off limits against UCRA civilians."

"Unfortunately he shouldn't have been crossing the river," Largo replies, a bit too coldly for the heat in the room. *He was dead already anyway if he wandered from the west side*, he wanted to add, but didn't. "I apologize for your loss. We will look into it."

The citizens before him start to talk loudly amongst themselves.

"We're permitting live rounds only while the Fulton Street Bridge and gate are down to keep you safe," the Treasurer adds, cuts Sutter off, talking close to the microphone in front of him, and raising his voice to keep the focus on him. "With the excessive heat and temperature affecting the Z-rations, burning off the sedative chemicals in the meat before it can be fully digested, we've decided to approve live rounds to protect our borders."

The council men and women alongside him start to turn and murmur to each other.

Councilman Sutter starts to open his mouth.

Largo cuts him off.

"*And* with the insurgent activity both within the city and without," Largo says as he casts an angry eye at his fellows on either side of him. "It's what I have discussed with Mayor Honeywell and is what we've decided to do in the interim to protect you and the citizens across the river."

The last statement draws bile into his throat. He hates referring to the local undead as if they were truly part of Grand Rapids. Doped into tranquility by the drugged meat byproduct they are fed (at the city's expense), the walking dead still aren't supposed to be here, taking up space, crowding out lands and livelihoods that were beyond their caring now. The land belongs to the living, and

Rupert is damned if he simply continues to watch it go to waste on the lost and wasted.

"Speaking about the insurgent activity, what're you doing about it?" a man asks sitting near the front of the audience, his bright yellow short-sleeved shirt draws the eye like a singular spot light.

Largo opens his mouth to reply, and then thinks better of it. Better to not play *too much* of his hand. "Mr. Mayor, would you care to answer this?" he says instead.

Even tall, gaunt, thinning gray hair Mr. Sutter must agree as he snaps his mouth shut.

The speakers in the room crackle, and then the voice of Mayor Dean Honeywell comes across the meeting room PA.

"First of all, I'd like to express my deepest sympathies to all the citizens and soldiers who have lost friends and family in this horrible attack both on our city and the UCRA. The city council, with the local authorities and the GRCC, have committed to focusing all their attention on investigating and bringing swift justice to the perpetrators both within and outside Grand Rapids City Proper."

The speakers hiss and pop, causing many in the meeting room to jump and wince and don furrowed brows. Largo just smiles, and absently scratches the corner flesh of his patched eye.

"Though I don't believe Loyalist groups have been fully ruled out, all reports appear to concur Reganshire is behind the Fulton Outpost attack and infiltration of the UCRA," the mayor continues. "For what reasons we do not know, nor fully understand…"

You haven't been listening then, Largo thinks. *They want what everyone else wants: freedom to do what they want and need to do to survive without having to depend on paying a premium for something they shouldn't have to pay for.* His eye scans across the GRCC soldiers lining the walls.

"…but we will get to the bottom of it. Mr. Largo will be contacting Reganshire and Mr. Regan today and try to understand

and smooth things out," the mayor says against the static. "But I can assure you, we will tolerate no further attacks upon any of our citizens. We will avoid all out war at all costs as I don't believe the outcome would deem good for us, them or West Michigan.

"Upon my return to Grand Rapids tomorrow, I assure you, I'll take very stern measures to protect our well-being and livelihood," Honeywell concludes.

In the audience, someone coughs: "Bullshit."

Largo fights a retaliatory smile and nods.

"What about this GRCC officer who appears to have gone rogue and killed a bunch of people?" Yellow Shirt asks.

Largo notices the busty female driver from Captain Billet's crew double up her fists and be quickly restrained by her two other crew mates. He casts a sideways look at the current GRCC commander, Colonel Lee Jackson. He smiles inside seeing the sour reaction scrolled across the man's face.

The Treasurer lets Sutter answer.

"All we know is that Captain Jacob Billet left the hospital. He was in a coma, and somehow, miraculously, snapped out of it, and appears to be somewhat addled because of it," the senior councilman says. "But I'll let Colonel Jackson comment further on that subject. Colonel?"

Oh, how the city's heroes had fallen. Largo grins.

The Huron's driver glares at Sutter, bearing an angry scowl and clenched teeth.

Largo steps back as Jackson rises from his chair. Jackson is taller than him but seems to droop, shoulders heavy with burden and concern. He runs a scar-laced, calloused hand upon his blond, close-to-the-scalp shorn hair, more silvery on the sides. His thick fingers rub at his temples. Bags under his otherwise shimmering blue eyes, he looks from the Treasurer to the audience before him. He inhales deeply. It does nothing to bring him fully upright. He exhales. The breath catches in his throat and he coughs.

Murmurs come from the crowd. "He doesn't look so good either." "Is he Turning too?"

Jackson hears, frowns deeper.

Usually a calm man and short worded, he can't help but lose one of his traits under current circumstances. Things have gone to hell in a hand basket, moreso as the incessant heat seems to have cooked the sense out of people's better nature. Sure, things have always run bumpy, he reflects. Considering the military has been there to help, Jackson cannot say he doesn't feel the same way a good majority of the Grand Rapids citizens feel about the GRCC: time to pull up stakes and get the hell out, leave the place to fend for itself. It is very tempting with all the finger pointing and ugly talk; "The military is doing nothing but policing us more and more, overseeing more of the city's functions." "The GRCC rolls through our streets and neighboring villages asserting their strength through their superior fire power."

Well, no shit, Jackson thinks. Grand Rapids is the biggest city remaining in lower Michigan. Canada teeter totters if it made the right move incorporating Detroit as part of Windsor; Michigan's at-one-time largest city still remains a sprawling ghost town. Lansing is still the capital, but he suspects it'll be only a matter of time before the governor relocates to the river city. After the Outbreak, everyone wanted the jewel of West Michigan viable and protected, the police force hadn't remained large enough in the aftermath so the National Guard had been called in, and then all various armed service units.

The city wants protection but it doesn't. It doesn't want the zombie populace on the other side of the river meandering into their midst, but shooting one or a dozen to save your skin is a crime. He has to hold his men and women accountable for every action they pursue within and outside the city. They risk their lives, and in some cases—as his thoughts meander to the goings on at the Butterworth Test Facility—risk their unlives for Grand Rapids and her neighboring towns and villages.

"Colonel?" the City Treasurer pulls Jackson from his thoughts. And now this event with one of his officers.

"From the reports we've acquired, the captain of the HTV Huron did come out of his coma. Reports are he left the hospital around the time the power went out when the outpost was compromised," Largo says, not looking at anyone specific in the audience but briefly glances to the remaining crew members of the aforementioned heavy transport. "It appears he attacked two civilians, and then three soldiers who were patrolling the UCRA enclosure. He then entered the enclosure itself."

"Killed them," someone seated in the crowd says.

"Yes, murdered them. Brutally from what we hear," Yellow Shirt responds. "What are you doing about this? How can we comfortably sleep at night knowing there's a rogue soldier who can walk in and out of the city as easily as me getting up and walking out of this room?"

There's commotion along the wall where Jackson's other HTV commander stands with the Huron crew. The captain of the Ontario clasps Lance Corporal Loutonia Phelps by the shoulders, talks in whispered but sharp tones, the woman scowls, grits her teeth and shakes her head. Jackson hears the driver hiss, "This is bullshit," then pushes her way by Captain Frank Forrester. She leaves the room.

"Well, what're you going to do about this?" Yellow Shirt says looking to the colonel, and then to the City Treasurer. "Colonel Jackson? Mayor...er, I mean... Treasurer Largo."

Largo frowns, his one eye squints with malicious intent at the man.

The colonel rubs at his face. "We're working on apprehending Captain Billet before he or anyone else comes to harm."

A flurry of other questions storms towards Jackson from the audience; people asking about the GRCC position on the insurgents, the Fulton Outpost incident, guarding of Grand Rapids, protection of the local industries, especially the meat processing plants, and Reganshire.

Jackson stands, nods at Largo, and leaves the meeting room through a side door.

Forrester, Stokes and Mulholland, and a few other GRCC soldiers exit also.

Largo steps to the podium again.

"We'll provide further updates on your questions and concerns as we ourselves acquire them," he takes up his pad with his notes on it. "I plan on taking an excursion out to Reganshire this afternoon to discuss the attacks on our city with Silas Regan and his daughter…"

"Looney," Yellow Shirt says with a grin. No one laughs.

"Mister Mayor, do you have anything else?" the Treasurer asks.

"No, Mister Largo, but please contact me after the meeting," Honeywell says against a pop and crackle of static.

"Meeting adjourned," Rupert Largo announces and shuts off the microphone. He leaves through the same door the Colonel exited and proceeds by Sutter and the other councilman, several GRCC soldier guards, including Tomes.

***

The last councilman leaves the Treasurer's office after a heated discussion regarding Largo taking on too much responsibility while the mayor is away.

"You'll talk to Honeywell about what you should be doing, yes?"

"Of course. I appreciate and respect you for your input, Leon," Largo says sitting behind his desk, hands clasped before him.

"Thanks for hearing me out," Sutter offers his hand.

"I need to call the mayor," Largo says lifting his desk phone without moving to accept the gesture.

The elder councilman looks at his hand, then at the Treasurer, not sure if he'd been outright snubbed or if the man is simply so busy—that responsibility thing. He turns and leaves the office without another word.

Tomes steps in through a side door.

"All transmission lines going down?" Largo asks Tomes, hanging up the phone.

"Men are already on it. Will have nothing but direct radio transmission in about ten minutes," Tomes answers. He wants to say the job would be done better than what Largo's little army of Loyalists had tried to pull off in April, but decides not to.

"Do me a favor, will you, Lieutenant?"

"Yes, sir."

"When you pay our friend in that disgusting yellow shirt his money," Largo says picking up the phone again, "kill him, and go ahead and keep the money for yourself. And my friend, Councilman Sutter who just left," he punches in the number Honeywell had given him to call him in Muskegon. "I think he needs a lesson in how not to speak to his superiors. Assure him his family will come in harm's way if he doesn't fall into proper rank and file."

"Yes, sir," Tomes says. Yes, that is the reason why he knows better than to chide his current boss.

***

"It's bullshit," Loutonia exclaims. She slams her fist on the plastic folding table next to her. The table rattles like it was hit with a sledgehammer, making the other people in the small 1st floor "GRCC Only" room wince. "It's all bullshit."

Jackson, Forrester, Stokes and Mulholland, and a few other soldiers stand in the small office on the ground floor of the City Admin Building. The room is sound-proof, and bug-proof, cannot be eavesdropped by outside eyes or ears. It is typically used for quick confidential meetings with the GRCC, mayor and city council.

Loutonia continues to rant: "The doctor doesn't have squat other than covering his ass saying no one noticed Jake leave when the power went out. Somebody had to. And then what went on with the guys who got a snag on his name patch. Hell, it could've come off, and they picked it up and ran into trouble and someone offed them."

"The police got fingerprints off the one victim's shoe, of all things. Billet might not have killed the two men, but he definitely had a run-in with them. Unfortunately the prints make him a prime suspect," Jackson says, leaning against the cool office wall across from Loutonia. "And with the current attitude towards us, that info disclosed to the masses doesn't help our cause."

Forrester sits in a chair next to the colonel. He rubs at his temples.

"And that's bullshit too," Loutonia blasts. "With all the things we've done and all the sacrifices we've made for the city, they take this one, as far as I'm concerned, unconfirmed incident and want to lynch the man who helped save them from one big threat, and now they don't care?" Loutonia paces the floor with hands on her hips.

Stokes watches her backside. Mulholland elbows him to shake him out of it.

"So we're supposed to go on a witch hunt and bring him in gagged and bound?" she says, turns her angry, frustrated gaze on Jackson.

Forrester speaks up. "It's better we do it than some wayward citizen trying to bring him in. If Jake is wandering around slightly unhinged from his coma, I wouldn't want any more casualties reported and him still on the loose. And with these Reganshire insurgents or Lettner Loyalists, whoever they are, I'd rather snatch him up versus him running afoul of any of those types. I don't see anything about him being armed. The grunts assaulted at the enclosure were shot but had their weapons still, and I don't know where Jake would've got his hands on a nine millimeter going from the hospital to the enclosure."

"If the Captain is looking to gear up, I'd assume he'd go straight to one of the safe houses," Mulholland adds, glances at a street map layout of the city and the west side of town hanging on the wall beside him. He traces his finger along the suspected route of his wayward CO. "If he went in somewhere near Bridge Street, the closest safe house is on Jackson Street."

"I'll call Largo and inform him we're sending a special team out into the UCRA to search for Billet," Jackson says, placing his hand on the land line phone. He lifts the receiver to his ear, pressing the office extension of the City Treasurer above. He holds the handset out before him. He looks at it as if he held a dead rat.

"Colonel?" Forrester asks, seeing Jackson's odd expression. The communications radio he wears at his belt crackles. He pulls the wireless earbud from the side of the radio case and stuffs it in his right ear. "Forrester here." He listens intently as someone on the other end of the comm relays a message.

The colonel hangs up the phone.

"Roger that. We're with the colonel now, and will get orders immediately." Forrester replies.

He looks at the crew of the Huron, and then at Colonel Jackson.

"Main lines are done again," Forrester says.

"What the hell?" Loutonia emits.

"Like spring time and the floods," Mulholland says, "But without the water."

Forrester looks at Stokes who sits in a chair, chewing the stump of a cigar. The sergeant sits with his thick hair arms folded across his chest and a scowl on his face.

"I'm going directly to Largo," Jackson says, getting to his feet. "Helluva time to have communication lines down."

"What's eating you, James?" Forrester asks the squat gunner.

"He's peeved because once we pick up Billet his time as Huron's commander is over," Mulholland cut in before Stokes can open his mouth.

"Shut up, Corporal," Stokes says like a kid caught with a secret and not wanting his parents to know.

Forrester humphs. "Sergeant, let's get a move on. I'm sure your captain can't be having a good time out there in his current state. Probably wandering about disoriented, regretting he left that hospital bed."

***

Leaning with back against door, Jake rubs his eyes and squints against the glaring sunlight coming through the window. He looks around his surroundings. His cobweb thoughts slowly clear. He sits in an old office on the upper floor of the old Old Kent Bank building at the corner of Bridge Street and Stocking Avenue. Dust motes sparkle like stars on the beams of sunlight coming through the crudely boarded windows. The air smells of moldy wood. He feels shaky, remembers the night before, entering the enclosure. He recalls the patrolling Gurks. Nothing like saying: "Hey! Follow me this way."

He tests his leg strength by climbing to them, using the door behind him as a prop. Like a newborn fawn, he wobbles a bit getting upright.

"Managed to make it this far. Four black last night before going spaghetti noodle," he says to himself.

Pushing with all his might, he stands. He grumbles. It is like his brain has switched off the signal to his lower body. He teeters like the UCRA civilians. Not good.

He looks around the old office, avoids the irritating sun beams. Luckily he found an open door and a secure place above ground before his body finally decided to crap out on him for the night. Avoiding the undead citizens wandering the streets, he didn't want to take any chances, unarmed and unprotected as he was in his Class A uniform.

Safe house, or the West Side Apostolate for a change of clothes and a weapon, or three, Jake decides.

Feeling the heat of the day seeping into the room, he pushes off from the door and moves to the outside hallway. No sunlight makes the corridor dark and dreary; he feels strength return and walks to the staircase. He blinks and jerks, startled, as the place is suddenly busy with bank tellers and office staff arriving for work. He blinks, back to dusty, dim old bank. A single female resident in a baggy, moth-eaten uniform, shambles by the bottom of the stairway. She pays no attention to him.

Fucked up. I'm really fucked up, Jake thinks.

He grips the stair rail and slowly, with wobbly legs, makes his way down.

The angry glare from the large windows on the main floor make his head hurt. Boards gone, extreme sunlight floods the place. He squints, turns away until his eyes adjust. Even then, there is an annoying flaring aura around everything, and staring directly forward, things have a fuzzy pastel patina to them.

His stomach grumbles as he reaches the dual glass front doors.

Behind him, there is the sound of shuffling paper and groaning. The rotting female resident stands behind one of the teller windows. She adjusts the name tag on her blouse with skeletal digits. The badge still hangs akimbo at her sagging pocket. *Does she think she's still at work?*

A sickly undead man passes along the front of the building. Jake has a sudden urge to run out and tear him limb from limb. Even behind the glass, he can smell him. The passerby smells of baked, rotting meat; a nostril-crinkling sulfurous scent. With the summer heat, Jake can understand why.

Jake watches the man as he passes and teeters beyond the building, heading towards the intersection at Bridge and Stocking.

"What… the…?" he says aloud, his voice hoarse and straining. He clears his throat as he slowly creeps from the confines of the bank building.

"Have a sparkly day," a female voice says behind him. He looks at the ragtag teller. Her head droops on weak neck muscles. Lower jaw hanging open, she drools upon herself a thick red-yellow intestinal syrup.

Jake nods his head at her.

She doesn't respond.

"Fucked up," he rasps lowly.

The undead, sagging carcass of a thing that has just walked by him now is dressed in a clean, light-weight short-sleeved shirt like he'd be wearing on days like these. The undead civilian glances over his shoulder and waves at someone across the street. Jake looks across the street seeing a man in khaki work clothes and a bright orange safety vest wave back at him with his free hand; his other hand holds a gleaming metal lunch box.

Jake begins to tremble as he looks up and down the street.

Cars and trucks and horse drawn wagons fill the intersection.

The buildings all around stand proud and freshly painted.

People draw in and out of the storefronts and factory buildings, getting on with their daily grind.

There is not an undead local in sight.

"Yeah, now this is kind of messed up, isn't it?" Lettner says, appears by Jake's side and pats him on the back. The Muskegon man wears a business suit and a brown 1950's fedora on his head.

A 1962 Sky Blue Buick Invicta rumbles by, heading west along Bridge Street. Behind the steering wheel: Jake's father, dead from prostate cancer since 2004, looks alive and well just as Jake remembers him. Billet Senior waves at Jake as he drives by.

"Come on, boy. Gotta keep moving forward," the man calls out as he draws his arm back inside the car window.

In the back seat of the huge old car, Jenna and a teen-aged

Joey sit; though, they don't appear to see Jake.

"You know what this means," Lettner chuckles as if stating a fact Jake should know.

Jake knows. He knows.

He doubles over, hands on the bank building's warm red bricks, and dry heaves until it feels his gut and intestines will spill from his mouth.

Chapter Six

Nearly 2,000 years ago, the Mound Builders flourished in the Grand River Valley. Each summer, these early people would gather on the west side of the river to fish, hunt and plant crops—and construct large earth mounds to honor and bury their dead.

Native American tribes, in more recent times of only a few hundred years ago, made their home and livelihood along the river. Like the Mound Builders long before them, these simpler people built their villages on the banks of the rolling rapids of the river they called Owashtanong, the "Far-flowing river."

Things changed for the People of the Rapids when the United States government acquired land in Michigan, south of the river, and opened it for settlement. A missionary and a fur trader established the first non-native settlement in 1825. The settlement grew into a village; the village grew into a small and bustling city. Louis Campau, the surly fur trader, and Lucius Lyon, another land owner who had moved to the area after a role as a U.S. Senator, were well known for their heated battles over their land plats established in the downtown area.

Why Billet looks upon the two men standing at a modern day street corner wagging fingers at each other, debating who could cross whose property and where, twists his mind. He wants to turn around and head back to the city proper. If rooms in the Spectrum Hill Hospital psychiatric ward are dark and air conditioned, it is tempting.

"You're almost like Bob," Lettner says, standing beside Billet. He wears period clothing like the two squabbling early Grand Rapids men. A black wool frock coat hugging his heavy frame, Lettner smiles at Jake like he knows some grave secret. Campau wears the same style outfit while Lyon wore a more regal Regency Tailcoat, also black, trimmed in black velvet. The heavy garments, incredibly hot in the heat, do not appear to draw any noticeable bead of perspiration from the three men.

Because they aren't actually here, Jake tells himself. He moves towards the street corner. The glaring sunlight makes him squint and his head throb.

A 1950's Black Coronet stops at the red traffic light on the south corner of Bridge and Lexington. It's big block 350 Hemi engine rumbles loudly, though it does not disturb the horse-drawn wagon waiting at the intersection beside it. Wood barrels fill the wagon. Emblazoned on the side of the wagon *Kusterer Brewing Co* stands out in boldly painted white letters.

The traffic light turns green. The Coronet roars off through the intersection, turning left onto Bridge Street. The driver at the reins of the horse-drawn beer wagon pumps a fist in the air after the car as he too turns his vehicle left, snapping his horses into a trot.

"The satellite zombs have their signal a lot more refined, dialed in, if you will," Lettner comments as they approach the street corner. They stand next to the still bickering Campau and Lyon. "But with time, I'm sure you can do the same and be a viable asset in a dead state of things."

A group of long haired young people, female and male alike, walk along the sidewalk across the street. They stop to share a smoke of a long white twisted cigarette. One of them holds a sign under their arm that reads: SAVE CITY HALL.

Jake knows he isn't long for the world of the living. He suspected it almost the moment he awakened in the hospital bed, knew his brain was warped and heading down the wrong path, especially when Lettner sat in his hospital room. He knew he was dying, if perhaps not already dead. It is a well-known fact, bizarre as it was, the UCRA civilians lived their unlife as they did in life. The chemicals in the doped meat they were fed, calming the usual killing rage, somehow brought things into perspective enough in their rotting brains to fire failing synapses, bringing memories of their former glory, ambitions and livelihoods to the forefront.

A parade materializes at the intersection and moves westward along Bridge Street. A high school marching band, in West Union green, red and white colors, Billet's old school, plays John Phillips Sousa's *76 Trombones*.

A banner flutters along the undercarriage of the rolling conductors wagon. Jake reads it. Groans. THE HERO OF GRAND RAPIDS.

There wasn't an actual parade for him when he and his crew returned to the city from taking the late William Lettner to meet his fate. The covert mission details had been leaked to news agencies, supposedly by someone in Grand Rapids own administrative office. It started a whole new big, bad, rolling ball of shit.

"No hero," Billet grumbles under his breath. "No hero at all. Following orders. Just doing our job."

He looks at the people seated on the float. He isn't surprised to see Jenna and Joey seated amongst the phantasmal images of Mayor Honeywell, Rupert Largo, Colonel Jackson and the crew of the Huron. His late navigator, Nate Parsons, even sits amongst the group. Loutonia is seated next to Jenna, both dressed in red and white gowns. Christmas? No. Pulaski Days.

Jake feels uneasy looking upon the two women, one his lost love, one his current.

"No shit *no hero*," Louis Campau snaps at Jake, sneering with an upturned lip. "You've brought chaos to this city. Assured death to all. Now, how I feel for Mr. Lyon here…"

Lyon cast his fellow a questionable glance.

A big gun booms from down the street.

Lyons head explodes.

"Shit." Jake runs across the street, in the opposite direction of the gun fire. The gun blast and UCRA civilian with its head missing brings him back to reality.

A liquor store on the southwest corner of the intersection offers its protection. Jake launches himself half-assed through the large, broken storefront window.

Another report from the gun. The sidewalk erupts in a spray of chipped concrete where his foot had just been.

He comes down within the store; sharp teeth of window slashes into his thigh, palms stabbed by broken glass on the store's tiled floor. He scrambles on hands and knees, too fast, off balance. He drives his head into the metal ledge of a liquor shelf before going sideways into the wet lap of someone reclined against the fixture.

"Sorry, buddy," Jake says, wrinkling his nose at the intense smell of booze, piss and blood wafting from the undead man he collides with. An island of empty bottles surrounds the fellow whose fleshless mouth opens and closes like a dying fish. If the drunk is trying to repeatedly sauce himself up, the red and gaping throat hole makes a futile joke of it.

Jake shuffles away as another shot rings off the metal shelving. The top shelf clatters down atop the civilian. Several bottles of Johnny Walker Blue Label land in his lap.

"Not good. Not good," Billet says to himself, finding refuge behind a defunct beverage cooler.

Gun report. Chunk of old drywall turns to its original mass of crushed gypsum.

Big gun, .50 Caliber, sniper rifle. *Either got some wayward shooter inside the enclosure,* Billet surmises, *or our friendly neighborhood civvies are turning marksmen.*

More gun fire, this time short, quick, three-bark pops. Semi-auto. Military issue M4's. "Some of ours?" Jake says as he soldier-crawls towards the rear door of the small shop.

Through the dirty and spider-webbed glass, three soldiers make their way up-street, leapfrogging behind cover, one at a time, one lays down suppressing cover fire for his brethren to advance safely.

Billet cracks the door open a hair, enough to get a hand out. He throws droplets of blood from his glass-embedded hand as he signals them.

And realizes he might be waving at the wrong guys.

One of the oncoming soldiers stops, squats behind the protection of a rusted automobile and scopes Jake.

Jake drops back inside the store as the glass and aluminum door frame thrums and pops against the assault of machine gun fire.

"Not ours," Jake curses, shielding his face as more bullets pound the glass. The pane shatters inward. Uniforms different; darker camo pattern. Ballistic helmets; smaller communications headset. No GRCC organizational flashes or insignia anywhere on person.

Shooter with high powered rifle the same as the grunts coming down the street? Maybe. Both gunning for him? Fucking definitely.

Billet peers around the shattered door to check the position of the trio closing on his rear. The big gun barks from the other side of the storefront, still from a Bridge Street-side building. The front man of the three—mercenary, Loyalist, Reganshire insurgent, Gurk-gone-rogue, whomever—takes the shot in the face, *hard*. The strike lifts the guy off his feet, arching backwards before doing a cranium plant on the asphalt. Dead before take-off and crash.

Big Gunner's got his own agenda, Billet nods. *Both appear to be me.*

"You gonna just stand there and wait for one of them to take you from this world?" Lettner says, now in the place of the in-store drunken zomb. He raises a bottle of Johnny Blue Label by a shredded, finger-bone hand. Still capped, nothing comes out as the bottle awkwardly tips towards chin.

Keeping low, Jake shuffles back towards the drunk. "Here ya go, buddy," he says, squatting before the man. He ignores another round from the sharpshooter as it hammers the wall and drops more plaster atop of them. Taking the bottle from the decrepit hand, he twists off the cap, winces, feels the bite of the glass shards scissoring into nerve endings. Jake takes a pull from the bottle, feels the smooth burn, comforted by the sensation and response of the alcohol. He shivers as the Scotch whiskey hits his gut. He feels… alive.

He gives the open bottle of expansive booze to the zomb who has regained the deteriorated visage which is *not* the late Muskegon regent. The citizen burbles something and tips the bottle; the contents chug all over its sagging chest.

Another round from the sniper rifle implodes one of the glass doors to the walk-in cooler along the store's west wall. Billet notices a light within though not electrical in origin. A gaping hole, big enough to crawl through, opens from the interior of the cooler to the old Kale's Tavern next door. He sees another hole that connects the drinking establishment to a defunct theater building and small urban apartment complex, and the old Kroger Food Store on the far corner of the block.

"Can't go out the way I came in," Jake says aloud. "And not going out the rear door."

Pushing through and stumbling over empty, crushed and smashed beer cans and bottles, he heads into the beer cooler and into the bar. A few more civilians cluster around inside, some sit at the dusty bar, some in booths, some on the floor. Two rot-face men, one chunky but missing huge sections of his midsection, and the other a skeleton with a flesh coating, sit at one corner of the bar. They peer up at a broken television monitor. They both slowly raise their arms and moan loudly. Billet almost stops in his tracks thinking he actually understands one of them as it exclaims: "Go Tigers!"

A saggy barkeep rubs a non-existent bar rag upon the debris strewn bar top. Only the stump of his arm makes the circular motion. His head seems too heavy for his neck; it rests at an angle on his shoulder. Fogged, rheumy eyes follow Jake as he passes.

"Stop for a drink. Make some new friends," Jake hears Lettner say.

He stops for a breath at the lip of the hole in the wall leading to the next building. Lettner stands as the bar keep, fully formed, scrubbing the polished wood bartop as a fat guy and his skinny buddy pump their fists at a Detroit Tigers game blaring on the television.

"You're gonna need friends if you plan on staying," Lettner says with a shit-eating grin.

Jake knows what he means. Still…

"I don't plan on it," he answers.

He takes a step back into the bar, steps up to Lettner.

With a snarl, he punches the barkeep in the face. The man topples, head pulverized. The scene returns to "normal." Red glop and bone fragments drip from Billet's fist. He feels a wave of killing anger rise, feels like ravaging all the undead civvies in the room. Tear their heads off. Rip their limbs off. Gnaw on their bones of rotted meat.

Gun fire snaps him back to his senses. He ducks into the hole in the wall.

***

"Head One, this is Tentacle Nine-Oh. We've lost visuals on the Rogue. Continue to be fired upon by L-Dog. Over." Another shot from a building on the north side of Bridge Street. The hood of the rusted car pops with a loud metallic thwack. The soldier clutches his M4 close to chest, and hunkers down lower behind his cover. "Fuckin' ay," he says though not over the comm.

Static, then: "This is Head One. Again. Do not engage the L-Dog."

Easy for him to say, thinks the mercenary. One of his team lays dead with his head blown off, and he and his partner under hard cover to avoid receipt of the same. He won't say it aloud, but he wonders when his boss would be sticking his neck out instead of sitting pretty with their client.

"Keep your eyes on the Rogue, Nine-Oh. Feel free to take your anger out on him if you get the shot," the radio crackles. "Just make sure you leave the usual calling card."

The merc looks down at the puffy pants pocket of his camos. Paraphernalia from the village west of Grand Rapids, Reganshire, fills the pouch.

"Ten-four, Head One," Nine-Oh replies.

"Nine-Oh, heads up. Operation Open Test is underway. You're free to engage if you run afoul of any of its inmates."

Thanks a fuck of a lot, Commander Tomes, Nine-Oh wants to say. The crazy undead asshole with the big gun is enough of a problem. Soon they will be running up against more rotting gunmen. He isn't sure if he's being paid enough for all this crazy shit.

"Fresh SitRep at 01100," Head One says. "Over and out."

"Roger that. Out."

Another bullet spacks off the pavement from the lone gunman down the street.

"Stay down, Rodriguez. Jesus H. I don't want to be running around here by my lone self," Nine-Oh says to the other merc across the street behind an old pickup truck.

Rodriguez shrugs, gives him a single nod and thumbs up,

understanding the transmission he also heard.

Nine-Oh counts off with hand raised enough for his partner to see. One. Two. Three.

The mercenaries rise simultaneously. Rodriguez fires towards the gunman. Nine-Oh hoofs it as fast and hard as he can across the street. He dives for the street's western side, finds cover of a house on the corner of Chatham and Lexington.

Rodriguez runs across without as much as a chunk of sidewalk spraying him in the face.

"Where're we going, Kincade?"

"We're following the Rogue," Nine-Oh, Kincade replies, waits for a moment. No further shots are fired from Largo's undead gunman. He looks at their third partner who lies by the curbside, head like a mashed tomato from the sniper's bullet. "We're going hunting for our own kill."

***

Jake sits under a tree on the corner of Chatham and National. His knees pulled up to his chest. His hands clasped to the side of his head. His eyes dart up and down the old neighborhood street. The safe house he aims for is just down the corner on Jackson Street. Cutting through some yards, he can be there in less than five minutes.

He can't move.

Up and down the street, everywhere he looks, something is going on but not in his time; the horse-drawn milk wagon rumbling along cobblestone; men in derby hats walking their lacey dressed ladies under lazily spinning parasols. Early 1900's.

A movement of eye brings a change of total scenery. Big black Buicks. Real American steel. Depression era. People in rags.

But then from the periphery, the people are in rags. They are the UCRA civilians, bodies worn threadbare as well as their clothing; unless they stumble into the arms of Sister Mirose's flock and into the West Side Apostolate.

"Hey, mister. You look like you could use some lemonade."

Jake looks up. A dirty faced kid stands before a rough built wood table.

The boy couldn't have been there before.

"I'm… all right, kid," Jake replies.

With his left hand, the kid holds a plastic cup. It is then Jake notices the right side of the boy's face is mashed flat, nothing but chewed and ripped flesh. Exposed skull bone shows where the flesh has been all stripped away, but even that looks broken and mangled.

The boy's right arm is bent at the wrong angle; elbow on the wrong side. His right leg amiss below the knee. He holds himself upright by leaning on the lemonade stand.

The boy's non-obliterated side changes between a ruddy face kid and the rotting thing he really is.

"You sell here often?" Jake asks the boy.

"Usually. I've tried going across the street to the other corner where it seems they have more traffic," the boy says as a big refuse truck rumbles by, going much too fast through the quiet residential street. "But my folks don't like me crossing the street."

Goddammit. Goddammit. Jake wants to scratch his eyes out. If he had a pistol, he'd blow his brains out. Insanity. Death. That's all there is for him, around him.

He feels the red rage grow. Hatred. Death. Tear. Shred.

Feast.

The Sky Blue Invicta rolls down the street. CCR plays on the radio. Billet sees a young version of his father and mother. His father in his army greens.

Jake looks away only to catch the gleam of the chrome bumper. It is like a sharp spear through the eye, but it snaps him out of his funk.

Getting to his feet, he starts away.

"Thanks, kid. I'll have to pass," he says as the boy follows him with the empty cup held out. There is liquid in the glass, looks like piss with a dollop something red mixed in it. "Stay out of the street."

The undead boy gives Jake a broken smile. Red pieces of meat drip off his contorted face.

Around the corner, the safe house. Change of clothes. Weapons and C-Rations. And something to quell his gnawing gut, both physically and psychologically. Something to feed the red rage he feels ready to consume him.

***

"Dammit, man. Do you think he saw us?" Rodriguez says, squatting, leans against the back end of a pick-up truck whose tires had long since gone flat. He watches two undead walking along the sidewalk. They see him and his companion, sniff the air, and continue walk-tottering ahead.

Moving eye from scope and lowering his M4, Kincade slings the carbine round his shoulder and reaches for the 9mm holstered at his side. "No. He's too busy talking to the dead kid on the corner over there." The mercenary replies, rubbing the back of his Gore-Tex-enmeshed hand across his sweaty forehead. "Definitely heading towards the safe house."

"It's cool though," he continues. "I've got the door lock code. The place will give us our own safe house should we need it in the days ahead."

"I'd rather be hooked up with the rest of the team when they let those undead soldiers loose," Rodriguez says as he did the same as Kincade; pulls his suppressed 9mm and holds it firmly in hand. His M4 already rests over shoulder but is in position to be retrieved quickly if needed. "That shit freaks me out."

They run up, Kincade leads. They easily reach the two undead civilians who had passed moments ago. Kincade chuckles as he presses the barrel of his pistol to one's head, pulls the trigger. What was left of the creatures decaying brain gushes out the front of its rotting cranium. Before it falls, he gives it a partner, doing the same to its walking mate.

Rodriguez laughs.

Another shambler comes out from between the houses as the mercenaries near the corner. A ragtag woman holds a dog leash. Something that looks like a mink scarf, collared and attached to the leash, drags behind her.

Rodriguez pops her as they run by.

They cross the street, keeping in the shadows of trees and protection of abandoned cars, wary of the man they follow in case he doubled back for some reason.

The rotting kid on the corner lifts his hand towards the two men as they near. His mouth moves, black tongue flops against loose teeth and red-black gums.

Kincade strikes the youth across the side of the head, sloughs off a large patch of loose scalp. The kid staggers, drops the dirty plastic cup full of piss and blood. The boy turns its foggy eyes upon the man who struck him, emitting a mewling sound with an expression of pain.

Rodriguez sees the boy's expression. "Oh shit, man."

Kincade's silenced pistol huffs.

A bloodless hole appears in the boy's forehead and he drops.

"Quit being a pussy," Kincade says as they move on, stopping next to a house whose porch faces Jackson Street. "Kid was already dead, just like the rest of these things in here. They ain't people no more."

Rodriguez doesn't reply.

"I got nothing," Kincade says, peeks around the corner of the house.

They move up cautiously.

The GRCC safe house, one of six within the UCRA enclosure, is a white, two-story home. The ground floor windows and front doors, one leading to the first floor and a second leading to the second floor, are boarded over. The boards look fresh compared to the paint-peeled, weather-worn siding of the house.

Kincade creeps around the side of the house, follows a narrow driveway running between the two story home and a smaller bungalow style one on its west side. He signals Rodriguez with a wave of his hand, and they slide along the side of the house, staying below the first floor window sills. Back steps lead up to a rear door. The security lock lays open, the door akimbo.

"I'm going up," Kincade mouths without words, gestures towards the second floor. "Wait for the All Clear."

Rodriguez nods, knows the routine. He unslings his M4, holds both weapons and scans the area as his companion moves up the steps.

Kincade checks the door, opens it a hair, checks the ascending stairwell. He goes in.

Sweat rolls into his eye as he slowly goes up the carpet-matted wood steps. He keeps close to the wall, away from center lest the wood sags and creaks. He relaxes then reaffirms his grip on his pistol, index finger gently on the trigger.

Gotta be a fucking arsenal of the city's shit up here, he thinks, almost drooling at the thought.

Top of the stairs: a door. Open. Guy isn't too worried about anyone coming up behind him. Dumb fuck.

Kincade slides through the door, back against the wall.

Something stirs around the corner in the first room. The sound of heavy tin cans hitting the floor, lids peeling open. Grunting, soft swearing.

Kincade swings around the corner, 9 millimeter leveled out before him.

Jake looks up but doesn't seem to focus. He sits on the floor amidst a small pile of white labeled cans. The can he holds is open, the index and middle finger stuffed inside and rising out of it with a large drooling dollop of rust brown meat slop. Smeared about his mouth is more of the same meaty gruel. He grunts and groans as he swallows hard, smacking his messy lips as he does.

The label on the can reads: Z-Ration.

"You sick fuck." Kincade snarls, raises the pistol at the soldier in the dirty Class A uniform slurping on food meant for the dead.

Jake suddenly becomes aware, eyes drop to the deadly end of the 9mm. His hand drops with the meat can.

The mercenary pulls the trigger.

Chapter Seven

A Blast Resistant Vehicle-Off Road, a Humvee-replacement on steroids, leads the way, rolling west along Fulton Street. Behind it, a secondary light tactical vehicle follows, then the HTV Ridgerunner-Class Huron. An old M60 Patton growls along in the Huron's path, while coming up on its rear another pair of BRV-O run single file as did the rest of the formation. Re-erected and fortified by a double wall of chain link fencing, the West Fulton UCRA enclosure gate shrinks into the distance as the patrol convoy moves forward.

"I've got nothing but civvies going about their day," the lead vehicle reports over the short wave radio. "No unusual activity. No one appears remotely agitated at our presence or the presence of anyone else."

"Ten-four, Michael-One. Nothing on our six. Peaceful and cool temperatures," the rear vehicle responds. With sarcasm.

"I'd give a year's pay to the rain gods if they'd hose this joint down," another grunt from the rearmost BRV says over the comm.

The road and sidewalks ripple under the heat haze. The local citizens hobble and teeter like tattered ghosts. The hot asphalt sucks at the tread of rubber tire and track.

"Hey, Noob, if you aren't from around here, welcome to our wonderful Michigan seasons," Michael One responds back.

"I got full open ports to keep my cargo from sweatin' and smellin' too much more."

"Thanks, Corporal. We appreciate the sentiment," another voice from the Huron replies. Lance Corporal Loutonia Phelps. A few other responses can be heard behind the main, mostly rosy expletives telling the transport driver where she can go.

"Sorry, Lieutenant. One of your boys didn't wear deodorant today," she responds.

"Let's cut the chatter, people." Stokes says, standing in his gunner's cupola. His helmet sits a few inches taller on his head, resting on a wrap of cloth standing in as a makeshift dew rag.

"Stay frosty, people." the voice of the M60 commander says, his already low, gravelly voice sounds rubbed by sandpaper through the short wave static.

"Roger that, Grizzly," yet another voice answers, Michael Two, from the second LTV.

"This is like our April excursion, just without the inland lakes everywhere," Stokes says over the Huron's closed channel system.

"Rather have the water than this heat," Loutonia glances at the soldier sitting next to her. He sits in the empty navigator's seat, rounding out the squad packed into the transport to eighteen. Seventeen hot, sweaty men.

Succumbed to the odor, the pine tree air freshener above her head is curled like a dead dry leaf.

The temperature inside the Huron was a balmy 80. Outside, much hotter. Another 14 degrees hotter.

Loutonia makes a mental note to fix the vehicle's A/C when they return; as long as they don't get thrust back out on the road.

With Jake being in the hospital, she paid little attention to extra maintenance of the Huron. When she hadn't been at his side, she'd been on duty: feed runs, excursions to the towns and villages outside Grand Rapids, rail line checks, city patrols. It hadn't left much time for her to do anything major on the vehicle other than general maintenance.

She can't believe what is going on now. Jake just up and

supposedly walks out of the hospital, and straight into the UCRA. What the hell was he thinking? What is he doing?

She will not believe the reports of him, in cold-blood, killing two city civilians or the soldiers on patrol the night before when everything else was going down. It isn't like him to lose control like that; well, wasn't much like him to do such things before the Lettner mission. THAT had changed him, she had to admit. Mulholland had brought it up first, and she hadn't seen it. Too close to him. But she knew, though Jake said otherwise, taking the mission with the man responsible for the murder of his family might have been the straw atop the camel's back.

But... There are a lot of things now pressing upon her conscience; this push for more support for the city by the City Treasurer, and Mayor Honeywell's excursions. Hell, she isn't sure but she thinks Rupert Largo might be swaying her to his view of things. Where is the mayor when all this crazy shit is going on? Honeywell seems more intent on maintaining the well-being of his Muskegon connections than the pot of chaos boiling and bubbling over on his city streets. What good would the open rail lines and freer trade lines matter if Grand Rapids collapses?

Are these city attacks the anti-zombie Loyalists again, or just a bunch of angry Grand Rapidians taking up arms? Or are these thugs they are hunting in the UCRA from Reganshire? What is the point if it is so? Silas Regan has always wanted more opportunities to be self-sustained and not dependent on the big city. But by calling a war down upon his head...

Loutonia shakes her head. It doesn't make much sense.

"Crazy times. Always crazy times," she says under her breath.

"Michael Two to all vehicles," the comm crackles. "We just intercepted a garbled message from the Butterworth Test Facility. We think it was Felder. We only got a few words." There is a long pause. "We think the BTF is under attack."

"We're going to try to send an emergency message back to

base, but we better head over there."

"Michael One is Oscar Mike."

"Grizzly concurs."

"Water Boy concurs."

Stokes's voice comes over the comm and behind Loutonia. "Huron concurs."

Michael Three and Four, the rear BRVs, call in their agreement to head towards the BTF.

"This week just keeps getting better and better," Stokes says, leaning his head into the cab. A stump of a cigar hangs from the corner of his mouth. Smoke curls in the air.

"Sit down and strap in," she says, one hand on the steering yoke and the other waving away the smelly cigar smoke.

"Anxious, Brannski?" Loutonia asks the soldier seated beside her.

"Lanski." the man corrects her. He turns his gaze from the view port in front of him, looks outside onto the city street. "And, no, just usually, um, on foot, doing recon."

She glances down at his crotch, where his snub-nose M4 lay.

"If anything gets in here, you're not going to want to use that," she says, nodding down towards the carbine. "Where're you from anyway? You're one of the new recruits from, where? Indiana?"

He doesn't answer right away, eyes back to looking out on the street, at the ass end of the water truck in front of them. "Yeah," he says. His attention on other things.

"Do you dab your toes in hot sauce and suck on them," Loutonia wants to ask, thinking she'd get the same reply.

She presses a button on the console to her left, checks outside air temp. 94 degrees, and it's not even noon yet.

"You might want to buckle up," she says, noticing the grunt hasn't harnessed himself in.

He looks at her. She can feel his eyes gaze her up and down.

"I don't like being restrained," he says, shifting in the

navigator's seat. "Do you like being... restrained, Corporal?"

"Excuse me?" Loutonia nearly hits the brakes.

He changes the subject, smirking. "Not a lot of these big beasts left, I hear. Kind of a specialty. No groups got these outside of Michigan. Like a wheeled Fort Knox, a rolling battleship if weaponized properly."

She asides his earlier comment, though answers haltingly. "Only five M213's made. Built in Detroit, joint Canadian-U.S. assembly. Only this one and the Ontario left unfortunately. Hard on fuel, but can go pretty much anywhere on the map."

The Huron thumps over something, throws Lanski slightly forward and sideways. She hears Stokes yell from within the cargo/troop area where he, Mulholland, and fourteen other Gurks hold up. He obviously isn't buckled in either.

"I'd buckle up," she reiterates.

He looks out the port again. "Where're we at?"

Loutonia leans over and taps the side of the navigator's HUD. "It'll tell you right there."

The soldier sniffs at her as she pulls away.

Phelps looks at him oddly. "You Turning or something?"

He ignores her, runs his finger along the thick green line going west and the intersecting line going north-south on the HUD monitor. The thick green is Fulton, which they are on. The intersecting street they are crossing: Deloney. They will approach Gunnison before the larger intersection at Lane and Fulton.

"So this is the vehicle which brought that Muskegon High Councilman to his eventual demise," Lanski says.

It is Loutonia's turn to ignore him. Instead, "I noticed you and some others in our convoy are wearing different uniforms." Different camo color. Different patterned ACU's.

"We just decided to wear our colors," he responds. "This rig hard to drive?"

She checks her area map. Drops a hand to chest and checks

her own seat harness.

"Takes a little getting used to. Not much different than driving an APC or AAV," she says. "Why? Are you planning on getting into the driver's seat?"

Out of the corner of her eye she sees the soldier slide his hand across the trigger guard of his M4, index finger starts to loop through it.

The safety clicks off the same instant she cranks the steering yoke a hard ninety.

The 40-inch dual front wheels bounce over the street curb, mashes the front end of a parked car, and clips a yellow fire hydrant. Slamming both feet onto the brake pedal, the Huron snaps to a stop.

Lanski crashes forward, face first into the navigator view port. His head bounces off the hard rubber port seal. He falls sideways into his seat.

"Fuckin' bit..." The dazed man starts, words clipped as the back of Loutonia's balled fist smashes into his face. His nose goes sideways with a crisp cartilage crunch.

Stokes yells, "What the fuck, Phelps!"

The lead BRV explodes.

"We're under attack," Phelps yells back as the comm erupts with chatter.

"What's going on up there? Wait a minute. What are you d..." Michael Four says as if he peers upon something surprising him.

Two sharp pops—pistol fire—and the radio goes dead.

The rear ramp starts to drop as Loutonia comes out of the cab, dragging the man from the navigator seat, his face red with blood.

Stokes leans against one of the steel side ribs of the Huron's interior, holds his head but starts to climb into his cupola. He sees Phelps and the unconscious soldier she drags behind her.

The other Grunts within the Huron are up, clambering

towards the dropping ramp. Mulholland is in the mix, working his way to his rear gunner position.

Something hisses over the street. The BRV behind them lifts off the asphalt in a ball of red-orange flames and black smoke.

The soldiers nearest the Huron's rear ramp fall back like pins hit by a bowling ball.

"Self-Propelled Penetrator Rockets," someone yells over the comm.

Loutonia sees three men step from Michael Four which had pulled off the road and stopped at an angle. The passenger side windscreen is tinted red. The soldiers wear the same color uniform as the man she roughly drops to the steel floor.

"They aren't with us," Loutonia exclaims stepping over her loosed human baggage.

Stokes and Mulholland teeter, stunned.

The three rogue soldiers from Michael Four point their mg's in the Huron's direction.

Loutonia tears the M4 from the hands of one of the fallen men at her feet, and fires through the gap of the partially opened ramp.

"What're you doing, you crazy bitch?" Stokes yells.

Loutonia ignores him, continues to send short bursts out the rear of the Huron. The three soldiers from Michael Four run for cover, two to one side of the street, one to the opposite.

"Compromised within and without," the Grizzly's TC, Lance Breckenridge, says over the comm, as if he'd heard Phelps over the chatter of machine gun fire. "Other tangos comin' in on foot."

"See," Loutonia yells at Stokes, points at the unconscious man at her feet. "See the uniform?"

"Just their get-up from wherever they were originally stationed. We all came on in different colors back in the day," Stokes reasons, trying to rise up through his open hatch. Whizzing bullets overhead keep him from his ascent.

The one man from the destroyed Michael Four runs back across the street to join his buddies. Loutonia fires again. This time a few grunts who'd picked themselves up off the Huron's floor add their muzzle flashes to the barrage. The running man goes herky-jerky. He stumbles, then goes down with several holes perforating his "different color" ACU.

"Would they be attacking us if they were our own men?" Loutonia snarls at Stokes.

The tank cannon roars. Caliber-.50 machine gun follow.

The men inside the Huron's belly pick themselves up. A few are still stunned from the BRV hit and slump in the nearest seat pan. The others open fire on the attackers who seem to have multiplied as the gun play ramped up.

"Where these guys coming from?" the voice of Michael Two says. "Shit!"

Another explosion. Static on radio.

"Michael One's down," Breckenridge, followed by several colorful words of how he felt.

The Grizzly roars again.

Mulholland scampers up into his rear gunner's nest, the only things visible are his legs. The familiar sound of his single .30 dully rings within the Huron.

"We've obviously been infiltrated. Who knows if the rest of them are coming in from other points outside the UCRA," Loutonia says as she looks down at the unconscious man who'd been riding shotgun beside her.

"Gawddamn Reganshire. We should've roasted their ass the minute we thought they were involved," Stokes growls.

"No one knows if it's them, or Loyalists," Loutonia explains as more bullets ping off the Huron. "Hell, the way the factions within the city are fighting, it could be citizens within Grand Rapids herself."

Another rocket hisses overhead. They wait for the impact. For death.

The Huron shakes as a blast booms from the north side of the street.

"SPPR shooter down," Mulholland says over the comm.

And as suddenly as the chaos starts…

…It stops.

"Tangos are oscar mike, heading back to their holes," Breckenridge radios.

"What the fuck?" Stokes says.

Loutonia's baggage rises from the floor. Blood runs from mouth and nose, the soldier staggers upright to his feet. A grenade in left hand, index finger of right through the pin loop. "You're fucked," the man named Lanski growls. "One of the last big transports, huh? Hauled the hero of West Michigan, huh?"

Loutonia backs up, stands beside Stokes. The other men lower their weapons.

"What's this about? Who do you work for? Reganshire? The Loyalists? Someone else?" Stokes blurts out.

Lanski grunts, humored, and grins. "Dead men don't talk I hear, but I ain't saying nothin'."

He backs up to the commander's stand. The light shines through the open portal above.

"You let that thing off in here, and you're as dead as us," Loutonia says, eyes on the hand grenade. She glances around her. There is no cover, not inside their tin can. She notices Mulholland isn't perched in his position any longer. He is gone.

"We're here to open this side of town again. Give it back to the living," Lanski says. "At least that's what my boss wants. I don't really give a shit as long as I get paid."

Everyone gasps when the pin is pulled. Lanski doesn't blink, just uses one hand to retain the explosive and handle; with the other he grabs onto the cupola column and raises a leg to step up.

A shadow falls across the commander's hatch. Something

flashes downward followed by a bone-crunching pop. Lanski stiffens, eyes wide. He collapses to the floor like a ragdoll without its stuffing; convulses a few times, a knife sticking out the top of his skull.

The grenade drops from his dead fingers; handle and body not falling far apart. Loutonia scoops up the explosive, quickly gets the handle back in place. Stokes picks the pin from the Huron's floor. She holds the grenade out. He holds the pin out but does not go to insert it, hand shaking.

"Jeezuz. Nice," Loutonia says, grabs the pin and finagles it back into place.

Exhalations of relief reverberate within the shell of the Huron.

Mulholland hangs his head through the open commander's port. "He down?"

"You almost blew us the fuck up," Stokes swears as the rear gunner spins about and slithers down the hole like a snake.

Loutonia shoves the harmless grenade into his hands. He jostles it like a hot potato before realizing it's safe.

"Blood all over my floor," she says as she grabs an oily rag from under a seat pan. She wraps it about the dead man's head, wipes her bloody hands on his uniform.

The rear ramp drops the rest of the way to the road. The soldiers spill out, fanning out, guns raised.

"Just tryin' ta help," Mulholland, in a small voice.

Loutonia and Stokes glare at him for their own reasons.

"Can I get my knife back at least?"

***

"Central, this is Fulton Patrol. We're rolling towards the BTF," Breckenridge says over the comm. It isn't even noon yet, and the TC sounds worn out, fatigued; voice low and slow like the words float on a molasses river. "Grizzly, Huron, Michael Two and Three online. The men that didn't make it have been… dispatched appropriately and left in a secure location. Sending coordinates now."

42°57'50.0"N 85°41'31.8"W go silently across the air waves.

"Grizzly out."

"Copy that," the voice of Captain Frank Forrester replies. "We're enroute. Jackson's on the horn, wants to talk to you."

Brief radio silence.

"Fulton Patrol…" Full voice, then mouthed away from mike, "Hell with it," before returning to full clear voice, "Commander. Lance. I'm damn sorry for the attack and losses. It wasn't my plan to send you peppered with operatives not of our group." Jackson says, radio crackling with static.

"We've gathered the remaining troops and are checking outposts. No other new hires. Must've all went out last night and with you this morning. Still trying to contact Felder at Butterworth, and our illustrious Treasurer," the colonel responds. "I spoke to Councilman Sutter, and he said Largo has all the paperwork on those new men."

Engine rumble in the background, someone in the convoy with an open mike: "Told you so."

Stokes stands at his quads. Mulholland in the rear. One other grunt stands in the other rear gunner's port, and one in the CO's stand… under the watchful scrutiny of Stokes next to him.

"Largo glommed onto some new Lieutenant when they came in. Nice lookin' guy. Cedric Something," Loutonia says breaking in.

"Captain know you checkin' out other men already," Stokes says over the air.

Loutonia pumps the brakes, reminds him who's boss, throwing the four men above against their individual coamings and causing shouts of dismay amongst the men inside.

"Lieutenant Tomes," Jackson says. "I've got a call to Lansing and Fort Custer to see what Intel I can get on him and the batch of recruits who came with him."

"Still can't raise the BTF or the M45 Outpost," the radioman says to all.

They creep up to the intersection at Fulton and Garfield, a block away from the old John Ball Park Zoo. Loutonia shivers, thinks about the last time they ventured into that place. Invaded and pilfered by the Valley State U. geneticists for their own insane experiments, the zoo itself has been doubly cordoned off, leaving the sprawling park grounds around it a vast, overgrown mess littered with weathered, rotting picnic tables, benches and silent, rusting playground equipment.

"Hold. We got activity ahead," Michael Two radios.

The convoy slows.

Loutonia focuses through her view port.

"Aw no, no. This is way fubar'd, man." Stokes says over the comm.

"Tangos at 10, 11 and 12 o'clock, comin' heavy from the southwest," Michael Two says. "Wait a minute."

Loutonia can see them: a small group of soldiers gathered about the intersection at Valley and Fulton. A pair of old traffic lights lay on one corner amongst the collapsed remnants of a west side home. A soldier armed with an assault rifle, one leg up and resting on the faded yellow traffic signal, points towards the oncoming motorcade. Uniform wrinkled, unkempt and untucked from baggy trousers, he waves the craggy stump of his left arm towards the convoy; the sleeve, shred to the shoulder, flaps with the action. The others in the amassing throng appear confused, looking hither, thither and yon. As he, they snap to when they turn attention on the approaching GRCC as each vehicle blusters loudly under the downshift.

"They-they are ours!"

More of the street corner infantry appear, stumbling through the hodge-podge piling of the house. More assault rifles, pistols, a bayonet or two.

Even from her minimalized view, Phelps sees the confused

expressions change to ones of pure unadulterated anger. Ragged fingers loop through trigger guards. Loose red jowls gnash. Soldiers that should have been dead and no longer standing, with bandaged heads, arms and stitched legs of gray necrotic flesh, slowly start to move their way. War-torn visages with red eyes that gleam like hot embers focus on the procession.

Stokes swears and racks his quad guns.

"Central, this is Fulton Patrol. We've found why Butterworth hasn't responded," Michael Two radios. "Someone's opened the doors and let the ZT's out."

"Poor bastards," Loutonia hears Stokes say. Does he mean the pissed-off undead soldiers blocking the intersection, or their own group?

Chapter Eight

Some bumping and thumping come from the floor above. Rodriguez backs up the outside stairs, keeps his eyes on the rearward yards between the houses.

A lone zombie walks along the street, passes between the opening between two homes on the other side of block. It staggers along like a drunk but does nothing than move onward.

Something thumps and crashes upstairs.

"You okay up there?" Rodriguez says into his commlink.

Nothing.

He backs into the door, looks up the indoor stairwell. All quiet above.

"Kink, do you copy?" Rodriguez asks.

He holsters the pistol, shoves it back into the sleeve with suppressor still attached. He hefts his M4 and flips off the safety.

The upstairs door is closed. He gingerly touches the doorknob like it might be a red hot chunk of coal, then full fists it, turns it, and pushes it open with the tip of his gun.

"Kincade? Hello?"

Something thumps deeper within the house.

"I'm coming in," Rodriguez calls out. He steps from the box-shaped entry way into a small kitchen. The tile floor is thick with blood. Kincade or the GRCC soldier, he cannot tell. There are no bodies, just several sweeping smears in the blood puddle from an obvious struggle.

Rodriguez notices the cans scattered about the floor. *Bram* it is jokingly called. Z-Rations. Doped meat slop the city feeds the undead residence to keep them docile versus their feral relatives who roam the lands between all the protected cities and villages.

The mercenary feels the hairs on his neck rise. Did they corner one of the undead civilians up here versus this "rogue" army captain?

"Kink? Nicky, you all right?" Rodriguez calls out, more urgent.

A cabinet directly across from the entry way into the gore-smeared kitchen reveals two fresh bullet holes.

Rodriguez warily steps into the next room. Old green-brown plush carpeting: something from the 1960's or 1970's, still awful fifty years later. The blood trail across the floor reminds him of dragging bloody deer carcasses through the field.

The trail, still wet, glistening, curves around from the main room to a small wood-floored hallway. He hears something dripping from the room beyond. A leaky bathroom faucet?

"Hurrk!"

Someone coughs and chokes in the other room off the main, beyond a partially closed door. Large splatters of blood end at the threshold to this other room.

Rodriguez nudges the door open with boot tip, grips his carbine tight, meat of his trigger finger tickling the trigger. "Nick?" he says, squints into the darkened room.

There's someone on hands and knees in the room. Ass faces Rodriguez, literally, as the camo military pants lie bunched about the man's knees. The shirt and pants are the same as Rodriguez. The man before him seizes, back arches and he emits a gargled bark. Something wet hits the floor, and the acidic smell of stomach bile and other offal permeates the air.

"Give me a second," the man grumbles in a low, hoarse voice.

"Right, right, Nicky. Take your time," Rodriguez says backing out of the room, pulls the door back to its semi-closed state.

Rodriguez looks around. He still can't discern where the other person is, zombie or GRCC grunt.

"Fuck, Kink. Who put up a fight with ya?" the mercenary says looking down at the floor. His eyes pop when he glances across the room and sees the stock pile of army green crates, weapon and ammo boxes of all shapes and sizes. Other, smaller crates have NON-PERISHABLE written across them along with their food contents. Another pile of crates is labeled Z-RATIONS.

"Shit, man, we hit the mother lode." Lowering his rifle, Rodriguez steps over to the crates. "If we can find the other safe houses where the fuckin' GRCC stores the rest of their stuff like this, fuck crop dusting this shit hole, we'll be fuckin' set to wipe out this whole area with boots on the ground."

The door to the other room creaks open.

"If you're done barfin', ya big pussy, let's check this stuff out and call Tomes. Let him know what's sitting here for the picking."

A throat clears behind him.

"You kiss your momma with that mouth?" Jake says with a cough.

Rodriguez spins around.

Kincade's suppressed 9mm phuffs twice in the mercenaries direction, held in Jake's bloody hand. The mercenary groans as the bullets bite into his shoulders, tear through flesh and muscle, destroying nerves.

The M4 thumps to the floor. Rodriguez follows, going down on knees, arms limp and dangling at his sides.

"That's for your buddy popping *me* in the arm," Jake smiles, his teeth drip like a wolf's after a fresh kill. Chunks of... something... limn his mouth and chin, drip from the tip of his nose. "But I appreciate you letting me get my britches up."

"Whatcha do with Nicky?" Rodriguez stutters, biting back the pain.

He looks at Billet's uniform. It is Kincade's. Blood drips on the left shoulder from the flap of cartilage that used to be Jake's ear. A widening dot of red seeps through the fabric near Jake's left armpit.

Jake grabs the mercenary by the collar and yanks him to his feet.

Rodriguez screams, his wounded arms jerk painfully.

Jake punches him in the face, and proceeds in dragging the semi-ragdoll man around into the wood-floored hallway, into the bathroom the next room over.

"I had to thank your partner for coming in," Billet says as they step into the bathroom. The room is small, consisting of a rust-stained toilet and a similar small sink. The largest piece of fixture in the room rests on grubby slate tiles: a large claw-foot cast iron bathtub.

Kincade lies in a heap within the tub, naked down to his skivvies. Head twisted at a sixty degree angle. Throat slashed. Multiple stab wounds to the chest and belly, his combat knife sticks hilt up in his bloody abdomen.

A bloody Class A uniform rests in the corner.

Rodriguez stands speechless as Billet continues: "I guess I didn't realize this location didn't have ACU's. Your buddy's uniform fits pretty good." Jake runs his bloody hands over the chest of the combat uniform. "Not quite the wear of my unit…"

Rodriguez snarls, tries to lift his arm enough to reach his holstered pistol.

Jake punches him again.

"Simmer down, buddy. Don't make me more irritated than I already am," Jake says.

His throat tingles. He coughs and swallows. The damn Z-Ration meat. *Never gulped down a bunch of it before.* His fingers tingle like ants crawl all over them. His throat feels fuzzy.

An old couch sits in the front room. Fabric worn through

in places; white fluff and springs poke through the seat cushions. Billet drags the man into it, slightly surprised at the ease of which he pulls the man along who is about the same height and build as he. He pushes the grumbling man into the chair.

"You got me curious." Jake rubs at his mouth to make sure there is no lingering meat slobber or vomit. "You aren't in normal GRCC garb. You talk about getting into our other weapon stashes. Getting back to Tomes? Crop dusting? Taking out this whole area?"

Jake leans in close. Rodriguez recoils, eyes squinting and nose wrinkling like he's gotten a whiff of ass. "What's going on here, soldier?"

"I ain't tellin' you shit," Rodriguez sneers.

He screams when Billet jams his dirty thumbs into the bloody bullet holes.

It is a peculiar thing. Jake knows it's the doped meat in his system. Part of him feels like raging, like simply ripping into his captive, pulling the guy's intestines out through his nostrils, strangling him with them. He knows that rage will overtake him when he becomes hungry again. He's been on enough UCRA feeding runs; a late drop of meat often meant the expenditure of a whole lot of rebuffing rubber rounds and fresh, painful wounds from frenzied denizens.

He runs a hand across his forehead, touches the long raised scar early last Fall when a Feral one-upped him out in the field. He winces, the healed wound still feels aflame when poked at, like a hot, dull knife dragging across his skin right to the skull.

Keep it in check, Jacob, he thinks to himself. *Keep it buried deep. Conduct business like you always have when you got hip deep in assholes and your enemy doesn't want to spill the beans.*

Jake pushes his fingers deeper into the man's torn flesh holes. The soldier's eyes start to roll up into the back of his head. Jake slaps him to keep him conscious.

"You're a stray dog," Jake says close to the other man's face.

"You've shit in my yard, and I want to know where you came from, so I can throw you and your shit in your owner's face if I get the opportunity."

"You're dead," Rodriguez says.

"He's got that right," Lettner chuckles, seated next to the man.

Billet ignores the apparition.

"Your fucked up little city is crawling with guys like me, more inside this little enclosure for the dead. In Chicago we just shoot anyone that's turned or shambles out of hiding, not cage them and keep them because you feel they have rights, that they're still of some value just because they're associated with your city or your lives somehow," Rodriguez says between gasps and gritting his teeth as Jake keeps gentle pressure on his wounds.

"You're Loyalists?" Jake looks at Lettner. "Or hired guns by a Loyalist group?"

Lettner's Loyalists had come out of the wood work since the Muskegon commissioner's capture and execution. They hold the same anti-zombie beliefs as the late regent, and their reach obviously goes beyond the lakeshore and deep within West Michigan's cookie jar.

Lettner smiles, shrugs.

Rodriguez winces. "Hired, but not your Loyalists or whatever."

"Mercenaries?" Jake says, surprised. Who would hire mercenaries? Why?

"You're dead, Captain Jake Billet." Rodriguez snarls. "Dead if you wander around inside this place. Dead if you go back into your city."

Jake's brow raise. "You know me?"

"Know you? Hell, one of our orders is to kill you."

Jake recalls the three soldiers and the rogue shooter who took out one of the three.

"It appears I've more than one rogue after me," Jake laughs. He feels a little loopy; the doped meat.

Rodriguez's eyes widen. "Don't know about that other fucker who took out Cafferty. He'll be dead too if he's running around inside here."

"What's going down *inside here*?" Jake can feel the red rage start to rise. He presses his hands more firmly on the man's wounds. He can feel the pumping heart; could almost hear the blood whooshing through his veins at every beat.

Rodriguez bites his lip. It starts to bleed.

A radio squelch from the other room. "Head One to all Tentacles."

Rodriguez looks down at his watch. 01100 hours.

"What's this about?" Jake says, a red haze filling his vision. He sinks his thumbs back into the gnarled bullet pits.

Rodriguez screams. Eyes roll up. He slumps.

"Damnit."

"You're not listening," Lettner says, lying limp with Billet's thumbs tucked into his bloody shoulder holes.

"We've moved the schedule up. Planes landed this morning, is being loaded for cargo dump. Dusting will commence at 01500," the radio voice says.

Billet stands, shaking. The rage boils up like droplets of gasoline teasing an open flame.

He moves to the room in which he had dragged and changed clothing with the other infantry man. The man's radio lies in the corner next to a pile of vomit. Jake can smell the bile-drenched meat that he hadn't quite been able to hold in.

"All personnel are to vacate the west side and any posts within the city. Meeting spot will be as planned. Head One, out."

Billet smashes the radio with his fist, ignores the dull pain and the shards of plastic that embed in the side of his hand.

He groans and staggers. His hands claw at the door frames of each room he passes through. He enters the kitchen, fights the urge but knows it has to be. Mixed in the blood on the floor, the

Z-rations ooze from their crudely opened cans, beckoning him. He drops to his knees and greedily scoops up meat and sticky blood, gooey acrid thick red gravy over the delicious meat.

"Death's coming," Lettner's voice says in his ears.

"Salvation is with the Lord's sister," another voice: Loutonia's.

Jake looks over his shoulder, meat and blood slop drip from his mouth and chin.

The mercenary stands there, gritting his teeth, M4 in hands, arms loose. He points the gun half-assed at Billet, bites back a scream at his next action.

Tat-tat-tat-tat.

The bullets slam into Jake's chest and legs like the fingers of God flicking at his body, punching him, throwing him forward onto the blood-slick floor. He goes down and rolls over on his back. He snarls, slips, tries to get up on his elbows.

"These are my type of people," Lettner laughs standing beside the mercenary, hand on his shoulder.

The soldier doesn't register the touch. He takes a step in Jake's direction, nearly boot to boot, levels his gun, curses in pain and anguish.

And pulls the trigger.

***

"Motion detector's gone off at the Jackson Street safe house."

"We're kind of in the middle of something here," Breckenridge responds back to the radio operator at Central Command. He stands in his turret hatch, holds tight to the coaming with one hand and his mounted Cailber-.50 machine gun with the other. His driver puts their M60 tank over a curb, the gunner swivels the 105mm M68 turret cannon towards the intersection of Valley and Fulton. If the Grizzly is going to breathe hell fire, he doesn't suspect the Huron would like a shell roaring over their head.

Loutonia breaks in over the air waves, "Could be our captain."

She looks through her view port. The line of undead soldiers continues to grow. She doesn't focus long on any one face. She fears she might know one, or twenty, or more, of them.

"We're not moving at the moment," Breckenridge responds.

The lead BRV sits at a slight angle with its three-man fire team locked and loaded. With the A/C on, the driver still looks as if he sits under a shower head, nervous perspiration more than the heat. He keeps the vehicle running and ready for next actions.

The Huron sits behind it, all roof-top portals manned, guns positioned forward towards the corner ensemble.

"What're they doing?" Mulholland says.

The undead soldiers continue to amass along the intersection. Some point at the military vehicles, some expressionless, dead eyes simply staring. Others snarl, growl, shaking fist or whatever weapon they hold towards their living comrades.

"Gettin' ready to open a big ole can of whoop ass," Stokes responds. "We're ready," he adds, hands on the grips of his quad gun.

"We'll not fire upon our own people," Breckenridge, tone threatening. "We might've signed up for that abuse after death, but I'll not have a hand in shredding those poor grunts any more than they've already been."

The Soldier Resuscitation Action Protocol, or SRAP, had been doled out by the government when troop numbers, both due to those KIA and "fresh hires," had dwindled to a dangerously low level since the virus came into effect. As one of the chief medical meccas of the Midwest, Grand Rapids was one of the few test facilities opened and sanctioned to "bring back" those service men and women who'd been mortally wounded but able to resuscitate. As long as the head was still attached, heart able to beat, and a replacement limb or two capable of being stitched on, the troopers were re-trained with the plan to bring them back into active duty.

The semi-undead "zombie troopers," or ZTs, were hardier in

unlife as they could take more punishment if they were shot. And as long as their brain case wasn't blown off, they could keep going indefinitely. They retained their skills and training for the most part, just with an intensified enraged and more deadly edge than they'd been in life.

The only problem—Breckenridge shakes his head—they took their orders via a chip embedded in their skull. There is no real "leader" for them as the majority are NCO's. And the way they mill about, angry and unsure, no one seems to be controlling them.

"Command, who's got the electronic leash for these men?" Breckenridge asks. If the soldiers are untethered and running amok, and armed to boot: trouble. Lots of trouble for all.

"Felder and the main physician, Rutkowski, held the reins when it came to these initial trials," Colonel Jackson radios back, his voice strained with tension.

"Felder's dead," comes the response from Michael Two.

Loutonia looks through her view port again. The small sea of ragtag undead troopers open and a limp body spills out onto the pavement. The near-naked, torn-to-shreds scarecrow of the dead man can be none other than Hank Felder. She shivers, if he would be put back together via his own program, he'd need all new limbs and a fresh coil of intestines.

"The experiment's a failure. Permission to open fire," Stokes calls out. His gut churns with the thought of being one of those poor grunts.

"Stand down, Sergeant!" Breckenridge warns.

The *whup whup whup* of helicopter blades slap the air, rising from the city. Heavy. Low.

"Bird in the air," Michael Three reports. "What's this now?"

"Better yet, who's in that thing?" Mulholland says over the Huron's closed circuit.

***

"Fly low. I want to see my handiwork," Rupert Largo says.

Our handiwork, Tomes thinks. He pulls back on the stick, angling the blades of the Apache helicopter. The aircraft slows. *Our handiwork and the blood of my men. Too many men, who didn't sign up for this resistance.*

He blames himself for not thoroughly researching the mission, the client, the area before accepting the job. The want and need for money may kill him in his current profession. Not today. Maybe someday.

The chopper drops to the height of four telephone poles. Tomes likes the feel of the old war bird, reminds him of Afghanistan. Which makes him feel suddenly very old and tired. He thought things were fucked up then.

Below, the GRCC convoy and the mass of *uncaged* undead soldiers. The vehicles lay staggered, a jagged spear. But the converging army of re-animated, rejuvenated soldiers—the GRCC's own people—form up like a beast that won't stand to be broken.

"Good work. Good work," Largo says.

Tomes turns to reply, "You're welcome," only to see the man in the co-pilot seat gloating. If not for the five-point harness keeping him nearly rigid, the City Treasurer would be patting his own back.

The helicopter drops another pole length. The downwash kicks up debris from the house, yard and street. A curling, tumbling gust of dust.

"Let's get going. You've hung me out here long enough," Largo says, ignoring the pumping fists from the convoy, and the same from the ruffled undead soldiers. "Silas Regan's waiting."

Tomes throttles up. *If this had an ejector seat, I'd put your ass right through the blades*, as the helicopter rises again, starting to move forward. If the service payment had been made in full rather half up front, he would've considered it.

Beep beep beep beep. A red light on the cockpit console flares with each bleat.

"What's that?" Largo bellows.

Tomes answers: "Your friends below are shooting at you."

And just when he was thinking about negotiating the bird as part of the contract.

***

Stokes lowers a burly, hairy, scar-crossed arm against the haze of the dirt squall. He tries to peer at the hovering helicopter. "Get the hell out of here, ya asshole." He's not sure who's in the chopper, one: it can't be any of theirs as the GRCC loaned their one remaining heli to the city, and two: HQ sure as hell better have informed them they were coming out before he threw a couple slugs into the chopper's metal underbelly.

Whizzt. From the dust cloud intersection, a chubby rope of smoke shoots up from the street.

Someone beats him to sending up a brutal payload.

"Who's firing the RPG?" Michael Two yells.

The helicopter moves away. The shooters aim is off. The gunships right weapons wing—empty—takes the hit versus the fuselage. The concussion tilts the bird sideways. The blast mangles the undercarriage, up the right side of the chopper. The rotors keen like someone's thrown a handful of rocks into a big fan.

"More insurgents?" Breckenridge comes over the comm.

The helicopter limps away, heading west. It might clear the tree line rising above John Ball Park. It will want to clear the heavily fortified, locked down, and human-abandoned John Ball Zoo. It coughs black smoke. Orange-red flames burp from the wound on its side.

But all eyes on the ground are on the undead soldiers emerging from the backlash of the critically wounded war bird.

Loutonia sees it from the driver's port as do Stokes and Mulholland above her.

Stokes beats her to it. "The troopers are armed!"

Bullets ping off the armor hides of the lead BRV and the Huron. Mulholland ducks as an errant projectile zips by. Stokes yelps as something bites his thick upper left arm, tearing the fabric of his sleeve away, leaving a fresh red stripe on his hairy limb.

"Do not return fire!" Breckenridge barks in everyone's headset. "Full reverse. Back up. Back it up, and maybe they'll stand down."

"They're pissed off grunts, probably mad at us living who didn't put them down the right way," Stokes says, his voice tight with tension. "I'd be shooting at me, too."

The Huron's hide chimes like a dinner bell as a hive of lead bees slam against it.

Michael Two rolls backwards, swinging around behind the Huron. Another rocket propelled grenade fumes in its trail, misses the vehicle, blasting a hole in the nearby weed-festooned parking lot of a defunct hardware store on the corner of Garfield and Fulton. Michael Three and Grizzly start to back away from the corner.

"I'm loadin' up non-lethals," Stokes says, dropping below deck to retrieve proper ammunition.

"Got you covered, buddy." Mulholland nods.

A woman's gasp. "Are you concussed? You're doing something responsible."

"Shut up, Phelps," Stokes replies. "Get this beast rolling."

Stokes pops up like a gorilla from a rabbit hole. Ammunition that can slice, dice and julienne flesh is replaced with non-lethal orange-tipped rounds. *Meat tenderizer rounds*, the Captain liked to call them.

A practiced pro, Stokes attaches the pair of canisters to his gun rack. Beefy, hairy-knuckled hands to grips, he makes the quad .30's bark like a pack of big dogs. The orange tips hammer into the dwindling dust cloud and the undead soldiers.

"They're turning back," Stokes growls; proud of himself. His teeth rattle in his thick square skull as he sweeps the quad gun side to side before the Huron.

With a live round, careful not to hit his target, Mulholland fires his M4 versus his mounted Caliber-.30. He has the precision, but doesn't want to chance hitting anyone. Already the name tapes on individual troopers stand out as stark reminders of a place he doesn't want to go. It is seeing those men and women in army green, in shambles, half-alive, that he had made a pact with Stokes. Lord forbid if he's mortally wounded, or starts to Turn, Stokes is to shoot him in the head. Vice versa if Stokes goes down.

Stokes laughs, squeezing off a few short loud bursts at the troopers. "I got them on the run."

Mulholland notices an undead soldier standing in the broken debris of the corner house. A M4 like his own is leveled to eye, points straight at Stokes.

Eddie takes a breath, eye to scope, fires once.

A charred board splinters beside the undead gunman, hits the soldier in the arm as it fires.

The shot goes over Stokes dense cranium.

Eddie breathes out.

"Turning about," Phelps warns as she guns the engines. A maneuver only for cramped spaces, as they are wedged between the zombie troopers and the vehicles behind them, Loutonia turns the big front dualies as far as she can to the right, locks the right track, and puts all power to the left.

Mulholland and the soldiers within the Huron brace themselves. Stokes yips like a bronco rider, still firing, as the Huron sweeps about in a near-perfect 180 to face the way they had come.

"They're followin' the helicopter and breaking up, headin' north and west." Mulholland returns to firing his .30. The shots throw up dirt and concrete before a few undead troopers who follow them. Name tapes read: McPherson, Ellis, Newberg. He wonders if they simply noticed their living comrades and wanted to re-join them.

The convoy treads east again down Fulton, slowly, eyes on

broken storefronts and alleyways. Any place dark, any hidey holes where either the undead grunts or living insurgents may fester.

The locals are the only ones who surface, coming out, attracted by all the noise.

"We gotta radio the M45 gate, and the Apostolate," Loutonia says hearing more bullets plink off the Huron. "Our boys at the outpost might be able to fend them off, but the Apostolate…"

"We're making the call, Huron." Breckenridge responds. Dead air. Hesitation. "M45's out. No response. Apostolate is on alert."

"Anyone ID the people in the chopper? Fine time to fly out when we're in the thick of things." Michael Three, sounding none too happy.

Jackson comes over the air waves from town. "Fulton Patrol. I've just got off the horn with Commissioner Sutter. Largo's left the city, heading towards Reganshire to negotiate."

"Or get out of the frying pan." Stokes wipes a bead of sweat from drooling down his brow.

Everyone knows the City Treasurer had stated he was going to visit Reganshire, interested in finding any connection to the Grand Rapids attacks. No one expected it to be so soon, him gallivanting off, especially in the midst of the shit going down in the city.

The man deserves a shot up his tail pipe, Stokes thinks.

"We're getting more intel on the Largo's right-hand-man." Jackson's voice sounds haggard, tired, like he'd just run a gauntlet and got his ass handed to him. "He definitely isn't from any Michigan unit or anyone sanctioned tri-state unit on record. Largo may have his hands full in more ways than one."

A sour feeling twists Loutonia's gut. It starts to make sense but she doesn't voice it. Largo the prick. Largo the thorn in Mayor Honeywell's side. Largo the controller of the city's cash flow. The Loyalists of Lettner hitting so close to home. The well-armed insurgents in their midst. *An inside job under Largo's tutorage*, she questions silently.

The heat outside nearing 100, the temp within the Huron a balmy 74, Loutonia can't suppress a centipede-crawl chill up her spine.

And her captain still out there. Jake wandering the streets with the locals, the insurgents and now the hostile undead troopers.

"Back up to Lane and Fulton. We're sending reinforcements, and tracking Largo's copter." Jackson says over the comm.

Loutonia glances out the side view port as they roll back towards downtown. The undead civilians stop at curbs and street corners, vacant eyes stare like they are watching a parade. Some even limply waved. A man in tattered work clothes takes a shot to the head and goes down. She doesn't know if it came from their group or someone, dead or living, pursuing them.

"Wherever you are, Jacob," she says under her breath, gut still twisting, "I hope it's somewhere safe."

***

Jake has more bullet holes in him than he's ever imagined; more than enough to stop a living man from walking and breathing. Air still fills his lungs, though it feels harder and harder to draw. He limp-walks: his right knee and hip lead-ridden, feeling aflame, stiff. He doesn't feel like checking, but perhaps a chunk of flesh hangs free, flopping within his tattered and bloody pants leg.

He holds the mercenary's M4. The man will no longer need it. The soldier had been in about as much shock as him when Jake got to his feet after being shot enough times to drop a small herd of deer. Jake had taken advantage of the moment, not waiting for the man to reload, not waiting to see if more bullets might put him down for good.

Though his hands and forearms, including the gun, are red with the man's blood, Jake can't recall how he killed him. It is all blanketed in a red haze, a crimson curtain when trying to recollect.

"Gotta get to the bottom of this," Jake grumbles. He swallows, tries to rid his throat of its dry soreness. "Something big is going down."

He lifts his hand to straighten the name tape above his right breast pocket. The hand drops as did his jaw when he looks up.

He stands on Indiana Avenue, not far from the corner where the side street met Bridge Street, a locale well-known to him.

It is Bob's place; an old Marathon gas and service station.

Old it is not. Not currently, though it should be.

Small, house-shaped building. Sitting angled towards the corner, towards Bridge. Painted white, with not a blemish on brick or mortar, roof or window. Big sheet metal Marathon sign hangs on a freshly-painted steel beam. Shiny red Coca-Cola sign. Flimsy marquee with removable number plaques: 29 cents for a gallon of gas.

A blonde haired, long faced man—young, perhaps in mid-30's—quickly steps from the service station. His 1950's era blue coveralls: clean, pressed, not a spot of oil upon them. It is Bob, a younger, livelier version. He looks at Jake, murder in his eyes; eyes of blue, not death-fogged. In his right hand: a black crowbar.

A painful nudge to the back of Billet's head: a gun barrel.

Jake slowly turns his head.

A black haired man. Tactical vest. *Baddage* on the name tape.

"Fuck." Raspy mumble; Jake's lips and throat still a-tingle from eating the doped meat.

"You are," the undead-though-looking-very-much-alive assassin rasps back.

Chapter Nine

Across the street, walking behind a baby carriage with his wife, Jake sees Lettner. Wearing a tweed suit, much too thick a garment for the season, the late Muskegon commissioner sports a slicked back pompadour. Jenna wears a full length dress, cotton, floral print, again much too much for the hot summer day. Her bouffant hair piled high; she looks like a blonde Jacklyn Kennedy.

Lettner drapes an arm over Jenna's shoulder. Her reaction, nothing; she stares ahead, trance-like. Like a zombie. He looks directly at Jake. His lips move slowly, forming words so they can be read from afar. Sorry. Can't. Help. You. Punctuated by a middle finger against Jenna's dress sleeve.

The rough jab of the gun barrel at the base of Jake's neck brings him back to the present situation.

"Can't hit you… from afar… Captain," the gunman, Baddage, says; speech halted. Either the man has a speech impediment, or he isn't one of the living.

An image forms in Jake's mental eye of perception and recollection. It comes like a candle sputtering to find oxygen. A light bulb flickering as electricity flows herky-jerky into it. Jake recalls the black-haired civilian, the loose mop of scalp hanging off its head like a disheveled toupee, standing in the mass of panicked UCRA civilians during the April storms and heavy rain. Staring at Billet, perfectly content as chaos boils around him.

"What do you need to hit me for?" Jake asks, clearing his throat. The damn doped meat. Feels like a coat of dry moss lining his throat.

"Damned gooks. Took my brother, not taking my friend," 1950's Bob snarls, steps closer with the black crow bar gripped tight in fist. "Damn Commie gooks. Get outta my country."

Black Hair, Baddage, yanks the pistol from Jake's side holster. Silencer tossed away. Bang! Close to the ear. Bob gets one in the cranium, staggers back, crashes into the new box shaped pumps. Goes down for the count.

There is no blood.

"You didn't have to do that," Jake says. His ears ring. He watches the pistol wing away, clatters and slides not far from downed Bob and the gas pumps.

The neighborhood goes hazy. Like a slide show where the pictures are intermixed, some of older days, some of current. He sees, first, Bridge Street circa 1950s. Big cars. American flags. Gas nowhere near seven bucks a gallon. Music playing: Elvis Presley, Bill Haley and the Comets, Bobby Darin.

Flit.

Post-viral pandemic Bridge Street circa 2013, beyond, and current. Rundown buildings and homes. Best time to sample lead paint chips if desired. The walking dead, Grand Rapids afflicted civilians retained, protected behind a barricade of concrete and concertina wire on the city's west side. A calm populace, fed doped meat slurry from the city's one large meat processing plant for that activity alone. The unliving people going about their days and nights, re-enacting days gone by in their former living, breathing lives. Living on and on, and on and on.

Jake feels tired, more tired than he's ever felt.

His hands touch his chest wounds. Sticky black-red blood stains his fingers. He knows he shouldn't be upright. If his stomach wasn't twitching from the Z-rations, it would be twisting with solid realization now.

"Move, Hero… of Grand Rapids." Black Hair shoves the tip of the long rifle against Jake's neck. Big sniper rifle.

Jake glances to the street as they walk onto the gas station property; the place flits from the past, then to the present and back. He sees the Huron, Loutonia and him talking to a tattered, floppy arm Bob. The memory, that image, vanishes.

People stand, stopped, on the sidewalk and street. They watch him and the gunman. They too flip-flop between bouffants and pressed slacks, to opaque-eyed decaying remnants of their former self.

Black Hair prods him on between the gas pumps, past the quiet form of Bob. New blue coveralls besmirched with oil stains. Tattered blue coveralls stained with blood, yellow drool and dabbles of dried meat.

"Hero of Grand Rapids? That what this is about?" Jake's words come out rubbed across 60 grit sand paper, his throat a dry pipe, tongue like wall insulation.

"Yes." Black Hair nudges Jake.

They move towards the station's single door: shiny aluminum frame with two panes of clear glass. Flit. Dirty, smashed-in door frame with two panes of broken glass: a maw of serrated teeth.

Jake chuckles, comes out as a phlegmy cough.

Hero. He hasn't heard that joke in a while. It stems from the Lettner mission. Ended up not being so covert once the man's head slipped into a noose. Everyone came out of the wood work. Anti-Lettner fanatics. Pro-Lettner Loyalists. Big congrats on bringing the man to justice. Parades. Parties. Molotov cocktails thrown at the Huron and crew. Death threats. Riots in the streets.

Hero? No.

Jake feels as if he's started a war.

"Why don't you just shoot me and be done with it?

"I… have been," Black Hair says. "Others have… always

gotten… in the way."

Another mental image. Seems like yesterday. Seems like a life time ago. Their new young navigator. Campau. Jake sees him, donning Jake's helmet. The navigator rising up in the command station. Huron's engines roaring. Guns barking like cracks of thunder.

Then a single report of a long rifle, and blood rains down Jake's hatch, where he should've been standing. In command. Not weak. Not failing his crew.

"Goes to show, aim sucks when you're dead." Billet tries to laugh. It feels like someone cracks him in the chest with a sledgehammer.

He is roughly pushed into the interior of the service station. Stumbles. Goes down on hands and knees.

"I should… leave you here… to see what's coming next… from Mister Largo," Black Hair says, standing in the open door way. He brings his long rifle up. He can't miss from this distance.

Jake stares at the gun barrel. Straight to the head. It is the way to go when one…is in this condition.

"Rupert Largo?" The words drip like venom. "You aren't the first today to try and nail me down. He's paying you to do this?"

The red haze starts to rise again. Jake fights it. He needs information. The puzzle pieces float in his mind's eye, but they don't come together. He knows they all connect.

"Payment… is life," Black Hair says. "He saved me. I… owe him. I do what… he says, though the others… are paid."

"I think I ran into a few of them."

A lot of blood in the Jackson safe house as evidence. And Jake recalls the merc's words.

"What's coming next," he repeats Black Hair's words. "A plane? A payload? Dusting at three this afternoon."

The light bulb of realization flickers. Its filaments grow hot, start to glow white. The puzzle pieces snap together like thunder claps.

An earthquake-like shiver wants to wrench Jake's spine from his body.

"I don't plan... to be in here when..." Someone rises up behind the undead assassin. "The cleansing... rain... falls."

Black Hair senses someone behind him.

Too late.

He spins, rifle snaps up.

Bob is there. Crowbar comes down.

There is a loud metallic clang in the same instant the gun roars.

Black Hair goes one way, stumbling. Gun droops in the aftermath of the crowbar's contact.

Bob goes the other way, toppling like a tree, right side of his face blown off.

Jake takes advantage of the distraction.

Joints pop as he rises. He throws himself at the staggered assassin. Red, hot anger, hotter than the air, prickles at his flesh.

He puts his fist into the side of Black Hair's face. The man goes down, rifle skittering away.

"How was I to know your City Treasurer was a man after my own heart," Lettner says, then laughter.

Jake can't see the man, but his chortles are like knitting needles stabbing his eardrums.

In the distance, the whup whup whup of helicopter blades punching the sky. They grow from the city, chop over the neighborhood. Lake Michigan Drive? Fulton Street? Start to fade—suddenly metallic cough, mechanical wheeze, losing steam—towards the southwest.

"He is on... his way," Black Hair says. A red-brown sludge drips from his mouth where Jake cracked him. "Tomorrow... this place will be... cleansed of diseased flesh." He turns to look up at Billet. Broken teeth. Black gums. "Flesh of the living... and dead."

Jake rolls off him, gets to his feet, but feels like falling over.

Across the street, on their knees, his wife hunches over their teenage son. Lettner laughing. Changes. Largo laughing. Jenna screams. Joey howls in pain. Flesh and muscle melt from bone.

Something punches him in the abdomen.

Sharp pain like a red-hot fire poker plunges into his gut. It brings him back to reality.

Black Hair stands before him. Fist wrapped about the leather-wrapped handle of a long bayonet-style knife, hilt pinning Billet's shirt to his stomach. The 16-inch blade sticks into him, through him, out his back.

Jake staggers. Black Hair can't get a shot on him so he wants to take it mano-a-mano.

"Fine, motherfucker," Jake snarls, ignoring the knife lanced through him. "Let's do this."

It is Black Hair's turn to stagger. His rheumy eyes stare down at his blade which he's let go.

"You… live?" Black Hair wheezes.

Jake launches himself at Black Hair. "Because I'm already dead."

***

"We're going down. Hard." Tomes yells over the bleating klaxon and wounded whine of the helicopter. The stick and pedals shudder so violently they threaten to turn his bones to powder.

"Have you called it in? Where're we at?" Largo blurts, coughing from the smoke inside the cramped cockpit.

Tomes's right leg sticks to the side of the cockpit. At seat level, a series of holes let daylight shine through, where leg and knee cap lean. The tangle of metal and wires, and the mangled flesh of that appendage is all he sees. He looks away, needs to focus on controlling the descent of the whirly bird, not on how bad he's torn up.

"Called it the minute we were hit," Tomes says, the earth coming up sideways at them. They have passed over John Ball Park (thank God), managed to get high enough to get over the hills, expressway and beyond the enclosure. Old, overgrown golf course on the other side of the freeway. Too close to the city still, and Ferals prowl relentlessly along the perimeters with all that scent of fresh meat. "If we can maintain a bit of altitude before totally breaking up, I'm hoping to set us down somewhere a bit more open and away from town."

Golf course shudders away underneath them, the view violently shivers with the helicopter. Tomes studied, in depth, maps of the area. They had needed to with coming up from Chicago and making forays out into the wilderness outside the confines of the city. Coming from a true concrete jungle like Chicago, Grand Rapids, if not for the undead and all, is a paradise to him and his men. In any direction, it is not far to travel to find oneself in the boondocks, in a dense woodland, beside the rushing Grand River on a grass-lined bank, or horizon lost viewing acres of open field and farm land.

The wounded helicopter jumps, making Tomes cry out in pain as whatever is lanced into his leg touches a nerve. He pushes the cyclic sideways in an agonized haze. The struggling rotors throw the chopper sidelong.

It is Largo's turn to scream as the Apache drops into a mass of pointy-topped pines.

Screech of tortured metal. Tree branches thrash, pop, snap. Tremendous crack as spinning rotor blade slaps into thick tree trunks. Rattle. Roll. Helicopter drops to ground, wood and metal debris flying everywhere.

Both Largo and Tomes gasp as the belly of the whirly bird slams to earth; breath blasts from lungs like an uppercut to the gut.

"Am I alive?" Rupert says, brain spinning in head.

Tomes doesn't respond. There is blood splashed on the glass

canopy where the darks-skinned merc sits.

Helmet radio squelches. "…we tracked your descent. We're coming to your location."

"Hello? Hello, this is Grand Rapids City Treasurer, Rupert Largo."

"ETA, ten minutes. Please respond."

The voice over the comm sounds vaguely familiar.

"We're here." Shrugging off the unfastened five-point harness, Rupert pushes on the canopy. The glass bubble resists, then releases and opens like a clam shell. "Who am I speaking to?"

"Do you copy?"

"We're here," Largo says again, going sideways and falling into a thicket of tall grass, wood shards and sharp metal splinters. He swears as he comes up on his knees, a finger length piece of metal embedded into the meat of his palm. Not thinking, he plucks at it, tears it out. His blood flows like water down his wrist.

"We're not transmitting on their frequency."

Largo looks to the front of the cockpit which rests at a forty-five degree angle. Tomes moves, but very slowly.

Holding his bleeding hand, Largo stands, teeters. Head clears. He steps to Tomes, sees the helicopter's side mingled with the wreckage of the merc's leg; the metal and flesh look as one.

Largo looks through the trees. They sit atop a slight rise. He can see a road not far: O'Brien Road, runs east and west from roughly the Butterworth Outpost, butts into Wilson Avenue. Reganshire property.

"You didn't get us too far from the city." Largo says, annoyed, and checks the pistol holstered at his chest.

Tomes tries to move. Sharp spears of pain rush from his right leg and try to pierce his pounding heart. "Motherfucker," he snarls. "You unappreciative motherfucker."

In the distance, coming from the southwest, the hum of two small aircraft.

"I'm a man on a mission," Largo says, peering out and around the wreckage. "You knew what you signed on for when you took your mission with me."

Two figures off in the distance, from the way they had come, move through the dense tree line. They move slowly, stopping, looking about as if they are lost also. Three more humanoid forms emerge behind them, one on all fours, like a dog, before standing upright.

Tomes sees the figures too, and growls deep in his throat. "You self-centered son of a bitch. You're no better than those poor dregs out there."

Largo watches the Feral zombs as they draw closer. They don't seem to sense the two pieces of living meat. Yet. Probably more inquisitive as to the noise of the helicopter crash.

"You're probably right, Mr. Tomes." Before the man can react, Rupert grabs at Tomes holstered sidearm, yanking away, and steps back. "I have a need to survive." He checks the pistol, a 9mm Beretta, pops the clip, inspected, palms it back into the handle of the gun. Satisfied. "Though I'm not quite hungry for the same thing they are."

The hum of the two single prop aircraft grows louder.

"Perhaps if your men are successful in purging the west side, giving me some city land back," Largo says as he watches the Ferals dip down out of sight behind a hill. They still move towards their locale. "I'll set up a little memorial for you."

Tomes tries to pull his leg free from the wreckage. He bites back a scream as his leg doesn't budge though blood and fresh pain weep from the appendage.

"I am sorry. I truly am." Largo says, slowly backing away from the mangled warbird and the mercenary, his eyes more on the Ferals who make the top of the hill. The two front most creatures stop, heads rise, sniff the air, and then the whole group starts a teetering skip-run towards them. "I did have great plans for you, but…"

"Motherfucker," Cedric swears again, hatred burns in his eyes at the Treasurer.

The Ferals a little more than fifty yards away, Largo turns and runs, pistols in his hands.

"Gawddamn motherfucker!" Tomes yells.

The sound of the twin planes draws closer.

The Ferals increase their pace. Dinner time.

Tomes fumbles with the headset cranked at an angle on his head. Every movement seems connected to his pierced leg. He grits his teeth, holds back a scream.

The smell of JP4 jet fuel makes his nose hairs curl.

Wasn't supposed to be like this, he thinks. *Take the job. Make some cash. Send it home to wife and kids.* His pursuits wouldn't put him or his men on any saints list, but it was an ends to a means in this life, this effed up world.

And if I'm not going to prosper, Tomes sneers, reaches for the radio dial, hoping it still works, *then you won't either, Mister City Treasurer.*

"Black Chief calling all Chi-town brethren," Cedric says as he watches the two zombs draw closer. The smoke and the small hot pieces of wreckage make the Ferals cautious in step. The "wild dogs" are smart, he thinks incredulously.

The cyclic still between his knees, the red bottom on the stick draws his attention. The chopper sits on its side, with its 30 mm M230 Chain Gun under its belly, hopefully still operational.

Tomes grips the stick, thumb on trigger.

"Black Chief to all," he says as the Ferals draw closer. "Mission compromised. We've been set up. Scrub all objectives. Head home or execute Final Stand Protocol Alpha-Niner-India-Two-Four-Two."

He sees two single prop Cessna's cut across the tree line in the distance, just making the outer boundary of the UCRA.

The two Ferals notice him within the broken cockpit. They

approach the nose of the helicopter, skeletal fingers flex. They hiss through black broken teeth.

"See you in Hell," Tomes growls into the mike, to his men if they are listening, at the Ferals.

He thumbs the trigger, inhales deeply. The smell of JP4 jet fuel thick, heavy.

The 30mm Chain Gun barks lead and flames into the air.

***

Largo steps onto the shoulder of O'Brien. No signs of Zees following him. He breathes a sigh of relief. Coming up the road from the west, a big Abrams and two rattle-trap Humvees. The tank looks familiar.

The woods suddenly explode behind him. No heat or direct flame, but the concussion pushes him into the street, almost topples him.

He looks back as he stands upright. Orange flame and black smoke flitter and flick through the trees in the distance from where he'd come, from the crash site.

"At least you weren't dinner," he says, saluting the fallen mercenary leader. "I'll save some money not having to pay your expenses at least."

He shrieks as he turns back around. The Humvees speed around him, one on either side. Brakes squeal as they box him in. The Abrams rolls up, stops, the front cowling a few feet from his chest. The 120mm cannon quivers above his head.

Rupert Largo sees the name of the big tank scrawled on the side of the turret. Red with drips like running blood, the word *Devastator* along with a drippy white skull with a combat knife punched through it.

The commander's hatch opens, squeals on tortured hinges. It doesn't go up all the way and is followed by cursing as a shoulder nudges it to full open. The man who eases himself up from the turret, rubbing his shoulder, wears a black beret atop his hairless head.

"Shit," Largo gasps.

"Have you forgotten me already, Mr. Treasurer?" The big TC smiles. "Pike. Major Jeremy Pike. I take it you need a new ride to Reganshire?" He salutes, grinning dangerously.

**

"Incoming!' Stokes yells.

"On the ground, in the air. What the eff? Has this whole place gone crazy?" The radio crackles, Forrester on the line.

"You just wake up to reality, Captain?" Breckenridge replies over the continued gunfire as the entire convoy rolls eastward towards Lane.

The ZT's follow but at a distance, some taking evasive maneuvers, spreading out and taking cover between homes and old, rusted vehicles.

The sound of incoming aircraft hums above the rattle and pop of gun fire.

Amassed at the Fulton and Lane intersection: Captain Frank Forrester and his M213 Ontario, the Huron's sister; two Bradley's; one of the cities two older Patton tanks, and a mix of BRV's and old Humvee's. The corner lots, save for the vacant Old Kent Bank building on the southeast corner, are free of habitation and now temporary parking lots for the reinforcement team.

"Don't have kids playing with radio-controlled again, do we?" Forrester, invoking memories of the flooded spring time, riled UCRA citizens, and a couple pranksters from downtown thinking it smart to buzz the neighborhood.

The answer becomes obvious as two small Cessna planes can be seen over the tree line. They emerge from the southwest.

Stokes won't let off his quad guns so Mulholland grabs a pair of binoculars below his hatch cowl and brings them to his eyes.

"Umm. This can't be a good sign," he says, his pronounced Adams apple bobbing furiously as he swallows quickly. "They are Agro craft."

"Speak in English, kid, not in Southernese," Stokes yells.

Mulholland drops the binoculars, gives the front gunner a sour look.

"Agricultural planes." The tall rear gunner peers through the field glasses again. "Crop dusters."

"Either way around," Breckenridge cut in, "They need authorization to fly in, over or around the city. And I didn't get any heads up."

The planes hum closer, low. Low enough for everyone looking upon them to see the sprayer pipelines affixed to their wings.

"Shootem' down!" Breckenridge orders.

***

A fist connects with a wet crunch against the mottled flesh of Black Hair's face. His nose, already semi-sunken, flattens, brittle cartilage crackling like dry leaves. He doesn't feel it even as his head snaps sideways against the heavy impact of Jake's blow. On his back on the pavement before the old gas station, he cannot move with the dark-haired furious soldier kneeling upon his chest.

"You can't kill what's already dead," Jake says, teeth grit, red rage like tinted glasses over his eyes. He drives another hammering blow to the undead assassin's head, further coating his knuckles with thick black-red blood.

In the distance Jake hears a humming sound, two distinct sounds. Single engine airplanes? His mind's eye sees two radio-controlled planes buzzing him and his crew and the rest of the GRCC unit standing before a teetering fence line of agitated undead civilians. Seems years ago, not months ago.

The thought is shattered by cannon and small weapons fire in the distance.

The distraction gives Black Hair his opportunity. He snaps his knees up towards his chest, connecting with Jake's backside. Jake tumbles forward, off the killer, and lands on his side beside Bob's prone body.

Black Hair wobbles to his feet. "Living… or not. I will… destroy you," he slurs, the right side of his jaw no longer fully connected to his skull, the necrotic tissue the only material holding things in place. "And after you… all that you care for… your family, your crew, your friends… anything… dear to you."

Bob lies on the hot concrete. His shell-shredded skull drools what looks like black pudding and gummy red-gray noodles. Jake's surprised when the undead man's arms and legs move, and it appears Bob is trying to roll to his side and get to his feet. With his neck and esophagus opened up from the close proximity gun blast, a bubbling burp of thick blood is his only utterance.

Black Hair reaches down, pale bony hands going for Jake's collar.

Jake notices the lopsided jaw line, and the blackened sharp teeth along the inside of the creature's mouth. He slaps aside the arms, grabs them as they try to return, springing to his haunches, and twisting downward.

Black Hair hits the pavement, on his back. Billet shifts and straddles him again. Opening his mouth to hurl insults at Jake, Jake takes the opportunity provided.

"Like any other of you sons of bitches," Jake snarls, jams his hands into Black Hair's mouth. "Remove the head, the spirit follows."

Fingers of one hand grip the top teeth, fingers of the other grip the lower as the assassin tries to wriggle free. Jake has the briefest image of how it must be to wrestle an alligator while trying to pry its mouth open.

Jake strains, pries; pries harder.

Black Hair tries to scream. Instead: a tearing sound, a ripe orange being torn apart. Heavy. Meaty. With lots of juice spurt.

With a bellow that echoes across the immediate neighborhood, Jake rips the assassins head open at the mouth. The heavy skull lid flips back. The mangled lower jaw goes sideways. Jake lets the body go, fingers, face and front splattered with Black Hair's gore-slop.

The body drops to the pavement.

A single engine Cessna coughs overhead. Piping and small nozzles are attached to the trailing edge of its wings. The plane's body beyond the shattered cockpit spit a line of black smoke and orange-red flame. It comes in so low Jake can feel the heat and the wind of its passing as the plane plummets from the sky, big as life.

A second plane follows—this one still in one piece. It buzzes over, bears due north as if trying to get out of the UCRA as quickly as possible. On one of the wings, an ornately sprayed tag: REGANSHIRE.

"Oh shit," Jake gasps, realizing the first aircraft's trajectory. He falls upon Bob instinctively, protectively, covering the squirming man's body with his.

The flaming Cessna clips the flat roof of the old Van's trophy store across the street from Bob's gas station. It flips and barrels into an abandoned two-story house behind the store, explodes, throws debris high into the air.

Jake gets to his feet, winces as he feels the now dead-dead assassin's blade touch a live nerve. He pulls the long knife out, drops it to the concrete at his boot tips. He presses his hands to the wound, both front and back. Slowly the blood flows.

From the surrounding houses stagger the UCRA residents. Drawn out by the explosion, by the noise of the crashing plane, by their strange undead nature telling them the chaos may bring "fresh meat." Dozens of bedraggled and rotting citizens move towards the old store and burning wreckage across the street from the service station.

Black smoke rolls towards the blue firmament, but Jake

notices a strange yellow vapor roiling beneath. Like heavy fog, it creeps slowly out of the flames, flows down over the roof of the dilapidated trophy store and into the street.

A man in tattered pants, bare chested save for layers of pale peeling flesh, stops and peers down as the thick yellow vapors coalesce about his bare feet. His head snaps upright. He spins about with more speed than Jake thought possible for the doped UCRA folk. The man seems to look to his brethren who continue to shamble towards him and the expanding ochre mist…

…Then he screams. He screams with dry tortured vocal cords, the sound like a bleating billy goat with its nuts in a vise.

His shriek, a mixture of surprise and pain, does nothing to detour the others of his ilk. They move faster towards him, to the further call of chaos.

"Gosh, Captain, this sure looks familiar," Lettner chuckles, standing beside Billet as the yellow ground fog rises up the legs and torso of the screaming zombie man.

Jake's heart pounds. It feels like the first time he's ever felt it beat. It beats too fast though, like a coked up kid playing a snare drum.

It's due to what he sees on the street.

"Yes, this looks very familiar." Lettner says taking a step backwards out of Billet's line of sight.

The yellow mist isn't rising; the bodies of the undead sink into it. Sink as skin sloughs and drools away like candle wax, as bones turn rubbery, and flesh and black organs turn to red paste.

Chapter Ten

There is nothing more agonizing to listen to than the bawl of the undead. It is like listening to a cow at slaughter, where the beast isn't quite dead and the chainsaw doesn't bite through in that first stroke. All you know is the poor creature feels every steel tooth of the saw tearing into its flesh. The horrible death knell increases on the street as UCRA civilians, once living, breathing folks, humans, turn to puddles of gore. They are unable to move, only able to dissolve like plastic in a hot furnace.

Jake loops his arms under Bob's armpits and lifts. For an emaciated bag of flesh and bones, the old boy weighs a ton. Ignoring the pain in his side, the gunshot wound to his arm, Billet lifts and drags Bob away from the spreading yellow fog curling and undulating toward the gas station.

"It affects healthy and unhealthy flesh," Lettner says skipping along excitedly beside Billet.

"Is this real? This can't be real," Jake says.

He spies a large garbage dumpster sitting behind the service station. It butts up against the wall of the one story building. "Who would bring this to the city? How could they without someone knowing. All the people we work with. We would've had Intel on this."

Black Hair's one word, one name, closed Jake's mouth, and then: "Largo."

Rupert Largo is well known for his contempt for Mayor Honeywell. Everyone knew, including the mayor, the City Treasurer bucks for his position. Rumors also abound there was a city commissioner leading an underground group of radicals looking to eradicate the zombie populace in the UCRA. GRAZA, Grand Rapids Anti-Zombie Association it was called.

With the activities of Loyalists well-known in West Michigan since Lettner's death, and GRAZA, and singular folk who take things into their own hands: the big city was hard pressed to really dig deep and pursue anyone in these extreme factions.

Now, adding hired armed insurgents—mercenaries—to the mix...

Jake's head spins with the endless possibilities.

"Quite the shit storm you're in, Captain," Lettner says as Jake drags Bob to the trash gon.

Lifting, pushing, struggling, Jake hefts Bob onto the steel trash receptacle. He climbs upon himself, then lifts the old undead gas station attendant to the roof line. A sack of potatoes would be easier to maneuver. He fumbles, almost drops them both back to the pavement below. The holes in his chest, arms and legs ache dully. His clothing sticks to his flesh, pulls away every time he moves, causes pain. He takes it, the only thing that makes him feel alive, motivated.

The yellow mist sweeps around the corner of the gas station. Lettner stands there, ground level, smiling, unaffected; it's an old friend to him.

"I see pretty clearly," Jake says, one last thrust upward, heaving Bob over the edge. He hears the crunch of gravel as the old zomb hits the flat roof top. Jake follows, starts to pull himself up and over. "Largo's involved in this somehow. Maybe the whole thing."

The toxic fog coils around the gas pumps, roils around and beyond, spreading like an incoming ocean tide. Jake sees the black haired rotter sent to kill him shrouded in the stuff, like a body lying just under a watery surface. Flesh melts away from skull. Clothing deflates as the body is eaten away. Red-black liquid gore oozes from shirt collar, sleeves and pant cuffs. A skeleton in ragged black combat attire is all that remains within a few heartbeats.

"At least he's better off," Lettner says, the first hint of glumness in his usually sarcastic jovial tone.

Jake ignores the man and pulls himself over the roof's ledge. He rolls, pushes himself upright, kneels, body crunching the gravel and tar-lined service station rooftop. The heavy fog doesn't rise any higher than the mid-way point of the big metal trash gon. Thankfully.

It's still a problem though as Jake peers down at the swirling, spreading mist. If it's the same stuff Lettner used on the West Olive populace years ago, the substance affects healthy, living flesh the same as necrotic, dead flesh; eats it down to the bone, all flesh, all muscle, tendons, organs. It turns one to sauce without the blender.

In the distance, from the city, sirens wail.

"They're bringing in the firefighting units," Jake says aloud, kneeling beside the still form of Bob. "They don't know what they're driving into." Taking his tattered and torn, bloody shirt off, he gently winds it about Bob's head to keep what's left of the ancient man's rotting gray matter inside his shattered skull. He ignores the deep gashes and puckered, weeping holes about his own uncovered body.

It will take the city several minutes to gather the protective convoy to flank the lone, special UCRA-designated pumper truck—an old converted MRAP the size of a school bus.

All the buildings west of the gas station are one story; Bridge Street Fluorescents, a short hop from the service station roof to it, then down and a quick jog across the lawn of the West Side Savings & Loans, Flamingo Lounge, a vacant lot and then Squire John's Fish-n-Chips.

An overturned Buick blocks the front entrance of the old

restaurant on the corner of Lane and Bridge, purposely situated, along with wood-plank and steel-reinforced front and side windows. The rear entrance, a steel door with an electronic sensor pad and video monitor above, keeps the contents inside safe from the local populace and then some.

"Radio in the Lane Avenue safe house," Billet checks one last time that Bob was secure.

Lettner looks up at him through the bloody shirt. "You better hurry, Captain. You don't want anyone else to die on your watch."

Unholy screams from below, Jake glances over the roof's side to see several more curious neighborhood civilians engulfed in the yellow fog.

"Help… us," his wife Jenna cries from the roadway, the ghost image of her and Joey starting to sink beneath the ochre waves.

"Fuck you. Not this time," Jake says back to Lettner, finding just Bob's shattered visage gazing up at him. The old boy lives, and there'd be plenty others if he can get to the Lane safe house, to the communications radio he knows is within.

He stands and runs for the west edge of the rooftop. He leaps the arm-length span between the gas station and the Bridge Street Fluorescents rooftop. With all his wounds, he expects more pain versus the dull throb.

On the opposite side of the lighting distributor store, a short drop to street level again. Jake stops, peers over the roof's edge. The heavy yellow vapors have flowed like flood waters further down the street, swirling around the West Side Savings & Loan, the Flamingo Lounge and further.

"How much did that plane carry?" he asks himself.

Never the less, he swings himself over the edge of the roof, and drops to ground level. He turns, standing on the grassy sward lining the old bank building ahead of him. The cloying yellow mist swirls about him, waist level, rolling up along his bruised and bleeding naked abdomen and chest.

He begins to scream.

Like a million razor teeth against his exposed skin, the flesh eating mists begin to feast.

***

"Quit screaming, ya big baby," Loutonia says across the internal channel. "Or turn off your mike."

"I can't believe our own mother fuckin' guys shot me." Stokes grips his hatch coaming with one hand and looks at his free arm he lets dangle at his side.

Mulholland leans forward from his rear hatch, able to view enough of the "carnage" his front gunner friend is making commotion about.

"You're just grazed," Mulholland says, exasperation in his voice.

The radio crackles. "We're at Lake Michigan Drive, heading to Lane and Bridge to assess the crash site. Other bogie is heading out of town," Breckenridge, voice pinched, short, agitated.

"Watch your step. We got Friendlies coming out on the street, attracted by the crash and all the activity." Forrester chimes in. "Next thing we'll get citations for noise pollution in the UCRA."

"Huron, what's your 20?" Breckenridge asks.

Stokes presses his throat mike closer against his skin. He winces, swears as the torn sleeve, sticky with blood, pulls at his arm wound. He sees Mulholland pretend to rub an eye with his fist, making a face: boohoo.

Stokes flips him off, then answers their convoy commander, "We're on Straight, coming up on the Jackson safe house. Lotta smoke and screaming rotters comin' from where the plane went down."

"Emergency vehicles are on the way. Don't shoot the pumper truck," Breckenridge responds.

Stokes makes a sour face, not sure if the tank CO is making a personal jab at him.

"Oh gawd," Loutonia says over the airwaves as they roll up to the corner of Straight and Jackson. The safe house is the second house from the corner. A body lies between the sidewalk and front lawn, torn in two, local civilians standing and kneeling about it, some unenthusiastically gnaw on leg and torso sections.

"Is it the captain?" Mulholland says. He tries to crane his neck and body to get a better view as they rumble up and stop at the corner intersection.

One of the BRV's behind them pulls ahead and up in front of the driveway. Some of the locals scatter, hop-hobble away, others stop their lethargic feasting and stand with jaws hanging open, drooling blood. They gaze about innocently like kids caught with their hands in the cookie jar. Two soldiers jump out of the BRV and approach the civilians and the mutilated body.

"It's not Billet," one of the soldiers radios, voice calm, normal to not further spook the undead civvies. "I don't recognize this guy, well, even in his current state. One of the infiltrators?"

"He's been here. I know it," Loutonia says on the Huron's internal channel.

"Throw a tarp over the body and secure it," Stokes says, "We have emergency vehicles coming in. Let's get ahead of them." Bridge Street is two short blocks away.

The men run back to the BRV, unload a large blue tarp and run back; covering the body and "staking" it down with a few chunks of broken curb and asphalt chunks from the street. The few locals still milling about stand there, looking down at the tarp, mewing and groaning: snack denied.

The Huron takes the lead, rumbling down Straight Avenue the few blocks to Bridge.

"What the shit?" Stokes says as they turn left onto Bridge. Indiana Avenue—zombie Bob's gas station locale—and the plane crash site a short block away.

The Huron turns into the tide of yellow fog which breaks and curls along the front of the big HTV as if it plows through a shallow wall of water.

Viewports open, Loutonia screams and coughs as the dense unnatural vapors flood the cab.

At that exact moment, a new voice breaks over the GRCC air waves. Coarse like speaking with a throat filled with sand and gravel, halting as if spoken between bouts of intense pain: "This is… Captain Jacob Billet of… the HTV Huron… downed plane was carrying bio-agent like that of… West Olive incident." The radio crackles. "Do not… enter area without… NBC systems fully engaged."

The Huron jerks to a stop, throwing Stokes and Mulholland against their hatch coaming. They both cough and wave frantically at the air as the disturbed yellow air rolls up over the top of the Huron.

"I repeat… engage all Nuclear Biological and Chemical systems before entering," Billet's gruff voice sounds.

"Jake," Loutonia says in a small voice, struggling to breathe.

The West Olive Township "cleansing" had been initiated by the late William Lettner, ex-Muskegon High Commissioner and ex-leader of the North Shore Coalition. Six years ago he sanctioned a chemical dowsing of the large lakeshore property in an effort to wipe out the undead "polluting" that land. The bio-agent was unproven and literally dissolved both living and unliving tissue, killing over a thousand innocent civilians, including Billet's wife and teenage son.

As Loutonia chokes on the thick ochre fog filling the drivers cabin, her exposed skin starts to itch and burn, she fears she will never see Jake again.

***

"Damn, this reminds me of a bad case of jock itch," Stokes says, scratching at his hairy arms and face. They itch and burn, but that's all.

The tide of yellow fog settles, cascades off the body of the big transport like dry ice "smoke" off a stage. Retaining its depth, coming up to upper rim of the Huron's front dualies and rear tracks, the M213 sits like a big metal box in a yellow stream.

Loutonia closes the ports with a flick of a switch and vents the guts of the rig, drawing in filtered but fresh air into her lungs. Her hands and face itch terribly. She checks herself in the small mirror dangling right of the steering yoke. No signs of flesh blistering or running, just a slight jaundiced patina on her brown skin that wipes off when she runs a finger across her cheek.

"Huron, Grizzly here. You folks all right?" Breckenridge, on the radio.

"Whatever it is, whatever the plane carried, wasn't the same stuff," Stokes replies, peering over the Huron's side. He can see the remnants of unfortunate UCRA citizens who had been trapped in the stuff. Amber-stained bones mix with a red-black goo beneath the surface of the dissipating yellow mists. The vapor flow down sewer grates like the ground is drawing a deep breath.

"The pumper truck has NBC analysis capabilities. We'll leave that for them," Breckenridge responds. "What's the crash site status? We're heading up to the Lane-Bridge safe house." Hesitation. "Captain? Jake, are you there?"

Loutonia's breath catches in her throat, though not from the current clean air.

Silence.

"I'm here, but in… pretty bad… shape." Billet's voice again, gravel-filled, cracking, stuttered. The last view words sound as if he struggles to emit them. "I've run… into a little bit… of resistance."

"Same here," Breckenridge replies. "We're a block away."

"I know… who's behind… all this." Billet's voice grows faint, fainter. Words garbled.

"Hold tight, Captain. We'll be right there," Breckenridge answers.

"Captain, we're be there shortly," Loutonia says.

"Negative, Huron. You'll wait for the pumper truck and secure the crash site."

Loutonia bites back further words as her frustration in not getting to Jake's side makes her want to curse her superior.

"Copy that, sir. Yessir." Stokes replies quickly.

"I'll have one of our trucks run Billet to the Apostolate," Breckenridge says. "We'll try to keep any further civilians from entering the contaminated zone. Do the same on your end until the stuff can be analyzed."

"Roger that. Huron, out." Stokes looks at the yellow swirl and the unmoving skeletal carcasses below it.

He spotted a few living zombs on the other side of the street, on the edge where the fog boils. They stop several feet from the roiling mists, appear to look about, and then turn and shamble away.

"Still a flicker of brilliance in their fucked up brain," he mumbles, fishing a stump of a cigar from his vest pocket. He winces when his torn sleeve again grazes his arm wound.

"Gawddammit," Loutonia swears off channel.

Stokes hears her from below, switches to the internal frequency. "We'll hook back up with the captain. No worries."

"We better," Eddie Mulholland breaks in. "Command is going to drag him in for questioning, unless the City Council gets their claws into him first."

"Speaking up now, Alabama? I thought you had something against the captain, all quiet and shit before his collapse." Stokes watches a re-furbed MRAP heading their way from the east, one of the emergency trucks from the city. It kills the sirens before entering the neighborhood, not wanting to put the locals in a tizzy. A pair of Humvees, not GRCC but GRPD, ride fore and aft of the big red vehicle.

Stokes turns his head, looks to Mulholland. Eddie peers back at him with furrowed brow, creasing his freckled face.

"I had some issues, not knowing the captain was sick at the time," Mulholland responds, words carrying from his mike to Stokes and Phelps ears only. "I had some issues when the captain went ape shit on Lettner last year. I didn't know the bad blood between them, what pain and anger the captain must've fought to contain that whole trip.

"I held that against him, that last act before they took Lettner away. I had issues with him right up until he collapsed. Bugged me, after he was comatose. I couldn't talk to him about it, realizing I should." Mulholland looks west down Bridge Street, where his captain surely is: alive but obviously still in rough shape.

"Boo-hoo. You're gonna make me cry," Stokes chuckles as he put the stump of cigar in his mouth. His chortle jiggles the piece of stogie from his mouth. It tumbles down, bounces off the top of the Huron and falls into the yellow pollutant. "Fuck," he quietly curses.

"He brought us through a lot," Mulholland snaps at the front gunner. "He's still deep in shit, and he's still our commander, and we're still his crew. What befalls him, we gotta be there for him, no matter what."

The pumper truck rolls to a stop before entering the swirling ochre ground cover as do the two Police Humvees. The driver of the lead vehicle sticks his head out the window and looks at a gooey body just within the perimeter of the yellow fog.

"You can head in. The stuff is non-lethal to us, so far." Loutonia radios.

"Copy that, Huron. We got orders to take samples and figure out what it is."

The MRAP fire truck rolls by the police vehicle and drives up and around the Huron. It stops in front of the defunct Marathon service station. Figures in HAZMAT suits pop up from rooftop hatchways and start shooting long geysers of water and foam at the fire just behind the old trophy shop across Bob's place.

"We'll be there for him no matter what," Loutonia says, returning to Mulholland's conversation. "Even if he's on his last leg, we'll be there for him." Visions of Jake in the hospital bed, all but dead to the world, fill her vision. She is simply happy he is still alive, awake.

"Hey, is that the wing from the plane over there?" one of the other soldiers says from a BRV-O parked beside the Huron. The grunt is out of vehicle, standing in the swirl, pointing at a mangled piece of metal hanging in a tree where the water and foam spray hits. "Is that *Reganshire* written on it?"

Loutonia comes up from below, stands opposite Stokes.

Mulholland brings a hand up, shields his eyes from the noon day sun.

"That's Reganshire tryin' to dump shit on us?" Mulholland, aghast.

"Didn't Jackson say Largo was on his way over there?" Loutonia replies, looks at the same thing everyone else is. The words on the crumpled wing, even drooling with water and fire-retarding foam, could be read. "Regan" stand out plainly, then a big crease in the tortured metal, then "ire." There is no doubt it is an aircraft from Reganshire though she doesn't recall any Intel of the small community having such vehicles.

"To find out if perhaps they're behind some of the attacks on the city," Mulholland adds.

"He might not be thrilled with their answer," Loutonia glances westward.

Chapter Eleven

"Big mess at site. Must've been a fuel leak. Charred bodies. Shell casings all around scattered amongst the debris. Some Swiss-cheesed Ferals on the perimeter," the radio squelches. "Fire burned white hot. Not sure if we'll find enough teeth to match dental records."

Devastator's tank commander, Major Jeremy Pike, notices the grin spreading on his new passenger's face, the face of Grand Rapids City Treasurer, Rupert Largo.

"You know they're talking about you and whoever rode down with you," Pike says, wiping a bead of sweat dribbling down from under his helmet.

Largo sits on the turret, two sandbags for a backrest. He wears the helmet of Devastator's gunner, Spc. Mitch Davison.

"Yes. It's very unfortunate I lost my right hand man in the crash," he responds.

"Someone local?" Pike answers.

Largo looks at him suspiciously through his one good eye. "What have you been up to, Commander Pike, since you… bugged out on your own." Changes the subject.

Thick woods hem O'Brien Road on the south side while deserted homes and properties blanket the north. Dark vacant windows stare at the big Abrams and its passenger as they roll by.

"I found Reganshire very accommodating, even with their distaste for anything Grand Rapids," Pike replies, watches the wood line as much as the desolate properties. His gloved hands grip the handles of a 50-Cal. mounted to his hatch coaming; the gun bracket looks freshly welded to the turret hatch.

"I hear they took you in with open arms."

Pike looks at the City Treasurer sideways. "You hear a lot."

"I have my contacts."

It is Pike's turn to cast a gaze of suspicion at the other man.

"They were happy for another piece of artillery, more armor, considering they've continued to work on their own to procure men and vehicles from outside West Michigan." Pike says, again wiping a droplet of sweat from his left eye with the back of his hand.

Largo notices a red raised scar on the TC's wrist, oddly in the shape of an R.

"We had to go a few days in lock up, being grilled by Old Man Regan's daughter," Jeremy shivers at the memory, "and some behemoth who now commands their military operations. But once we made amends with that gent, all was good."

A voice from below speaks up, "Except we got the crap jobs. Like being sent out into the boonies to pick up a big ole piece of sh…"

Pike jerks at the waist. Something thuds below. "Riggs," he growls at his driver.

"If you want to change out Larsen's position due to insubordination, Major, I'd be glad to take up his seat," Corporal A.G. McGraw says from below.

"I know now. A.G. stands for Ass Groveling…" Gunner Mitch Davison says from within the turret and the open hatch next to where Largo sits.

"Enough!" Pike booms. "You assclowns'll be walking back to camp if you keep this bullshit going." A leaky faucet seems to be under his headgear, he wipes another dribble of sweat from his brow.

Devastator's crew apologizes in unison; twisting, overlapping statements of "Sorry, sir" and "Won't happen again, commander, sir."

Pike clears his throat and resumes what he had been originally saying about their new tour of duty under Reganshire's guidance.

"They keep us up on deck for all their major runs since the incident at VSU in Allendale last year." He recalls Captain Billet and crew talking about their foray near the communal of mad scientists and experiments-gone-dangerously-wrong animal mutations. "We've not run into anything that fun. Just been doing small, run-about town missions keeping the place intact."

They roll past Collindale Avenue, an intersecting street that butts into and ends at O'Brien. The road dips into a gentle trough at the two streets before gradually rising again.

"Gathering ahead. We're almost to the spot," Driver Rigley "Riggs" Larsen says over the comm as the tank begins to slow its climb with the rise in the road.

"Copy that," Pike says, digging down on the left side of his commander's station as his gunner does the same. Davison pops up with a long rifle in tow and positions himself on his hatch cowling a moment before Pike does the same; slips a scoped, long-barreled hunting rifle from somewhere beneath him inside the turret.

Both men crank back the bolt of their respective gun, checking to make sure it's loaded. Largo thinks he sees a strange-colored cartridge in Davison's gun chamber.

"And what's your business heading to Reganshire?" Pike asks the Treasurer who starts to shift uncomfortably against his steel and sandbag turret seating.

Largo watches both men as they rest the butt of their guns before them on the turret and stare straight ahead. The tankers lean the barrels against their shoulder. Sleeves that had been rolled up to elbow are now worked back down to wrist. The City Treasurer says with a nervous stutter to his voice: "To see Old Man Regan, and come to some agreement on restoring pleasantries between Grand

Rapids and Reganshire."

Pike laughs. "Good luck with that."

Davison climbs fully out of the gunner's hatch, bumps into Largo but says nothing.

Another tanker, with McGraw on the name tape of his tactical vest, pops up like a big prairie dog in the gunner's wake. He climbs past Davison and the City Treasurer to the rear of the tank, untying a pair of large cloth tarps. Cloth tarps: something that can be used as a makeshift body bag.

"Oh shit," Largo mumbles under his breath. His one good eye starts to look for an avenue of escape.

"I'll say," Pike responds overhearing the man's gasp, "I've been trying to get audience with him since I got there. I only get to talk to his whacked-out daughter."

The Devastator makes the rise of the roadway and stops abruptly. The tank crew ready, they move little. Largo, on the other hand, jerks sideways into Pike's thick arm.

"For all we know, Silas is dead and Rebecca Regan runs the show," the TC concludes.

"Wh-what're we doing?" Largo finds the question hard to ask. His view shifts from McGraw quietly unraveling the tarps, shaking them out like bed sheets, to Davison, grinning at Pike, re-arms himself with the big rifle, and Pike who does the same with his weapon.

Pike places his big mitt of a hand atop Largo's helmet and turns his gaze forward.

The road dips deep again, deeper, into an almost valley-like depression. Another street intersects O'Brien from the south. At this intersection, crowding about… something… in the middle of the road like crows on a car-mashed rabbit carcass, a small group of raggedy Feral zees stand or squat. Focused now, Largo's ears pick up their hungry growls as they feast on something in their midst. They dig their hands into it, claw and scoop up something red and meaty into their terrible maws. So intent on their morbid meal, they don't appear to notice the massive Abrams tank perched above them at the top of the road.

"Like my driver so poetically said," Pike speaks. "We get the shit jobs. See those fine folk down there." He points at the feasting Ferals. "Two of them get a trip back to Reganshire for some… re-educating so-to-speak."

"Re-educating?" Largo says as both men with the rifles lift and takes aim. It is the first time he notices vented suppressors affixed to the end of each gun.

Pike tsks with eye to scope. "I know you weren't born yesterday, Mister Treasurer." Largo puffs up his chest a bit with the title statement. Pike grins, knowing. "Reganshire's been amassing folks—undead or otherwise—for some time now. Diversifying, I'd say. Soldiers from other outposts, some ZTs even," he says with a sudden growl of anger, "vehicles, a few nutjob scientists from VSU. Hell, I think they even hired some mercenaries from somewhere."

Largo's eyes widen at this, and then a smile lights his sweaty face. This was the reason he was going to see Old Man Regan: they appear to work on the same level. If he put Reganshire on his side, pull Grand Rapids and them together, and get rid of Mayor Honeywell in the process; more land, more opportunity.

"We dart the strongest of the Ferals, then haul them back to Reganshire," Pike explains, dialing in the scope atop his gun with sausage-sized fingers. "They got some concoction they shoot up the uglies with, makes them a bit more controllable. A bit, not like the UCRA citizens, just enough to leash and train them to use them for their own personal attack dogs. Pretty fucked up."

Ingenious, the City Treasurer thinks. He makes a mental note to ask Silas Regan about this.

"All right. Let's do this," Pike says as his finger slides into the trigger guard and loops around the trigger.

"Beers on you if I bring mine down first," Davison says, eye to scope, finger on trigger.

"Get your wallet out, buddy," Pike replies.

A whistle blows shrill and loud beside Largo's ear nearly throwing him from his seat.

McGraw smiles like a kid caught with his hand in the cookie jar as he lowers the whistle from his lips.

The six Ferals lift themselves from their grisly feast, leaving the remnants of a small shattered crate and mutilated canisters of red puree. Their heads tilt towards the Devastator's position.

Largo jumps again as Pike and Davison's rifles go off. Bang! Bang!

Versus a deadly bullet, purple tufted darts fly from the guns. Pike and Davison's darts hit their targets within an eye blink of the others.

Pike's hit a broad shouldered brute in the neck, diving into the rotted flesh that must have been a bit too rotted as the projectile blows through, in one side and out the other, to hit a smaller FZ on the other side of it. The dart hits the creature in the chest. The zomb peers down at the quivering thing in its right breast, and then collapses like a puppet that's had its strings cut.

Davison's dart hits the other big Feral of the group. The purple tailed projectile slaps into one of its gray-skinned arms. The burly beast glances down at the dart, snarls with broken teeth and black gums at the object, then fumbles backwards as if hit by a sudden strong breeze. It twists, slowly twirls like a drunken behemoth ballerina, then falls onto the gravel and weed-festooned side of the roadway.

"Hey! Hey!" McGraw shouts behind Largo, again too close to the Treasurer's ears. The loader waves his arms, gathering the attention of remaining FZ's who seem, surprisingly, slightly dazed and slower than usual.

The meat is doped, Largo surmises.

The standing Ferals start an uneven trot up the road towards them, leaving their fallen brethren and the meat slop for freshly, livelier food in the big armored tin can at hill top.

Pike and Davison put their rifles down.

Largo jumps yet again as McGraw brings up an HK416 and fires into the four advancing creatures. Pop! Pop! Pop! Pop! A hole appears in dead center of each advancers forehead. Still a soft one, Pike's original target's head snaps backwards and falls off, leaving a torn round of dark and black bloody flesh and throat guts.

The shell casings bounce off Largo's helmet.

All four FZ's drop into a state of final, and forever, lifelessness.

"Beers on you, commander," Davison smiles, puts his rifle down into the tank.

"Mine hit first," Pike snarls. "It just didn't… stick."

Davison smiles broadly.

"I did say something earlier about walking home, didn't I?" Pike warns.

Davison's smile turns to a frown.

"Now the fun part," McGraw says placing his assault rifle in the rack behind the turret and scooping up a pair of unfurled tarps. He grabs a rung on the top of the turret as the Devastator's twin turbine engines growl to life, and the big tank lurches forward, starting down the hill.

The tank crunches over the bodies of the dead Zees. It stops at the bottom of the hill, tracks mashing the drugged meat remnants into one with the cracked pavement.

McGraw jumps down from the tank, tarps flapping behind him. Davison climbs from his turret hatch, follows. They go to the downed brute on the road side. The creature still groans but does not move.

With one gloved hand on the grip of his mounted 50-Cal., Pike looks at Largo. "Well, Mister Treasurer, get down and help them secure our prizes."

Rupert Largo glances at the TC incredulously, then his brows knit into a stern disapproving look. "I'm not…" he starts, then his words fall short as he sees Pike's hand drop to the chest-holstered sidearm. The City Treasurer growls and climbs to his feet. He spreads his arms out to keep his balance as he moves to the side of the turret, then steps down to the hull deck.

"If you're on my rig, you're part of my crew and pull your weight," Pike says to Largo.

Largo eyes the TC venomously, suspecting the traitorous man would have no issue putting a bullet in his skull and leaving him there for another scavenging Feral or two. He drops to the roadside without a word, and goes to assist the Devastator's two crew men, who are already wrapping and binding the big doped brute Davison had dropped.

"And wait for the burden you feel when you venture into Reganshire, ya piece of shit," Jeremy Pike says under his breath. He watches the Grand Rapids City Treasurer get his hands bloody, and suspects the man is used to it, figuratively if not literally.

***

Reganshire, formerly the village of Standale before things went to hell in a hand basket, sits roughly fifteen miles west of the big city of Grand Rapids. When Silas Regan, a prominent business man in the area, took over after the mayor of Standale "lost his head" after Turning, Old Man Regan not only changed the name of the place, but changed the town and town's stance on the outside world.

Intent on keeping his people close and protected, he literally bulldozed everything along the perimeter of the village. He utilized the scrap material to build a bric-a-brac enclosed community and central living quarters where a large supermarket and its expansive property had stood.

Grand Rapids, still maintaining industries after it too walled itself up, was the main provider to many of the smaller towns and villages in a 30 mile radius. Distributing goods and services without asking for much in return, after some years of doing so, the big city requested "payment" in trade with the smaller communities. Southwest of Reganshire, old fertile farmlands stretched. Old Man Regan controlled these, and trade of edible crops for weapons and other essentials to survive did Reganshire well.

Protecting his community had always been paramount to Regan. When Grand Rapids suspended further trade of arms, vehicles and personnel, Silas kept bringing those items into his fold: some illegally, some with bribery, some with good ole American know-how under the principle: you scratch my back, I'll see you rewarded properly.

"This is Rover-One. We're bringing meat for delivery," Pike says as the Devastator approaches the intersection of O'Brien and Wilson.

Still on his turret-top perch, Largo doesn't see any fencing cordoning off this section of Reganshire land. Surprised to say the least, all he notices are two guard shacks sitting atop a bundle of banded telephone poles roughly fifty feet off the ground. One stands on the southeast corner, and the other stands on the northwest. Dark mirrored glass lines all four sides of the small shacks. A pair of small rails run along the entire bottom edge of the shacks, and a large electrical box with a pair of small transformers rest beneath the small lofts. Small satellite dishes, a trio of them, stand upright on the rails, slowly traversing the perimeter of the small square box of the guard shack.

"What're those? Where's Reganshire's enclosure?" Largo asks as he looks about. He can now see what stands at ground level: a wide concertina-wire and fenced barricade large enough to park a Humvee inside. Such a vehicle stands parked inside each post he can see. "I know they've expanded their territory all the way down Wilson to the river. Grandville and Jenison are up in arms about it. I'd think they'd have at least corralled their holdings this short a distance from the village."

"You don't get out much, do you?" Pike says with a snort. "Or privy to much Intel on goings-on outside your posh little place in GR."

"I know plenty." Though some things I don't tell traitorous lowlifes like you.

They roll closer to the strange guard posts.

"We have you in sight. Please confirm the heat signature next to you," the radio crackles in everyone's headset.

"Friendly," Pike glances at Largo. The Treasurer sweats like a water hose is running down his head, and it probably isn't just the heat. "Grand Rapids City Treasurer from crash site."

"A couple FZ's on the perimeter, but you're clear, Rover-One." The lead guard shack closest to their approach responds.

Pike notices Largo staring up at the oddly configured structure with the broadcasting dishes and a guy hanging out the window of the post waving them on.

"Giv'er a little gas, Lars." Pike says.

The Abrams lurches as brakes are applied the same time the turbine engine loudly growls and huffs. The noise reverberates along the densely wooded roadway.

"Rover-One, what're you doing? I got FZ's coming in on your six." The tower says.

"Oops." Pike feigns innocence.

"Jesus, what're you doing? Get this thing moving!" Largo yells, glancing back, seeing four Ferals slash their way out of the thick underbrush several yards behind them.

"Wait for it," Mitch Davison chuckles next to Largo. The gunner hunkers down at chest level in his hatch looking at the same thing the Treasurer is.

"What the hell? Move or shoot at those damn things or something," Largo says starting to rise from his seat. If these clowns don't move, I'm bailing and running for the guard post.

"We can't just shoot them. Mr. Treasurer, they might be

someone's—hell, say it ain't so—lost family member or something."
Davison grins.

Brow furrows, Pike sends daggers at the squirrely gunner.

"Giv'em heat. Our spectator wants a demo," Pike calls to the guard post.

Largo watches the small satellite dishes move along the track on the bottom edge of the guard tower. They form a line of four, side by side.

"Roger that," the tower replies.

"I didn't bring my suntan lotion," Davison chuckles. He drops below the hatch cowling into the tank's interior.

Largo looks at the gunner disappear. He turns to Pike, seeing the TC do the same down periscope maneuver.

Glancing over his shoulder, he sees a group of Ferals break from the tree line and stumble out onto the roadway. They are several yards behind them. Still too close. A few stop, baggy-fleshed faces peer upward as if looking ahead at the guard posts. The others hasten their gait.

Largo rises to his feet, nearly falling. Foot asleep. The rest of his body is fully alive though suddenly feeling an intense, agonizing heat—hotter than the already scorching summer's day—push against him, makes his flesh seem to cook within his clothing. He screams, not able to take the pulsing wave, fears he'll burst into flame at any moment.

Pike reaches up from his gopher hole and pulls the City Treasurer down, drops the man on his butt.

Largo swears as his ass glances off a thick iron rung on the turret, but notices the intense heat lessen.

The advancing Ferals slow their gait towards the tank and outpost. A few instantly stop, turn and hop-shamble in the opposite direction. Three stop in mid-stride and appear to check themselves. Gray-skinned hands claw at their tattered clothing and exposed flesh. They act like they want to get out of their own skin.

Four FZ's continue to advance, with struggling steps. They lean forward like they battle a strong breeze though none exists.

Largo yelps and goes down on his belly as another searing wave of heat threatens to cook his skull inside his borrowed helmet.

Three of the advancing Ferals slow to a stop, arms sluggishly rising, slapping themselves as if they try to extinguish invisible flames about their body. The fourth "wild dog" zombie pushes forward, mouth open, broken teeth bared, black tongue wagging. Largo can't exactly tell, but damn if the thing isn't viciously smiling.

"That's a resilient one," Pike says raising his head just above the hatch coaming.

Wisps of smoke start to rise from the lone Feral.

"That's what we need, one tough walking carcass starting a forest fire." Pike lifts an arm, pistol in hand, aims, pulls trigger.

The top of the stubborn Zee's head flies away in a spray of meat and bone. It drops to the pavement, dead-dead, at the same time the intense heat dissipates against Largo's own skull.

Looking confused, the remainder of the small Feral horde turn and depart back into the woods.

Largo's lower jaw hangs as if unhinged. It's the first time he's seen commonly ferocious, unyielding Feral-type Zees retreat from a living human snack.

"You're clear to advance, Rover-One." The guard post acknowledges. Two of the scooped dishes retract around to the other side of the lofty shack.

"Roger that. Thanks for the show." Pike responds and rises back topside, helps Largo sit upright again.

"Whatever," the tower replies, annoyed.

With a jerk and rev of its turbine engine, the Devastator starts forward. It rolls past the guard towers, turning right onto the cracked and rutted roadbed of M11, Wilson Avenue.

"What the hell was that, Major?" Largo says, looking back at the towers and the intersection. Nothing else moves from the woods.

"It's an Active Denial System. Military grade 95 gigahertz of microwave heat," Pike answers.

Heading north on Wilson, Largo can see the west side of the road and a 15-foot cyclone fence: Reganshire lands.

Pike inspects the fence line as they pass and proceed up the hilly road. "The living don't like it, nor do the undead who still have a scrap of nerve endings. Reagnshire's got ADS towers running up and down the road, and around the perimeter of their property. A few bigger ones, single systems, mounted on a truck or two."

"Great when you got a whole horde bearing down on you." Davison says popping back up in his gunners hatch.

Loader A.G. McGraw responds in everyone's headset: "Not so good if you don't like feeling your sub dermal skin layer cooked."

"They also have some AHDs," Pike continues, "I don't know what is worse; that burning, itching sensation or going deaf with bleeding eardrums." He chuckles seeing the effect the new knowledge has on the City Treasurer, knowledge he knows the man did not know. Admittedly, when he arrived in April, he was even surprised to find Reganshire had such technology. The GRCC in Grand Rapids, or anyone else in the area, didn't have it.

"AHD?" questions Largo.

Davison pulls a piece of jerky from the pocket of his tactical vest, bites off a big hunk and starts chewing while looking back at their undead captive cargo strapped on the tank's rear. "Acoustic Hailing Device." A line of brown half-chewed jerky drool creeps from the corner of his mouth. "Like the early warning systems the city uses when its defenses are breached…"

Unless the attack comes as a surprise from the inside, Largo thinks to himself with an internal grin.

"…but this one tries to blow your eardrums out at fifty yards," Davison continues. "Even irritates the dead folk enough to call them in, or, if the tone's maintained, slows them enough in their tracks to put a few slugs into them."

"Where'd Silas get this technology?" Largo asks. They roll over a deep rut in the road that makes his teeth rattle. "I'm surprised our military doesn't have it."

"The tech's out there," Pike says, "but they only field it in the big, big cities like New York and Los Angeles. Honeywell did have a connection to get some of the hardware, but turned it down due to cost. It's not cheap."

Another thing I can further announce to my city constituents to damn Mayor Honeywell's career, Largo thinks. Honeywell's ignored the fact the city needs further resources. The city needs to expand, not be all trussed up and tied down to the confines of the downtown area. The lands to the west should be theirs also, not the blight hole of undead civilians who add no value, just cost to Grand Rapids for upkeep and continued military presence.

And while shit hits the fan in town, ignore the fact of my string pulling, he continues. Good ole Dennis Honeywell, off chumming it up with the NSC Muskegon high councilman, working on trade and transportation deals to stretch Grand Rapids resources thinner and add more cost.

"You're not even out here in Reganshire seeing what our neighbors have that trumps our great city."

"What was that?" Pike asks.

"Nothing." Largo says quickly, not realizing he'd spoken aloud. The damn sweltering heat is making him loopy.

Over a rise in the road, another row of high-rise guard posts stand, two abreast on either side of the two lane roadway. Beyond the second row, more tall fencing which cuts off the avenue from further advance. Pieces of sheet metal and berms of sand bags line the inside of the fence line. Purposely cut-out wide rectangles in the metal barricades reveal armed men behind them, men who watch the Devastator's advance.

"You didn't answer me, Major, how did Old Man Regan

acquire such technology?" Largo asks as he spies the same radar-like dishes mounted on the towers ahead of them.

There is no doubt Regan has money. His great-grandfather on his father's side had owned the underground mines in and around Grand Rapids and outlying areas. Oil drilling and finds on these lands also dumped greenbacks into the Regan family kitty.

To not stay connected to Reganshire is pure stupidity, Largo thinks. He adds it to the long list of why Honeywell needs to go.

The Devastator's exhausts huff.

"…more than geneticists there." Pike was saying before Largo's attention drew back to him. The tank begins to slow as it approaches the Reganshire's south gates, though the village proper is still a mile north.

There is activity on the other side of the enclosure. Three Humvees roll up flanked by running guards, all armed.

"What was that?" Largo asks Pike to repeat himself.

"The Valley State University communal: it's not all crazed geneticists, but also electrical engineers, folks working on military grade items not just trying to mutate local livestock for…God-knows-what."

Largo's one good eye opens wider.

"After VSU imploded last Fall, Reganshire swooped in and picked over the remains. They acquired some of the surviving civilians—scientists and engineers—from the place," Pike explains as the Abrams slows to a stop four car-lengths short of the main gate. "The Allendale communal wouldn't take any of them, so a tough lot of them were more than happy to get back behind a protective wall, and Regan was happy to offer them a home if they shared a little of their doings in place of paying rent, so-to-speak."

Largo nods. "I look forward to finding out more and taking the information back to Grand Rapids." Brilliant, brilliant, he thinks, more excited than ever to meet Old Man Regan. If he can bring about a deal of new trade and peace between Reganshire and

Grand Rapids, and this new technology, he can surely dethrone Honeywell.

Largo envisions himself giant-sized, overlooking downtown Grand Rapids, arms enveloping it, enclosed around it. He embraces the city's buildings like stacked pokerchips, meaning money, power and land, all for him. And the West Side, the blight of Grand Rapids; he sweeps his giant arms outward, dragging across the land on the west side of the river. He wipes away the UCRA, the enclosure, the undead. More land for himself.

And the God-like arms keep sweeping outward, taking down Grandville, Wyoming, Jenison, Reganshire, Allendale—everything from Grand Rapids to the lakeshore. With the right people in place, the right men at his side, the technology and military might if he deems to use it; he can have all of West Michigan.

And on this day, meeting Old Man Regan, will be the start. No barriers ahead.

The enclosure gate squeals open along dry rollers on steel rail.

From the opening, a tide of people flow. The barrels of assault rifles and shotgun barrels wag upright like reeds rustling in a mild breeze.

A giant of a man in a tactical vest, the vest looking barely able to hang on about his wide chest and broad shoulders, wades to the front as if pushed. He wears a dark tan t-shirt under the chest piece revealing darker perspiration stains about his armpits. Though he holds a big gold-plated Desert Eagle that glints in the sunlight, his muscular arms are as thick as the Devastator's 120mm cannon. They look to be made as the same material just covered in flesh. The name tape on the behemoth's vest read: LaRouge.

The big man and his armed entourage stop a cars length away from the Devastator. A dozen men run from the pack, around to the tank's rear with long poles wrapped in thick cloth. They unfurl the material as they go, revealing what appears to be two large stretchers.

"Hunt go well?" LaRouge asks, eyes going to Largo.

"Without a hitch," Pike responds. "Bagged three pieces of meat."

Largo sees Pike look at him, and his return gaze darkens.

A slender pale hand appears on LaRouge's upper arm. The big man's initial calm gaze flees, replaced with one of shocked revulsion. He step-stumbles sideways as if shoved aside by the willowy hand.

"Shit." Pike mumbles under his breath, loud enough for Largo to hear.

A young lean woman dressed in white linens draws around the giant Reganite. At first the City Treasurer thinks he looks upon a ghost or ghoul, so white is her flesh—at least that which is revealed. Wrapped in a thin veneer of flesh which reveal black veins beneath, her skeletal hands end in red-painted fingernails; talon-like in their length and file. The white gossamer gown she wears flows all the way to the ground. Largo would suspect her as being a true ethereal spirit if the bottom wasn't caked in dirt and mud, perhaps the only earthy weight keeping her tethered to the ground. Her long thin arms are wrapped in gauze nearly to shoulder blade, dappled with large patches of red and yellow stains. Something weeps from beneath the bandages trying to get out. Her porcelain face is made up with too much red rouge about her high cheekbones, making her look like a ridiculously powdered dandy from some other century. Her hair, possibly long silky and blond in healthier days, wafts behind her, white as her flesh. It waves, tiny tentacles teased in a phantom breeze where it clings in patches about her balding scalp.

"You!" the apparition shouts, voice loud and clear like emitted from a bullhorn.

Largo looks at the crimson talon pointed at him.

"You're a spy from Grand Rapids, come to take my father's secrets."

The haunt is real, Largo realizes with a sinking feeling. Old

Man Regan's insane daughter: Rebecca.

"Miss Regan, I assure you as I called ahead, I've come here to discuss new trade and other opportunities with your father. I…"

"I heard you. We all heard your intentions just a moment ago," she screeches, still shaking the accusatory finger at him. "I look forward to finding out more and taking the information back to Grand Rapids."

Largo's eye widens, and he peers at Pike.

Pike shrugs, feigns innocence. "I didn't know we were talking on an open channel." The smirk on his face betrays him.

"You're under arrest, Mister Rupert Largo," Rebecca Regan says, gritting her teeth, yellow teeth jutting from horribly receding gray-black gums. "Drag him down and put him in the stockades."

A half a dozen men jump at her command and rush to the tank, clambering upon it like ants.

"Commander, you're to be commended for your catch," LaRouge, finding his voice and stepping back beside Rebecca—but not too close. He salutes the man with two fingers quickly to brow.

Largo scowls at Pike as the Reganshire men clasp him by arms and legs.

Pike shrugs again, a look of pure innocence this time.

"I didn't know," the TC replies with a sidelong nod and wink at LaRouge.

Chapter Twelve

He awoke in a long box. He can sense the four corners, top and bottom.

And it is dark.

And his back rests on fabric, and his head lies upon a soft pillow.

His arm lay at his side while the other lay across his chest.

"Dead," Lettner says appearing over him, face down close to Jake's. "Just give it up. Be dead. Why push yourself any further? What's the point?"

"Don't listen to him, Jacob," his wife, Jenna, whispers to the other side of him. "You have much to do."

Billet realizes he lies upon a cot. His fingers can feel the stiff weave, the thick canvas.

"You'll have to tell all your military buddies about me, won't you, Captain?" Rupert Largo says, replacing the image of Lettner. "Send them all after me. Get me good."

Jake's eyesight begins to adjust. The images blur, still talking but now fuzzy silhouettes.

"Come home to me, Jake," Loutonia says close to his ear, then Jenna's voice. "Come home to me and Joey before you go."

He wants to scream.

The box lights up. Not a box, a room with wood paneled walls.

Jake clasps his hands to his throat, sits upright on a blood-stained cot. His entire body hurts, aches, feels on fire. His heart pounds like a bass drum submerged underwater.

A fuzzy form bends towards him, a stubby tube with a needle at the end draws towards him.

Get that away from me, he tries to growl. Only a strained jumble of nonsense words emits from his aching, dry vocal cords.

He slaps the needle-tipped tube away, connecting also with the hand holding the apparatus. Both items snap. The form with the damaged fingers screams then pulls the hand to chest.

A new face drops before him. A hard faced woman with short cropped dark hair and a large wood cross hanging from her neck. Jake recognizes the face frowning none-to-happy back at him. Hands as strong, callused and scar-striped as his own slam him down on his back onto the cot.

"Make sure Terese hasn't suffered any broken bones," Sister Mary Mirose says, her dark eyes not leaving Jake's. "And we won't have any more outbursts from you, correct, Captain?"

Billet cranks his head side to side. *No, ma'am.*

Another nun—a squat white-haired old woman—checks the hand of the small nun he had struck. The young one wears a different colored "tactical habit" than the two older women. Versus the darker colors, her clothing is a brown and cream colored habit tied at the waist with a slim cord. She dons no sidearms like Mirose but a secondary belt hangs lopsided at her waist with ammunition packs. And unlike Mirose who wears no cap and veil upon her home-cut close-cropped hair, the young nun does.

"I'm fine, Reverend Mother," the young girl says to Mirose. "Just cracked my knuckles."

Jake's brows rise. "Reverend Mother?" But the words come out a series of dry pops, like dry leaves crunched under foot.

Mirose sees the look on his face. "I've taken over the diocese since Father Pettish passed. You remember Father Pettish, don't you?" She asks as if testing him.

"Yes," Jake replies, a clipped hoarse bark. He nods again. It hurts to move his head.

The young girl steps back towards Billet. No Epi-pen in hand this time. She gingerly checks the bandages about his arms, waist and legs.

"This is Terese, a postulant of mine," Mirose introduces the young girl of probably thirteen years. "A nun-in-training. Another urchin like the two young men you delivered here to work this past spring. However, unlike them returning home, Terese has come and decided to give her life to the good Lord Jesus Christ, and to aid the poor and afflicted."

The behemoth nun hesitates at the last word. Her coarse mood seems to soften. She kneels beside Jake, as does her postulant seeing her mentor's actions. Mirose gently places her hands on the sides of Jake's bandaged arms; her arms like thick rippled tree limbs.

Jake can smell her; smell the blood in her veins, the strong heart pumping liquid vigor through arterial canals.

His lids flutter with the inhalation. When he opens his eyes again, he tenses on the cot and snarls.

Both women give off an annoying luminance.

Mirose shines like a spotlight, yellow around the edges but bright, an old bulb still able to exude its brilliance. Her postulant, Terese, dazzles like a welders torch, bright white, crisp. There is no heat, just the blinding glare, but Jake can smell, see and hear their blinding life aura.

It makes him angry. It makes him want to rend their flesh, tear them limb from limb, to sup from that magnificent essence.

He begins wailing, a loud, long hoarse bawl, and thrashes in place on his cot. The agony, the unbearable agony doesn't come from what he is feeling but the pain of realization, hard and honest, of what he's becoming. Perhaps what he already is.

"Be calm, my friend. Be calm by knowing the love and care of thy Lord Jesus Christ is in you and with you always," Mirose says, voice cracking.

Jake feels droplets of moisture fall upon his face. So seething with rage and death, he thinks little wisps of steam rise where the cool drops hit his flesh.

Mirose places her hands to either side of his head. Big, rough skinned hands. Cool hands. For a moment Jake fears she might crush his skull like an eggshell.

"Be calm," she repeats, pressing firmer.

Jake screams: a loud, low, ragged bellow. A thousand volts of electricity rage through his body, or so it feels. His back arches off the cot, his entire body rigid.

He collapses, loose, a ragdoll man. The seething rage and bloodlust is gone, blown out like a hurricane wind through a pile of leaves.

Mirose releases him, sniffs as Jake opens his eyes. She gasps, stumbles backwards, nearly bowling over her young postulant.

Terese steps forward, peers in silent awe as the look on the big nun's face stands out in fear-filled surprise. "Did you heal him, Reverend Mother?" the young girl asks.

Mirose bites on her words. "I… I didn't…"

Jake looks up at Mirose. He tries to speak, to thank her, but cuts himself short as his ragged voice starts to come out in a dry hiss. Instead, he nods, which hurts like hell. Muscles and bones battle against his brain as it tries to command their obedience.

Thick drapery hangs across the door to the small, dimly lit backroom in which Jake lay. It suddenly parts, metal rings clang against the aluminum crossbar spanning the door frame. Loutonia rushes through the entry and, before the curtains have a chance to settle, drops to Jake's side.

"How did you shake your coma?" Loutonia asks, strong arms wrapping around Jake. "What were you doing out there by yourself?"

Her heated concern is cooled by teardrops against Jake's flesh. He feels her warmth, can hear her heartbeat like a lightning stroke in his ear. Her blood courses in the network of veins and arteries like heavy surf with each beat. Her life aura, bright as a white light strobe, makes him gasp more than her crushing grip.

The terrible rage wells up within him. He fights it down, the urge to break his driver's—and his lover's—grip, then crush, rend, tear her apart until her life light blinks out, and her beating heart ceases to mock him.

It was the last thought, *his lover*, which makes him fight harder to regain control. It is like a child fighting a towering grizzly bear, a grain of sand fighting for a foothold against a tsunami. But he wills what is left of his human living, feeling, caring side to break from the unliving monster threatening to consume his body and soul.

Moisture rolls down his cheek. He tries to speak, a hoarse gurgle.

Loutonia loosens her grip and pulls away though keeps her hands upon his upper arms. Her brown wet eyes gaze upon him, and he wants to push away and have her not look upon him. She looks at his bandaged arms, the bulge of wrapped gauze under the fresh uniform the Apostolate nuns have clothed him in. A small white patch of linen is taped to the side of his head, already growing red about the ear and torn scalp.

Jake snaps his eyes closed as her gaze meets his. *Don't look at me*, he says in his head. *Don't look at me. I'm not ready.*

"She knows. They all know." Lettner stands behind him. "You've lost. Give it up. Give in. Let them be finished with you."

Loutonia draws down and hugs him again, holds so tight she might be trying to crush what little life he has out of him.

"I'm just glad you're…" Hesitation. "…all right, Captain."

"Come to us before it's too late." Another voice. Jenna's. "Come to us before all is lost."

Jake slowly sits up, lets Loutonia move aside and assist. Every nerve and muscle, bone, heart and thick blood scream at him to lie back down and not move. He grits his teeth, growls fiercely. *Bullshit.* 45 years: been through a lot of shit. Fuck if this is going to keep him down. There are still things to do; the main: find Rupert Largo and bring the son of a bitch to justice.

"Gonna try to see him swing?" Lettner mocks Jake, standing beside Sister Mirose and her postulant, both women oblivious to the apparition of the late Muskegon High Commissioner.

"You bet your ass," Jake says. Mirose's young postulant steps behind the big nun as he gets to his feet. His words in his head sound as a guttural grunt and hiss.

Jake is sure the young nun-in-training has never seen a dead soldier rise.

***

"This is an outrage!" Rupert Largo bellows. He digs his heels into the gravel pathway so his captors have to struggle. The small procession walking behind and alongside him appear ignorant of his shouting.

The big man in military garb, with LaRouge on his name tape, walks behind Largo, frowning. Erik LaRouge, aka Lucius LaFleur, can do without the man struggling and carrying on so.

Pike also walks behind the irate Grand Rapids City Treasurer. The Devastator parked in the background, his crew and several other Reganites carefully remove their unliving parcels.

Unlike LaFleur's frown, Pike smirks and chews the butt of a freshly lit cigar. He's not a smoker, but the stogie quells the stink of Rebecca Regan who walks several feet before them with her own retinue of guards.

"I contacted you ahead of time," Largo yells. His handlers grit their teeth, irritated. "You knew I was coming. I demand to see your father."

Rebecca stops abruptly. Her half dozen bodyguards stumble over each other. She pushes two of them aside as she spins and stomps back towards the City Treasurer. His two handlers grip grows slack and he half expects them to let go, a wide-eyed, clenched jaw look of nervous terror on their face.

"Oh shit," LeFleur says as he watches Rebecca advance, cold fury burning in her cool pale eyes.

Largo's retainers let him loose as she stops before him.

"My father is… occupied… at the moment." Rebecca says, leaning into Largo's face. With heelless shoes, she stands roughly an inch taller than the Treasurer's 5-foot-8 stature.

Largo turns his head as her foul breath snakes up his nostrils. It's more than a bad case of halitosis. Smells of meat too long in the noon day sun.

"He's busy running our meager little town," she continues, "which your mayor should be doing with his own versus sending his commissioners to spy on us."

If Grand Rapids wanted to spy on you, we wouldn't do it by walking straight in here, Rupert thinks, taking a precursory glance about the area.

The center of Reganshire consists of a renovated Meyer supermarket. It had been a massive store, the biggest shopping center in what had been the village of Standale. When Regan took the reins sometime after the initial virus swept the countryside, he spent a considerable amount of time re-purposing the outer edges of town to build up the headquarters and living quarters he planned for the old store, on the western edge of the village. Besides making a cathedral-like homestead out of the center of the large supermarket building, he built small residences for the rest of the Reganshire populace within and around the building. Smaller shops about the main grounds became barracks for the woodshops, metal shops, Reganshire militia and a host of other small manufacturing works to enhance and sustain the small town.

An old Starbucks coffee shoppe made Largo lick his lips. Even in the unrelenting heat, a good coffee sounded… good.

"If you haven't heard," Largo starts, "our 'good' mayor's been out of town visiting Muskegon. While shit hits the fan, he's nowhere in the vicinity."

"I'd heard he wasn't about, at least that's what Papa said," Rebecca says with a seductive hiss. Mood changes, her eyes drop to the City Treasurers lips. Her black tongue slithers from her mouth and runs about her pale full lips.

LaFleur shivers.

"Fucking gross," Pike mutters very softly standing behind the towering Reganite.

A mischievous smile curls Largo's facial features. "Honeywell's out cavorting with the Muskegon regent, making plans to further connect Grand Rapids with Muskegon and the lakeshore, further extend the city's influence westward." Cavorting, maybe not. The rest is true though.

Rebecca's left brow rises in suspicion. "Extending influence westward? What do you mean exactly?"

Something small, white and wriggling drops from her wispy hairline and hits the ground at her feet. One of her retinue puts a boot tip on it, grinds it into the pavement.

"Standale used to be a Grand Rapids suburb," Largo says, using the villages prior name before the pandemic and Silas Regan's emergence. "Your father has always been suspicious of… Honeywell…" Almost saying *us* which might doom his plan. "Of Honeywell wanting to extend the big city's interests back out to the suburbs."

"That's why we've worked hard to be independent," Rebecca says balling her fists, blue veins bulge through semi-translucent flesh. She knuckles her sides, stands proud, thrusting her skinny chest out. She sees the Treasurer eye her breasts through her near-sheer top. (He sees shriveled, mangled pancake-like breasts under her too-sheer top.) She smiles wider, knows he wants her. "Why, we've just finished construction of a new metals manufacturing plant, and a new meat processing facility a little southwest of Fennessy, and…"

Her guards steps side to side nervously.

LaFleur clears his throat loudly, glaring at Regan's yammering daughter.

Rebecca looks up at him towering behind the Grand Rapids man. "Do you have something in your throat? Do you need me to rip it out?" A gangly fist rises, and she opens her hand, flexing the talon-like fingernails.

"N-no, ma'am," LaFleur answers quickly. "But he *is* from Grand Rapids." *Don't tell him all Reganshire's secrets, ya stupid psychotic bitch.*

Her eyes narrow, then widen, falling back upon Rupert Largo.

Between them and the massive store-made-living quarters, a small group of Reganite soldiers run behind collared Ferals. One can tell by how unkempt the wild Zees garments—if they actually have any—hang in age-old rags from their scar-striped and dirty bodies. Their handlers hold long flexible poles which are attached to the creature's collars. The poles are stiff enough to keep the things from looping back on them, and the men jerk them roughly forward if the FZ's try to go their own way.

"To the stockades, spy!" Rebecca shrieks, dropping her open hand and pointing at Largo. Her nail nearly clips the tip of his nose.

Largo's captors grab him again.

"Wait, wait!" Largo struggles.

His retainers halt but only because Rebecca isn't moving from their path and glares at them all.

"I have information," Largo says, voice cracking, bleating like a lamb who *did not* want to be led to slaughter.

LaFleur moves aside to let Pike step in closer. Pike taps his earbud as he moves behind Largo's containment retinue.

"There are more… opportunities, should we say…" the bleating voice changes to sly fox. "I want to discuss with your father a few things. One, if we work something out together, that is, he and myself, I can guarantee a mutual benefit for Grand Rapids and Reganshire. I know there are many things Reganshire would like to have but are out of reach due to location and limited resources. Standale, back in her day, was not a factory town like Grand Rapids. Yet you have acres of woodland and vacant field, things the city doesn't have."

Rebecca listens with creased brow and a dangerous frown.

"Second, and the main, I mentioned Honeywell is in Muskegon and on his way back to town. I know his route. I know the retinue of guards and a… soft spot… along the newly re-established rail lines where a contingent of well-armed men…" Rebecca's frown deepens, and Largo quickly adds: "And women. They can easily ambush the train. Take out Honeywell. Hell, even wreck the rail line which would sever the artery again to the lakeshore, leaving better opportunities for trade between Grand Rapids and Reganshire, versus bypassing and going straight to Muskegon."

Largo smiles within. If he laid it on any thicker he'd surely drown in his own scheming.

Rebecca's frown disappears but the seriousness remains. She takes a step closer to the City Treasurer. One of Largo's handlers gulps loudly behind him. Largo stiffens inwardly, expecting a savage strike from the crazed young woman.

"What're you saying?" she hisses. "You want us to kill Mayor Honeywell?"

Largo works hard to unlock his fear-frozen jaw as the woman leans nose to nose with him. He notices her hairline move about her temples. Pale maggots squirm about the pale follicles.

"Th-that's what I'm saying," he replies, fighting back a wave of bile rising in his throat. "It's the only way I can guarantee a new mutual relationship between Grand Rapids and Reganshire. Take out the head. I'll fill in for the body.

"Honeywell's train is due to stop at the Lamont Depot

early afternoon tomorrow." Largo says. His body shivers with anticipation. "I'm one of the few who is privy to his time table and whereabouts, including the rail car he'll be riding in."

"But there is a GRCC garrison there," Rebecca says still suspicious. "We kept tabs on Honeywell's departure and activities of the Grand Rapids Central Command. Daddy isn't blind to these types of things."

"The garrison and what few men are actually part of the city's military is under my control," Largo responds. "I have a group of my own there."

His thoughts go to Tomes. It is a shame the mercenary leader died. *But then orders should have been coming straight from me anyway. The man seemed to be growing soft. I don't need people like that in my cabinet.*

"You won't have issues at Lamont. I can assure you of this," Rupert smiles, best politician face.

Pike steps back from the throng. "You get all this?" he whispers into his throat mike.

"Affirmative, Stray Dog." A voice replies in his earbud under a slight crackle of static. "Stay close to Largo."

"Roger that," Pike says. At least keeping tabs on the City Treasurer seems a better activity than his failed attempt at keeping an eye on Old Man Regan. Silas Regan is an elusive bastard. So much so during the short time the Devastator, he, and his crew have been in Reganshire; it often seems the old man simply sends orders down through his daughter. *Overly cautious,* Pike suspects, *or something else entirely.*

"Now may I speak to your father, young lady? Obviously there's much planning to do," the City Treasurer says. His chest rises high now, though his paunch of a belly still sticks out. He is on fire now, stoked and resolute in his purpose here.

Rebecca raises a wicked finger nail and gnaws on it, deep in thought with those dreadful pale orbs upon him. For a moment, her concentration seems thrown as she discovers something under that nail and the tip of her red-back tongue flicks, trying to dislodge a piece of meat stuck between teeth.

"My lovely Miss Regan," Largo says, attempting to go down another avenue with the woman. He tries not to cringe, or expunge the bile still knotting his throat, as his one good eye roams up and down her lithe form. "I assure you my intentions are honorable. Our two great towns cannot progress without each other. I would like to see us all together—Reganshire, the Grandville-Wyoming conglomerate, Comstock—unified, on equal playing fields, building a better tomorrow together."

LaFleur winces.

Pike fights a strong desire to exclaim: "Bullshit."

Rebecca's finger pops from her mouth, a smile pulls her pale flesh taut. She leans into the City Treasurer's personal space, nose to nose again. Pasty maggots drip from her hairline like drops of pearly sweat.

The smell of tar and rotten meat hits him hard; Largo struggles with an urge to turn and run, or vomit in her face.

"I believe you, Mr. Largo," Rebecca coos, sniffing at the man's face. "But I'll still have to talk to my father on your requested meeting. Daddy's been so tired as of late. I think this entire life-style's worn him down. I hate to see him suffer."

"Of course," Largo stutters, tongue tripping over the words. Sweat rolls down his brow and his armpits feel like dripping caverns, and it isn't just from the scorching heat wafting over them all.

"Mr. LaRouge," Rebecca shouts.

Lucius LaFleur pushes through the few people before him to stand beside the Grand Rapids City Treasurer. He smells the faintest scent of urine in the air.

"Let our new friend get cleaned up..." she says, smiling like a sudden love-struck teenager.

Largo sighs with relief; though his gut still knots with her expression.

"Then put him in the civilian stockades. Perhaps father will offer him an audience this evening."

"What!" the City Treasurer bellows, hands ball into fists. His retainers grab his arms to keep him from attacking the tittering Reganshire woman. He wants to say more. *The insane, deceitful bitch*. It's not his intention to stay the night in this cesspool or be treated like a criminal.

He decides to change his tone as her laughter turns into a raging snarl. "I should be getting back before th…"

"You shall wait to see father when he is ready to see you, not a minute sooner, not a minute later," Rebecca interrupts him, her tone winding down a threatening path again.

She looks to LaFleur. "Learn what he knows of Mayor Honeywell's trip back to Grand Rapids tomorrow, and ready the militia. Use force if he changes his mind about telling you."

"Now wait a second," Rupert starts.

LaFleur looks at him, shakes his head. *Leave it alone if you know what is good for you*, his gaze says.

"I'll send someone to gather our new friend Mr. Largo when daddy wants to see him." Rebecca finishes.

LaFleur nods.

"We'll be in contact," she says to Largo, backs up a step, gazes the man up and down, licking her lips. "Welcome to Reganshire."

"Fuck," Largo says under his breath.

"Fuck," LaFleur says to a man beside him who draws deeply on a cigarette.

The man nods, inhales, makes the tip of the lit cig hell-fire red. Still gently nodding, he glances at Pike.

The TC makes eye contact, then stares straight ahead as Rebecca Regan and her armed retinue march towards the built-up supermarket/reinforced fortress that is her and the old man's home.

It is the first time he questions himself on the decision to take the mission he is on and going AWOL from the GRCC and Grand Rapids.

***

Pike sits on the Devastator's turret munching an undercooked hamburger. Grease runs down his stubble-ridden chin, catches on the short coarse hairs and winds down jagged little scars etching his lower jaw. If stars shine in the clear night sky, the spotlights glaring down upon the busy compound make them impossible to see.

The Devastator rests behind a wide and long line of other vehicles, some military issue, some regular cars and trucks welded up, souped-up, into rugged and battle-ready off-road vehicles. An M978 HEMTT—Heavy Expanded Mobility Tactical Truck bulk liquid transporter—stands in the vehicle mix; the rear half of its 2500-gallon tank cut down and fitted with a row of three Caliber-30 machine gun placements on both sides.

A post-apocalyptic movie from Pike's youth comes to mind. He inwardly shudders: the world has become stranger and more chaotic, *madder*, than anything on the old silver screen.

Between the field of vehicles and the massive Regan living quarters and a good chunk of the Reganshire populace, Rupert Largo kneels in the village stockades. After a shower, meal and fresh clothing, they had tossed him back outside in the muggy evening air to stew and curse. Pike is sure the man is probably re-thinking his position on bringing Reganshire back into the main city fold.

He chuckles, takes another bite of the undercooked burger—better than the MRE's stowed below in the tanks bowels—until a wisp of cigarette smoke assaults his nostrils.

Pike frowns and peers down at the gentleman standing beside the front left skirt of the big Abrams. "Sergeant Aikens," he nods at the man.

"Haven't heard that in a while. Ha. Sergeant." The man says then takes a long drag from his cigarette. He holds it, then slowly exhales a billow of white smoke. "Would rather not have you use it around here though." He says glancing about, wary of any Reganites standing close by.

"I know all about you, Vesper," Pike replies, popping the last bit of burger into his mouth. His teeth crunch on something hard—a small bone? He leans and spits over the side of the tank.

William "Vesper" Aikens takes another puff off his cigarette, brow furrows and eyes shoot daggers at the TC. The tank commander might as well blab it to the whole place. Asshole.

Pike grins, using his tongue to check his tooth and make sure it isn't busted by whatever he'd bit into.

"I was close to the late Commander Neilsen, and with Jackson." Pike explains casually, also glancing about to verify no one he doesn't want to listen cocks an ear towards them. "I know all about the GRCC… emissaries… in villages outside Grand Rapids." He glances around again, speaks a little softer. "You're good with me, Sergeant."

"Just tone down the name calling, Major," Aikens reiterates.

Pike wipes his hands on his dusty tankers uniform, slides from his perch, turns as he hits the tank deck. He climbs down to ground level; a move as smooth and practiced as if he could do it in his sleep. He avoids stepping in the small wet pile of spit burger laying upon the cracked and crushed concrete drive.

"What do you think about this hot mess?" Aikens says drawing on his cigarette.

"State of FUBAR," Pike replies looking upon the rows and rows of men and war machines. "The City Treasurer," he nods towards the civilian stockades, where the locals are punished, versus the outsiders who spend a day in chains near the north entrance before finding their head on a pike. "Largo's really putting his beloved city in a tight spot."

"Largo doesn't give a shit about anything but his own ambitions from all I've kept abreast of regarding the idiot," Aikens says. "At least Honeywell has always made a go at standing up for the common wealth, decency and survival of everyone. Old Man Regan has done the same, though you wouldn't know it with the animosity he stirs up against Honeywell and the city."

Pike leans in close to catch every word. His eyes go to the north gate and the rotted heads lolling side to side in the warm evening breeze.

"Speaking of which," Pike starts. "I've been here roughly three months and haven't seen hide or hair of old Silas," he looks towards the hodge-podge cathedral-like structure in the center of the compound. He realizes it looks like a giant middle finger pointing towards the sky. Appropriate, knowing what he knows of Silas Regan, the patriarch of the place. "I hear his orders through his daughter and her fledgling commanders, but I've never seen a sliver of the man himself."

It is Aiken's turn to look towards the Regan compound. A large window, shuttered now, overlooks the central plaza, over the old store fronts used for more housing and small trade shops, onto the vehicle square, and the small fenced in pen in where captured Zees are held and kept as "blood hounds."

"I've seen him, but not lately, not down here," Aikens responds. "We had a pretty rough winter this past season. Lost some of the meat cattle. An outpost and small communal down on Fennessey froze to death, two dozen souls, men, women, children, turned into popsicles, and then we brought them back and..."

Aikens looks down at his shoes.

The bright glare of spotlights made everyone's face white as a ghost. Pike looks upon Aikens, a GRCC Spec Ops man who's probably been stationed in Reganshire way too long, and sees a pale, sour frown cross the man's face.

"I didn't partake," Aikens voice sounds far away and small. "I couldn't eat human flesh. I wasn't gonna be some freak like..." He looks up at that large picture window again, takes a drag off the little stump of cigarette left. He drops the butt to the ground, stomps it out while withdrawing another white stick from his dingy shirt pocket.

His hands shake as he lights the fresh smoke.

"Anyway, I heard the old man got really sick. The crazy wet spring we had didn't help matters I guess. Rumor has it he had a bad case of bronchitis and some other shit laying him low. He came out a few times. That got less and less until he just stayed inside, giving orders through Rebecca.

"He used to sit at that big window up there and keep tabs on what was going on here in the village proper. Can't say when I saw him up there as of late." Aiken takes a deep drag from his cig. "Hell, might've been right before you got here."

Pike feels his chest tighten as his mind turns things over. "The old bastard ain't dead is he?" His thoughts go to Regan's twisted daughter. If the old dog is down and the young rabid bitch is at the helm: *major* state of FUBAR.

"Not from what I hear," Aikens returns, takes another puff. "Rebecca and subordinates bring down orders from him. Well, mainly Rebecca. But I don't poke around much on the subject. I don't want to end up in Largo's position, or worse."

Pike's eyes go to the rotted heads wagging on the poles.

A commotion in the midst of the battalion of vehicles draws both men's attention. Taunting shouts and cheering rise in the humid evening air along with fist slapping flesh. A small fight has broken out within the massive Reganshire convoy.

"Must be anxious for the fight," Pike comments, brow furrowing.

Aikens's cigarette glows fiery red, crackling as it burns down with a deep inhalation. "I'm out of here if this ordeal goes south."

Pike climbs back up the skirting of the Devastator to get a better view of the scuffle. "I'd think about heading out anyway," he says. "Whichever toilet the shit drops, either Honeywell is going to bring down all hell on this place, or Largo, if he gets into power, is going to bend both father, daughter and rest of Reganshire over backwards and screw them the same as he's trying to do to Honeywell."

The Devastator's gunner, Mitch Davison, pops up from the turret hatch. Mumble-swearing as he digs a finger into the side of his mouth, he looks at Pike and spits a half-chewed dollop of hamburger.

"Don't know where they got that burger, but they obviously don't know how to process their beef," the gunner grumbles, again with finger in mouth, checking his teeth.

Pike recalls Aikens comment about the winter beef shortage and the Fennessey outpost. He decides not to mention what Davison might be eating.

The yelling and fighting amidst the amassed vehicles stirs the "blood hounds" in their pen. They press against the tall fencing, rotted fingers looped through the chain link. Rattling the cage, they squeal and bellow along like spectators at a prize boxing match.

"This's fucking insanity," Jeremy Pike mumbles to himself.

And tomorrow is only going to be worse.

Chapter Thirteen

"…fucking insanity." The voice of a perturbed Tank Commander Lance Breckenridge. "We're spread too thin."

A dozen-plus replies follow.

"…should wait for reinforcements from Holtrop and the NCS. If he's going to send any. Does anyone know how the mayor's visit went?"

"Where's the Wyoming-Grandville coalition forces? We've covered their asses enough times."

"Who came up with radio silence when someone of importance is cutting right through hostile territory? Honeywell's got a cell phone, doesn't he?"

"No. He's old school. If rotary phones still existed…"

"Quiet down." Captain Frank Forrester, commander of M213 HTV Ontario. "Let the commander talk."

Breckenridge clears his throat. Heart pounds. Blood rushes through veins and arteries like a river undammed. "Captain Forrester and I have spoken to Jackson. We're stretched thin, he acknowledges this. He's sent police and soldiers to the BTF and the Butterworth gate to re-secure it and try to round up any troopers still meandering about. The M45 outpost is a mangled mess, no one's coming or going out that exit. The city's on lockdown, city officials, in light of Honeywell and Largo being out, have put Sutter in charge. Commissioner Sutter and Jackson are working together to make sure there're no other insurgents in the GRCC or the town.

"We've gotten word Reganshire's gathered their militia and marches on Lamont to intercept Honeywell's train. We're moving out at first light, along the 8th Avenue corridor, to get to Lamont first." Breckenridge takes a ragged breath. "We've had no contact with the garrison there and suspect the insurgents have taken over the area also."

The night hangs in the heavens like a heated blanket above the West Side Apostolate and Quadrant 5 of the UCRA. Temperature still in the 80's, no one needs a heated blanket.

Bodies stuffed in a warm room. Lots of blood, flesh, hearts pounding. Bright lights, soul lights, or whatever it was. Battle-weary. Fatigued brothers and sisters, tired, frustrated from a long day of fighting insurgents, the heat, planes dropping on their heads, fighting their own undead battle brothers.

Still, they push on.

"We should be heading out now." Stokes. Always speaking before using his brain. Still, a good goddamn soldier. "Reganshire is going to have a 15 mile lead on us."

"You better make sure your rig is ready to depart full throttle then, Sergeant." Forrester's voice again. Not serious, poking a bit of fun at the hairy little man.

The smell of stale cigars, oil, gun powder, perspiration: normal road stink for the squat tanker.

The little gorilla needs a bath, Jake grunts, adjusting the deep tinted welding goggles resting upon the scarred bridge of his nose. He sits in the dark, atop the Apostolate building, avoiding the glare of the single farm light hanging over the front of the place.

"How do you like this existence?" Lettner says standing beside him. The late NSC commissioner scratches at his neck line, at the rough, red, rope burn skin. "Too bad they took my head off after your father-in-law put me to the gallows. I could walk this path with you."

"Fuck you. Shut up," Jake growls. It is a literal growl. He can't get his vocal cords to harmonize and bring forth normal words.

Billet feels deep within himself, tells his brain and senses to tell him if he is really, well, part of the undead or not. His fingers still feels the coarse brick at his ass. He can feel the cloying heat and humidity at his flesh but he doesn't perspire. It hurts to breathe deeply, yet he can smell the faintest scents: a bowl of rose water, its droplets rolling down a brass crucifix and the perfume of young fresh blood pumping through a postulant's veins.

"Messed up, isn't it, Captain?" Largo now, taunting him: the broad-chested, one-eyed sonofabitch.

"Not as messed up if we catch you in Lamont with your lackeys," Jake growls, caring less what the night heard.

Below him, out of earshot, Gurks walk a freshly erected chain link around the military vehicles standing idle along Bridge Street and Valley Avenue. They are packed in like an Old West wagon train defending against attackers. Though the UCRA civilians will cause the soldiers no trouble, still, no one wants to sleep or have to meander around their vehicles, in the pitch of night, in any form of Zee territory.

"If *you* get that far." Lettner again, chuckles.

Jake can't catch the transition between the apparitions—but he knows they are things from his fucked up brain. They flit like pale hummingbirds in and out of existence within an eye blink.

"I can't find my baby. Where's my baby?" A woman's voice wails in the darkness.

A male voice calls out from the night; a hoarse growl. "Johnny? Karo? Stephen Roy?"

"Mom! Dad! Don't leave me!" A young boy's voice, high and shrill.

"Shut up!" Jake snarls, gnashing his teeth. He cups his hands over the sides of his head. An ocean roar, and then his hands drop as new sounds come to his ears.

It's a usual thing, when out on night patrol in the UCRA: the wailing, growling, high and shrill cries of the civilian undead within the retention area. Now, he can make out their voices, their garbled words, their cries of frustration, loss, confusion.

He feels a fresh understanding regarding why the living civilians felt so strongly about keeping these poor, unfortunate souls cared for, clothed, fed, safe; though he wonders if even the living folk—other than, say, Loutonia who understands zombie dialect—understand what their neighbors on the west are actually saying, or going through.

"Jacob?" His dead wife, Jenna, says beside him. "Jake?"

Jake turns and throws an arm to his eyes, blocks the radiant yellow light trying to spear his eyeballs. For a moment he feels like launching himself at the light, kill the light, crush the beating heart and tear the flesh until warm pure blood flows.

"Jake, what're you doing up here?" Loutonia says, stops for a breath, noticing Jake's position and hearing a soft groan from him. She can't tell if it's in agitation or surprise.

The welding goggles reduce the glare as his eyes adjust to her presence. Like the wailing UCRA voices, his brain seems to click, changing frequency like a radio so he can look upon her in some form of normalcy. Through the dark lenses, the woman's solid curves are limned in yellow-white spurs radiating along the silhouette of her body.

Jake feels a longing to pull the Loutonia to him, embrace her, and hold her.

He feels the longing to crush the breath from her lungs, tear the life from her body.

He presses his fingers, hard, against the coarse brick surface beneath him, breaking the calloused skin of his fingertips.

"You probably shouldn't be up here. You've been through a lot today, hell, the last three months," she says, her boots crunching on the gravel rooftop. She turns her head to listen to the wail of a nearby UCRA citizen somewhere in the darkness.

How easy it would be to simply open his mouth and speak to her. She would know then what he's becoming. But it isn't so much her knowledge, but his fear. Would he remember her, or his crew, his family, his life, himself if and when he truly becomes one of the undead?

Rage bubbles up like lava, red and hot. Loutonia's form and the night take on a crimson hue.

Jake closes his eyes, clenches his teeth, fights it down.

Cool calloused hands touch his face.

The building eruption simmers to a glowing ember in the pit of his knotted gut.

"However it happened, I'm glad you're back with me, with us," Loutonia says.

She draws close, her lips brush his, press firmer.

Picture frames of memories flash through Jake's mind: Jenna and Joey in their glass tomb, never to return; Loutonia battered by her Turned husband, burying her children killed by the same man; Jake and her together, tangled in sweat-moist sheets, laughing, loving again amidst their tragedies and chaos of the world.

He wants to scream. He wants to cry.

Boots crunch on gravel, far down the street. The sound moves towards them, along an alleyway which runs parallel to Valley Avenue.

Jake takes her by the arms and pushes her away, turning his head aside, looking down at the rooftop.

I'm sorry, but only in thought.

"I understand," Lou responds, not backing down, placing a hand on his shoulder. "You've been through a lot. We'll…" She hesitates, swallows hard. "…we'll work things out."

Lettner and Largo appear behind her, shaking their heads, laughing.

Billet stands, fists clenched. It is the only way to contain his rage.

He puts a hand to his throat, rakes his fingers gently up and down it.

"I know, you've lost your voice," Lou says.

Jake points at himself, and then taps his head. He goes to his mouth, opens it silently, rolls his hand outward. Loutonia looks at him, stumped at first.

"You know things." She says.

He nods.

Digging into the pocket of her tactical vest, she withdraws a folded piece of paper. She pats her hip pockets, withdraws a pen.

She hands him the paper and pen. He holds them loosely until he can feel them in his grasp. The reaction time seems painfully slow for the sensation of touch to connect with his brain. He palms the folded paper, presses the ballpoint down and scrolls one word cleaner than he expects to write in his current state.

He passes the paper to Loutonia.

More heavy footfalls crunch gravel down the street, from the alleyway. Jake turns, pulls the goggles down enough to peer over the frame. The dark neighborhood beyond the Apostolate takes on a fuzzy gray sheen, like looking through night vision goggles but without the blue-green glow. Civilians shamble about, moving away from forms which move quickly, hunkering down behind retaining walls, dense bushes and old cars.

Loutonia turns, holding the paper so she can see it better against the glow of the farm light. "Largo." She nods. "Yeah, we know. He went out to Reganshire about the same time their planes tried to crop dust the enclosure. Jesus, it's like Lettner is alive and well living in Reganshire."

Lettner stands beside the Huron driver, points at her and smiles. "I do like this girl."

"We fear the worst though. One of the troopers from the BTF tagged his helicopter. It went down just west of Butterworth. They sent a team out. Didn't find anything but a pile of burnt metal and a few dead Ferals. We're thinking maybe he and the pilot got out, but they didn't come back to town. Command is thinking, with all the insurgent activity, perhaps Reganshire was waiting for them."

Those insurgents aren't Regan's, Jake wants to say. Badly.

He lifts an arm that suddenly feels like dead weight. He waves Lou to pass the paper back to him.

A bolt clacks open and closed from the alleyway. It is too far away for Loutonia or the men down below to hear. Jake hears it as if the action was done right next to his ear.

"We're moving out in the morning," she says. "You should come down and get some rest. I don't know how you're still standing." The last words come out halted, like she'd just taken a 2-by-4 to the back of the knees.

He presses pen to paper, but turns his head, looks back into the darkened neighborhood. The gray haze. The forms limned in a dull yellow glow, faint but discernible to him; men on the cusp of death yet virile enough to heft weapons. The civilians hurry away as fast as their flimsy, ragdoll legs can take them, revealing their own aura, faint ochre, barely visible even to him.

The unliving still burn with a vapor of life.

The muzzle of a sniper rifle stands pointed upward at Loutonia and him. The way Lou beams like a nightlight, Jake knows the shooter likely isn't aiming for him.

"Go down. Will join in sec." Jake writes on the paper, hands to her. He wants to write Largo is a son of a bitch behind this recent chaos.

Metal on metal sound. Shell being chambered. Bolt being drawn into place.

"Go… down," Jake rasps, surprised his voice sounds so clear as he speaks the words to Loutonia. He gives her a half smile, almost feels like work to move his facial muscles.

She takes his hand, squeezes it, brushes it weakly with her own, and returns the smile. She turns and heads towards the stairwell.

Jake immediately turns towards the shooter down the street. He puffs up his chest, one foot on the raised lip of the rooftop. The gunner will have to put a bullet through him to get to her.

A soldier at ground level hears the crunch of Jake's boot on the roof lip, looks up, shining a flashlight up at him. A flashbang of light in his face, but Jake doesn't wince though the initial pain is intense. He blinks the light flare away, stares straight out in the direction of the shooter. There are others out there, other figures in the darkness. Not local civilians wandering the night. Not hardy living folk meandering outside the protection of the Apostolate or wanderers who have slipped into the UCRA.

These are ZT's. Undead troopers, soldiers, men and women he has known. Restrained from entering the afterlife, these grunts are stitched up, kept alive by science and the chemicals.

Jake can understand their rage, their rage against the living.

But they are still soldiers.

"Stand with us, soldiers. I understand your plight. I understand your reasoning, but until we can stand no more, you are still in service to your country, to your brothers and sisters in uniform. We stand together, or fall and fail all and everything." Jake says this in his head, staring out into the darkness. He can see the raging red eyes of the fallen and resurrected.

"If you want to stand alone, strike me down," he commands with the grunts and groans of tortured vocal cords. He clears his throat, like trying to dislodge small stones. His last words come out audible, intelligible.

"If we stand alone," he ignores the surprise at his own voice, as coarse and gravelly as it comes to his ears. "If we stand alone, we will let this uncivil war conquer us. Self-less pride, duty and honor, the heart and soul of a true soldier, *will* be lost."

He stares into the darkness. He can see nothing. It's like the blanket of night has grown deeper, denser. He pulls down the goggles just enough to peer over their dark rims. Where just moments ago he could make out figures in the darkness, he only sees fuzzy silhouettes disperse into the ebony mire, heading away from their location.

"Captain," one of the living grunts from below calls up to him, "did you say something? Are you all right?"

Jake looks down at the soldier, the bright white glare of the soldier's life aura is faint as an eclipsed moon at midnight.

Jake clears his throat, hopes he won't revert to the choking guttural grunt and rasping.

"I'm fine," he says, giving the soldier thumbs up, the action of bringing his arm up makes his joints pop and crackle.

***

Below, at the base of the steps leading to the roof, out of earshot of all, Loutonia quietly weeps. Teardrops roll from cheeks and drop onto one of her .45 caliber pistols in hand. *Fine?* She knows different about her commander, the man she cherishes.

And it breaks her heart to pieces.

***

Morning washes over the city's west side like hot bath water. Sweat dripped from the underside of helmets, berets and habits. At 7 am, the soldiers readying up outside appear to have showered in their clothes.

"Gonna be a scorcher," Breckenridge says as he stands beside the Grizzly, his crew preparing the tank for its jaunt out of town.

Beside the TC, Frank Forrester inspects a set of county street maps. His green fatigues are dark with perspiration. "Everyone's got the route we're taking to Lamont. We haven't heard from our Reganshire contact yet. He's going to call just before Reganshire moves out, so I'm hoping they're still gearing up."

Breckenridge holds his helmet under his arm. He pulls a rag from the bottom of it and wipes it across his brow. "We have more or less flat roadways to traverse versus Reganshire if they take the traditional route through the Grand River valley. We should be a few paces ahead of them." The TC turns to Jake who stands looking up at the sky behind a pair of dark goggles. "You agree, Captain?"

Billet clears his throat, the gravel not loosening. He rubs at his neck, massaging it with gloved fingers still tingly from a dip of Z-ration he partook of before everyone had risen from sleep. He's almost glad to feel his body resisting speech and feel the cold prickling sensation from the doped meat on his flesh. He casts a glance at the dozen or so UCRA civilians already lined up outside the Apostolate doors, waiting for morning grub. They moan and growl and swat at each other, oblivious as it were to their plight and condition, while he... he is *well aware* of his situation.

"Captain?"

Jake turns back to the TC. He opens his mouth. They'd never understand him. "Na..." he coughs, hand still to throat.

"We've discussed the mission," Loutonia says coming up behind them. Stokes and Mulholland follow. "Jake inhaled some of the chemical mess. I'm surprised it didn't eat his insides straight out. He and I spoke last night, through pen and paper. Whatever we have to do, we're all in."

Jake looks at Loutonia. She casts him an affirming smile. He turns back to Breckenridge and Forrester, nods. Yes.

"She's always got your back," Forrester says towards Phelps.

"Hoo-ahhk," Jake says though it sounds more like someone clearing their throat. He motions to Forrester to hand him the map.

"Other thoughts on our route?" Breckenridge asks as Jake takes the map.

He follows the 8th Avenue route he heard them speak of last night. It is the flattest and clearest route, roadway-wise, between Grand Rapids and Lamont—other than taking the I-96 corridor.

But the interstate swings too far north of Lamont. The small rural village sits about fourteen miles northwest of Grand Rapids, and the route from where they are positioned currently consists of twists, turns and trading outposts where they'd have to stop, not blast right through. Even if they head out now, and if Reganshire does the same a few minutes after, Reganshire will get to Lamont first.

Jake pokes his finger at a spot on the map, 8th Avenue and Remembrance Road. Breckenridge and Forrester look at the map then at him. He shakes his head and then traces a route from their present location then to Leonard Street half a klick south. At Leonard, he traces his finger west along that route which offers minimum turns and detours.

Loutonia looks over his shoulder, and Stokes and Mulholland draw closer.

"Leonard Street route would be faster. Roadways are clear from what I recall," Mulholland speaks up, hesitates as Jake glances at him. Jake nods his affirmation. Huron's rear gunner carries on. "We won't lose as many minutes or miles and as long as Reganshire doesn't take the same route, we should be a bit ahead of them and get to Lamont before them."

Billet nods. He smiles at his gunner. His jaw froze mid-action, probably looked more like a tight lipped scowl. Mulholland drops his eyes to his boots and Jake quickly gives him a thumbs up and nod again. The tall thin gunner understands, gestures back and gives a weak smile of thanks.

"Let's ready up and get this travelling circus rolling," Breckenridge says, waving his fist in the air.

He wipes a line of sweat from his forehead and looks at Jake. "Damn, Billet, you got an air conditional under your vest? You look pressed, dry cleaned and fresh as a daisy while I'm sweating my balls off."

Jake shrugs.

"Tell him to look around at the local rotters." Lettner

recommends, standing beside Jake. "The dead don't sweat."

Jake ignores him and shrugs again at Breckenridge.

Forrester signals a grunt with a radio set strapped to his back. The man steps up to the Ontario commander. "Contact Command. Let them know we're taking Leonard Street versus 8th Avenue."

"Sir, yes sir," the radio man salutes. He looks up at Forrester as the radio operator stands several inches shorter than the five-foot-ten HTV commander.

"And find out if any more of the GRCC's finest are going to be coming in behind us, we could use a few more troops," Forrester finishes.

The radio man nods, spins on heel and plants his face smack in the center of Sister Mirose's chest.

Mirose chuckles, grips the soldier's shoulders so he won't fall as he rebounds with reddening face. She turns the grunt back around facing Forrester, Breckenridge, and Billet as a score of armed nuns in full tactical gear draw up behind her.

"The Sisters of the Apostolate are here to serve." Mirose says, her thick calloused fingers digging into the radio man's shoulders.

Jake inwardly shivers as the big nun stares straight at him.

Chapter Fourteen

"Is this a good idea?" Breckenridge says over a secure channel. "Hell no, it's not a good idea. Who suggested they come along?"

A M3 Bradley Infantry Fighting Vehicle and a pair of BRV-O Light Tactical Vehicles take the lead of the convoy as they head along Leonard Street, three miles northwest of Reganshire properties. The IFV leads the three vehicle advance guard team. Each Light Tactical Vehicle boasts five men, one of those manning the big 50-cal machine gun turret on vehicle's roof. All scan the roadway, what is ahead and to the sides. Roughly five minutes behind them, another Bradley, Breckenridge and his M60 Patton tank, the HTV Ontario, and another pair of BRV-Os, with the Huron closing up the procession's rear. The steep banks on either side of the road keep the formation in a tight straight line.

At the hindmost flanks of the military convoy, the Sisters of the Apostolate follow. Nuns with helmeted heads: one even with a pith helmet, ride behind the GRCC on quad runners. Within the mix, two Ram 2500 heavy duty pickup trucks rumble down the cobbled-up road.

"Wasn't my idea," replies Forrester. "You did mention we could use more troops, sir."

"Nuns? Old ladies and kids?" Breckenridge exclaims, voice filled with tension. "I can't wait for the City and Central Command to get their hooks into us for this one."

Billet looks down from his commander's perch riding high atop the Huron. It feels good to have the cool armored hide against him, and the mounted 50-Cal machine gun at his fingertips. Stokes stands within his own gun pulpit, weapons slowly swivel, barrels sweeping the neighborhood beyond, vigilant against any foe—living or unliving—creeping about. Mulholland mans the vehicle's rear, focused on where they'd been, making sure no one tries to sneak up their ass.

"They'll always blame us for something," Jake says out loud. He surprises himself, not only by voicing the thought but speaking it clearly.

Breckenridge jumps in. "What was that, Captain?"

"Nothing, sir." Jake's words more akin to the taut rawness of his throat. He coughs.

"Captain. A moment?" Loutonia cut in on a different channel. Breckenridge would've been up his ass instantly if she didn't.

"Go… ahead," Jake growls, coughs again. *Dammit, go one way or the other, will ya?* He curses himself.

"Sister Mirose and I talked the other day, when you were out of commission," Loutonia starts.

"The good sister wants to preside over your funeral. That's so sweet," Lettner says seated on the roofline, smirking.

Jake glares at the haunt.

Stokes turns towards him right as he does so. "What? I didn't do anything. Yet," the sergeant, forlorn, exclaims.

Jake shakes his head and looks over the other side of the Huron.

An Apostolate nun on a quad glances up at him as she rides along beside the big transport. Her veil is tied back. She doesn't wear the traditional habit but a long slit skirt with black athletic pants, military issue knee protection and black combat boots polished to a sheen that makes Jake envious. The good sister carries a muzzle loader strapped to her back. Sister Veronica, Jake recalls her name.

A tiny slip of an older nun who reminds him of Betty White hangs on to Veronica's waist like her life depends on it. Probably does to the frail little holy woman. The only real oddity: the Pith helmet adorning her white-haired head.

Sister Veronica catches his glance, nods, and speeds up. Betty White Nun latching tighter and screeching something unlady-like as they pull ahead.

"Mirose cares about you, as do I." Loutonia continues. "She said you've been there for her, and, now, she wants to return the favor."

"Not going to sit real well with Breckenridge," Jake replies, voice returning though still gravel laced.

"You said you needed more men, Commander sir," Mirose breaks in as if on cue.

"What? Ma'am, this is a secure channel. How did you—?" snarls Breckenridge in everyone's earbud.

"We're here to assist. Our calling is not only to God but to support our city, not just caring for the UCRA civilians who happen across our doorstep."

Jake finds Mirose in one of the big Ram 2500's. She sits in the back, in the truck bed, leaning against the rear window with in-cab radio extended out the small open window. She wears no veil, letting her roughly shorn dark hair thrash in the hot breeze. She's discarded any flowing adornments, now in white short-sleeved blouse, black tactical vest, dark athletic pants, and combat boots.

Sitting beside the big nun, her young postulant isn't as such adorned. She wears the traditional habit of a nun in training: tan veil and brown vestments. A wisp of blonde hair flutters from beneath her head gear. The tactical vest upon her small frame rides up to her chin; she looks like a turtle ready to pop its head back into its shell.

"It's our calling to be here for all the city's inhabitants in their time of need."

Mirose turns and looks straight up at Billet. A sudden lancing pain rockets through his temples. He groans, snaps his eyes shut tight. He brings his hands to his head, fights the shakes trying to overtake him. He takes off his helmet, stuffing it between the hatch coaming and himself.

"She knows." Lettner's voice rings in his head like a tolling bell. "They all know you're not long for *this* semblance of life."

"Gawddamnit! Why… don't… you… shut up!" Jake barks.

"Come home," a voice in his head. No, on the street: Jenna's.

Jake opens his eyes, stares through the dark welding goggles, down beyond the flanking caravan of nuns.

Standing on the edge of the street as they pass; Jenna, holding the hand of a toddler-sized Joey. They wave at him weakly, with feeble sad smiles. Jenna blows him a kiss then her flesh drools away from her raised hand as do all clothing of both her and his boy, all drool away until dripping yellow bones, standing erect, wave at him. "Come home before it's too late." Jenna's skeleton pleads.

His heart, thumping in his chest every now and again, starts to increase its strength. It feels like someone pounds a sledgehammer against his ribs. He feels an ache throughout his body as the muscle works to push the thick sludge that is his blood through vein and artery again. It makes his head reel. He grabs the hatch coaming to keep himself from falling over or buckling to the strong inner convulsions threatening to explode from him.

He blinks. The scenery changes; flitting at first like an old movie, frames scrolling slowly then picking up speed as the landscape comes clearer into view.

The sound of automatic weapons fill his ears, taps painfully at the inside of his skull. Fire. Explosions. Men and women screaming. He's on the ground, outside the Huron, the Huron with black smoke roiling from every opening. He notices a road sign, bullet ridden, leaning, half folded on the ground before him. He can make out the words: Welcome to Lamont.

Lamont was a small village in its day, smaller village after 2013.

The only reason why it hadn't passed away into complete oblivion like some of the smaller communities in West Michigan was due to its train depot, and the rail line running between Muskegon and Grand Rapids. Garrisoned by a small GRCC contingent after Allendale reeled its militia back into its own town, it stood as one of the furthest, and one of the most important, when the trade lines had been re-established between the lakeshore metropolis and Grand Rapids.

But now it's war.

Black-painted Reganshire vehicles fan the perimeter in which Jake stands in the center. Pickup trucks, modified cars, stolen Humvees and wheeled armor stand and direct their fire at the surrounded GRCC convoy. Roughly scrolled red R's drool down the side of each ebon vehicle, as if they've soaked up the blood from the battlefield and it drips from them.

"You die now!" Jeremy Pike howls from the turret hatch of the ebon-hued Devastator.

The turret rotates. The 120mm tank cannon points straight at Billet. The tank rises within the midst of hundreds of Reganshire infantry, a size Jake finds hard to believe they have. Beyond them, coming from every direction, over hill, up from valley, rows and rows, hundreds, thousands—a legion!—of black garbed and armed Reganites march, an endless sea stretching miles into the distance.

"No going home. No seeing wife. No seeing kid. Lost forever," Rebecca Regan shrieks beside Pike, standing within the turret gunner's hatch. A phantom breeze blows her sheer black gown against her upper body. The near-transparent material reveals a ribcage of bone and glowing ember within that frame, pulsing strongly: her evil heart.

Billet reaches for his sidearm. It's not there.

He raises a foot to take a step and finds something restricts it. He looks down: bodies. The street and surrounding area is covered with bodies; battered, bloody, bullet-riddled bodies. Heaped side by side, twisted into unnatural positions, ragdoll bodies litter the ground all about him.

There are no Reganites among the dead and broken, only GRCC troops and Apostolate nuns. A bloody hand lifts from the carnage before him. Mayor Dennis Honeywell draws himself up, clothing shredded, exposed flesh bullet-perforated and weeping crimson.

"You finally failed us, Jacob," the mayor says, teeters on legs straining to keep him upright. "You failed your crew, your outfit, and your city. You've failed me. You've let me die. You've let Lettner and my treasurer win."

Honeywell raises an accusing finger as a man appears behind him—first Lettner, grinning, then Rupert Largo. Largo pulls a long knife across the mayor's throat. "You've failed us all."

A new voice, familiar voice. Far away. In Jake's ears? In his head?

"Commander, we've got your AO. Orders, sir?"

"Private Wills?" Billet says, turning around, eastward.

Tunnel vision. Everything hazy, out of focus except for direct center. Far, far in the distance, but Jake can see them: a line of men and women in army green, tattered, torn, looking like they've been through Hell and back, march towards him. Private Wills marches front and center, sloppy with mud and blood, just like Jake remembers him from the April riverfront fracas when the enclosure had fallen atop the young soldier.

"I've got a good bunch from fire team's Charlie, Epsilon and Romeo, grunts from 1446th transportation company and a few from local Wyoming-Grandville, Comstock and East Grand Rapids units," Wills says loud and clear. "Sir, we're waiting on your command, sir."

Jake looks about: Reganites all around, standing, firing into troops who already lay dead and dying on the bloody ground. The Devastator's 120mm cannon roars: sends armor and body parts skyward where its fiery round explodes. The enemy sea keeps coming, wave upon wave to drown the GRCC, Honeywell, Lamont, Grand Rapids, Muskegon—all of West Michigan for all he knows—once and for all.

"Hump it, soldier," Jake says turning back to the fuzzy image of Wills and an army of troopers. "Double time. As fast as you can."

"Aye, Captain. We're Oscar Mike." Wills replies, and then yells, "We're taking fire! Take cover, Captain!"

Jake snaps his head around. Metal rings off metal close by, yet he stands surrounded by bodies.

"Get down, Captain? Jake!" Wills voice changes to another: Stokes.

Jake blinks, finds himself back in his commander's hatch, on the Huron. The only scene of chaos: the harried ground units disembarking from vehicles, hurrying for cover as bullets spack at their boot tips.

An errant slug tings and vibrates the upright hatch in front of him. "Shit," Jake exclaims as he ducks.

Stokes stands across from him, quad 30's hammering ahead.

"Lamont's been compromised," comes Breckenridge over the comm. "Mayor's train is a half hour out if he's on schedule and, sonofabitch, we got no way to reach him."

A lone Humvee rushes up, slows as it gets behind the 72 ton heavy transport. Decked out in heavy camouflage, the rear scout vehicle adds its dire news.

"Commander, Reganshire's mobilized and coming up behind us. Roughly three klicks away."

Billet takes a chance, rises up and looks eastward as if he might see the Reganshire army.

Lettner sits on Huron's roofline behind Jake. The late NSC commissioner smiles. He says as in the same breath Stoke's speaks: "Prepared to die, Captain?" And Stokes: "Prepared for orders, Captain."

Jake unlatches the folded 50-Cal machine gun, pulls and locks it into position atop his hatch coaming. He ignores the bullets ringing off the Huron's hide, yanks his black gloves tight to his hand, and grabs the weapon grips.

"This is it," he says to both, the irritating apparition and the squat gunner. "Prepared to fight."

***

A group of Reganites hunker around a communications radio under the protection of a large tent flap. Electrical cords from radio and a small battery of other electronics, including two large upright area air-circulating fans, lay upon the hot concrete. A man wearing a grease-stained shirt and dirty, sagging trousers, an eye patch over one eye, leans close to the radio speaker and holds the remote push-to-talk microphone.

"Roger that, Patch out." The dirty clothed man hands the mike to a gaunt faced man chewing a piece of jerky like a dog gnawing a bone. "Here ya go, Edmond. I'll go and tell Miss Regan the news."

Gaunt Face growls from the corner of his mouth. "Patch, you're the biggest kiss ass."

"If it keeps my head from the noose and wiggling on a pole," Patch shot a glance to the tall fence line encircling Reganshire and the line of rotting heads swaying upon the uprights, "then I do what I have to." He smiles, revealing red gums and gaps where teeth have been removed and never replaced. "Besides, I don't see anyone else with the balls to nuzzle up to her."

"Mainly because I want to keep my balls," Gaunt Face says, rousing a round of chuckles from his compatriots.

"Meh," Patch scowls, waves the man off with his middle finger. "I like to keep my friends close and dangerous crazy leaders closer."

Patch pats his sweaty forehead with an already perspiration-moist handkerchief and trudges away from the guffawing group.

"Hey," a voice comes from a lone tent he starts to pass. "Hey, is someone out there?"

Patch stops before a tattered green tent. A blue nylon tarp hangs over the peak of the small enclosure, secured on all four sides with rope; the rope tied to metal O-rings permanently set in orange 5-gallon buckets. A 50-gallon plastic drum stands beside the closed tent flap, lid open; water within. Bugs and a fine film of dirt float on the water's surface.

"I'm here," Patch replies to the occupant in the tent. He takes a plastic bowl from a stool beside the water barrel. Scooping up a splashing portion, he slips inside the tent folds.

Grand Rapids City Treasurer, Rupert Largo, sits inside the musty, muggy interior. On the edge of a canvas cot, he is shackled at ankles and wrists. A ceramic dinner plate rests on the ground, covered with breakfast remnants and flies.

"Whoo! Sure is hot in here. Gonna be another scorcher today too." Patch hands the other man the bowl of water. He withdraws his hand quickly as Largo takes the drinking utensil. He doesn't want to tempt the bigger man. Regardless of how bedraggled the Grand Rapidian looks, it wouldn't bode well for him to get nabbed by the man. "Nice eye patch. Lost mine to an, erm, errant screwdriver."

Largo growls but brings the bowl to his dry lips and gulps down the contents, spilling half of it onto his dirt and sweat stained shirt. He doesn't seem to mind the rinse.

"Where's Rebecca Regan?" Largo says, holds the bowl out, spitting off to his side some grit in his mouth. "Better yet, where is Silas? We had plans to talk last evening and—"

Patch waves Largo quiet. "Yeah, yeah. Things happen when they happen round here. We don't have the convenience to move all rank and file like you do in the big city. We follow protocol round here." He slips a dirty finger under his eye patch and digs at an itch.

"Protocol?" Largo's brow rose.

Patch reached back outside the tent and draws another bowl of the dirty water. "Yeah," he hands the bowl to the City Treasurer, "when the Regans say so, we march."

Taking the bowl again, Rupert brings it to his mouth and starts to sip. Something buzzing and the size of small kidney bean enters his mouth. He leans and spits again. A fat brown June Bug hits the pavement on its back. Little legs flail at the air. It rights itself and takes flight, hitting the ceiling of the tent, falling to the ground again. The one-eyed Reganite mashes it with boot tip.

"Well, I don't work for or under the Regan's. If this is how he wants to strike a deal with me and the city, shackled up like some miscreant who's stumbled into your properties..." Largo looks at the contents of the bowl before he draws more water from it.

"We have stuff going on today," Patch says as the other man takes one tiny sip then hands the bowl of rancid water back to him. "If you're requested to see anyone, I'm sure they'll yank you out of here."

Getting nowhere with this buffoon, Rupert thinks. He squints, tries to see out the slit in the tent flaps, see what's going on outside. He checks his watch: 11am, and it's already hotter than Hell. He'll roast away if he stays in the tent all day. He is glad at least they removed him from the stockades during the night. Perhaps Old Man Regan realizes he might be pushing his luck a bit treating the big city man like a common churl.

Still, the tent isn't much better. They keep him in shackles. The heat and the metal doesn't play well together, his ankles and wrists rubbed raw. He hasn't been given any food just water, and the water does little to drown his gurgling belly.

Largo shakes his head. Even if they make a deal together, he'll make sure the Regan's got the short end of the stick.

"Stuff going on today. Yeah, heard the ruckus," Largo says. "Circus in town?"

Patch grins, reveals a line of toothless gum. "Circus going out of town. Three-quarters of our militia is nearing Lamont."

Largo perks up. "That's wonderful. Any news?"

Patch looks the City Treasurer up and down, debating if he should say anything. He decides. "Miss Regan's sent out our forces to take Lamont and Mayor Honeywell's train when it comes through."

Largo checks his watch again. Perfect timing. An hour and half from now Honeywell's train will put him smack into Lamont. "I'm glad I could be of some assistance," he replies. "There'll be many opportunities ahead for Reganshire and Grand Rapids once Honeywell is out of the picture."

Patch peers wistfully up at the tent ceiling. "I wouldn't mind living in the city. Apartments are air-conditioned, aren't they?"

Largo nods.

"And decent jobs versus scrounging and working in the fields."

"Well, there's still required work like that, but…" The City Treasurer doesn't want to disrupt the man's dreams. "…I'm sure things are much easier than here."

Patch grows silent, staring above and beyond the small tent.

"I could make sure a man of your specialties… um, whatever you do… would live easily in the city, say, if you get me out of these bindings and bring me to Regan," Largo offers, honey sweet.

The Reganite's far-off stare crashes back to reality. His face sours like he's just quaffed a glass of lemon juice.

"You kidding me? My pretty little head would be waving on one of them pikes outside if I let you free." Patch says, backing away from the City Treasurer. "I'll make my own destiny when and if the opportunity presents itself. Always have," he rubs at his tooth-amiss mouth, "Always will."

Largo's honey pot boils away. He snaps upright off the cot, hands out. The one-eyed Reganite tries to back further away, stumbles, goes sideways instead. Largo catches him, fisting dirty shirt, some hairs and a bit of skin beneath. Quick thought through Patch's brain: they need to use shorter chains for prisoners.

"I don't know who you people think you're fucking with." Largo snarls, nose to nose with the man in his steely fists. He hasn't slept worth shit. Hot, literally, and pissed. Being chained like a stray dog in a cesspool like Reganshire… "I'm going to be running Grand Rapids, and you and the Regans are either going to be onboard like I'm offering, or you're going to continue to be a boil on my ass that's gonna get pinched and cauterized.

"I've got big plans and risked my neck coming out here to be treated like this," Largo continues, giving his captive a few hearty shakes for emphasis. "You go tell Silas and his crackpot daughter the time for talking is now, or do whatever you plan with me and be done with it, and you can see how the future works out for this place."

The Treasurer abruptly loosens his hold on Patch. The Reganite stumbles backwards, grabbing the tent flaps to steady himself. His sweaty shirt remains crumpled where the other man had held him. He falls partially out of the enclosure to more shouts and laughter from his compatriots.

"Your brother get mad at ya?"

Eye patch reference. Patch waves his middle finger at the knee-slapping crowd.

One of his brethren withdraws a menacing .44 Magnum from his waist belt and aims it at him. "Blow that dirty finger off, Pa…" The man starts, goes suddenly quiet and quickly holsters the big pistol.

"And blow that out your ass, Morteson. That little popgun doesn't frighten m…"

Patch sees the sudden downcast looks of his compatriots. Some jump back to what they were doing, or pretended to do, suddenly busy with a mundane task. Others look around as if there is something suddenly in the sky, start whistling, and nonchalantly walk away—then hurrying away.

"Shit." Patch says in a small voice.

"You're going to go talk to Old Man Regan and tell him what I told you, right? Hello?" the irate Grand Rapids City Treasurer calls from the tent.

"Yeah, yeah," Patch frowns, slowly starts to turn around back to his route to Regan's compound. "I'll be sure they see you somehow." Disemboweled in the stockades and head on the fence line.

Turning 180 degrees to face the big building again, he finds what he suspected and why his friends had suddenly hurried away.

"Hello, fellas." He says to the two towering Reganites standing before him.

Regan's guards were a hand-picked lot of giant men who would've been more helpful in heavy construction projects versus trip-stumbling over the heels of Rebecca Regan whenever she was about. No gent under 6-4, each man sport a shorn head with "R" brand on the sides of their head, the scar tissue painted bright red so it stood out. Regardless of the season, they donned black shirts, rolled to bulging biceps. Black tactical vests, heavy with pepper spray, combat knife, brass knuckles, and adorned with two sidearm holsters, threatened to erupt from their broad chest. Some wore black baggy cargo pants, while others wore camo fatigues. All wore black boots, scuffed, bloody and besmirched with grit showcasing their stomping brutality if ordered to do so.

"Hey, Patch," the dark skinned behemoth on the left says. Tone non-threatening, sounding actually quite bored. The big man frowns at the heat, wipes his sweat-beaded brow with the back of his black-gloved hand.

"Hey, um, Lawrence, right?" Patch responds. He knows most of Regan's guardsmen, but one never wants to know them too well. "What's up?" the words bouncing and stuttering off his nervous tongue.

A big pasty skinned gent with a chin chiseled from granite, Lawrence's partner grins, reveling in Patch's uneasiness.

"There's word you have Intel on LaFleur's convoy converging on Lamont," the big black guy says. "Miss Regan would like to see you."

Patch glances over his shoulder, looking for the sell-out who'd mentioned his name. Bastards. "Okay. Yeah, yeah, sure. I'll go with you. Beats standing in the heat."

"Hey! Hey out there. Don't forget our discussion," Largo's voice comes from the closed tent.

Lawrence and Chiseled Jaw peer at the tent, then at Patch. Looks become more dangerous as narrowed eyes drop upon the smaller Reganite.

"What?" Patch shrugs innocently. "He was thirsty. He called me in. I gave him a drink. He wants to see the Regans."

"His funeral," Chiseled Jaw says under his breath though loud enough for Patch to hear.

"Conspiring with a prisoner?" Lawrence accuses, turning his back and starting the trek to the building roughly a hundred yards away.

"High ranking Grand Rapidian at that," Chiseled Jaw snorts, a grin lining his sweaty face.

Patch knows they are both chiding him then. The big bastards.

He holds his tongue and rushes to keep up with the long strides of the big guardsmen.

The inside of the converted supermarket building is pleasantly cool versus the blazing summer furnace outside. Patch nods at the small crowd of Reganites setting up fruit and vegetable stands just inside the doors. They line up carts, tables and crates along the area where the cash register lanes had been. Other vendors, who most likely paid or traded handsomely to set up their wares indoors, pepper themselves amongst the produce sellers. The smell of fresh baked bread nearly grabs Patch's nostrils and drags him to a young woman setting up her stand. And a fine healthy female she is, Patch thinks running his tongue along his ruined gumline.

"This better be quick. I'm supposed to be off duty and in that givem-hell-wagon-train to Lamont," Chiseled Chin groans loud enough for Patch to hear as they walk before him, heading to the rear of the store where a huge cathedral-like add-on had been built for the Regan family.

The guardsman speaks as if he blames Patch for all the nuisance. And Patch knows if the man is truly offended by him, right or wrong, he'll hunt down Patch and take his frustrations out on him another day.

"I didn't think LaFleur and you were good enough buddies for him to consider you," Lawrence responds. "Hell, he took a handful of guys and gals with him, loyal to him, anyway.

"Good riddance, I say. Maybe the big oaf will catch a bullet and one of us will get a shot for the position," the big black man continues. "I'm…" he looks around to make sure no one important stands near, "…about done with being that crazy bitch's toy soldier."

They pass several re-furbished store areas. Thin pre-fab walls stand, long rows of box-like apartments take up spaces where grocery and sporting good departments had been. Most are large one-family dwellings, boxes within the boxes. Most of the inhabitants inside the store area work the fields and new industries on properties outside Reganshire proper. Their wages are spent on rent but they have a place within the secured confines of the massive Reganshire building. Narrow concrete floors run down center aisles, patrolled by the RPF, the Reganshire Police Force, a division of the larger military force housed in barracks on the north side of the building. The RPF utilize electric golf carts and segways for indoor duty.

Patch looks at children playing tag upon Astro Turf lawns, avoiding plastic flower beds, hiding amongst the fronds of fake poplar trees. An old woman works the soil in a wood trough of vegetables within a hydroponic shed. She glares at him as if his gaze molests her tender sprouts.

Meh, who needs this. Patch thinks as they proceed. Real men live outside with the breeze in their face and real grit.

They pass a young woman hanging laundry in short shorts

and a tank top.

Course, there is that, he smiles.

Those who cannot afford to live inside, or decide not to for financial purposes or otherwise—Rebecca Regan is known to stroll the corridors—they stay in tents, rudely constructed wood shacks and, if an opening presents itself, one of the small shop buildings around the immediate property. Patch enjoys being out of doors, enjoys his small mechanics shop just behind the old Meyer gas station. In the southeast corner of the compound near the southern gates, it's a decent place. He makes a good living repairing ramshackle vehicles the Regans allowed the outdoor working groups to have. The big military vehicles are serviced by others, though he often gets to squeak in and tinker when possible.

And with his workshop so close to the southern gate he gets to see all comings and goings of both workers and military groups; the workers heading down Wilson to the farms and fields Regan has acquired; the town militia off to acquire new men, weapons and vehicles to add to Reganshire's growing armed arsenal. On occasion, a small group of soldiers, equipped with heavy packs, leave and do not return for many months, if at all. Patch never asks but he's sure these are folks sent out as Regan's spies to infiltrate other towns and outposts.

Patch breathes easy, realizes he isn't sweating out all the coffee he drank that morning. There is something to be said about having a place inside the massive Reganshire fortress. The thought also makes him realize he has to piss quite badly.

He slams into the back of Chiseled Chin.

"Hey, what the fuck?" the big guardsman says spinning around. He elbows Patch in the chest, nearly knocking him to the ground.

They stand before the entrance to the Regans.

Patch fights the need for his bladder to relieve itself in his pants.

Old Man Regan has built a massive complex for himself and

his family when the shit hit the fan back in the day. Silas Regan got the people of the former village to come together and build the huge enclosure on the west side of town, build up the big shopping center into a living complex grander than any place else outside of the sprawling metropolis of Grand Rapids. He had taken anything and everything and built his base of operations: lumber, sheet metal, concrete, stone, steel and wood beams; they'd all salvaged from the old neighborhoods around the area, amassing it in one location, adding onto the old Meyer supermarket and department store.

The mile long storefront complex was impressive, Regan's home and bunker were the pièce de résistance.

Painted black recently, the interior entrance to the Regan's palatial estate stood with heavy stone block and mortar. Something that Old Man Regan's late minister wife had influence upon no doubt, masonry from a smattering of churches around the area had been taken and re-built into this cathedral-like structure. Stained glass windows two stories tall ran to the ceiling of the supermarket building and beyond.

A glass atrium stood overhead so natural light could beam down upon the front of the estate and its massive double oak doors. Torch sconces stood on either side of the ebon-hued doors; light bulb sockets on the mock-Medieval artifacts void of bulb but looked sinister just the same. Carved into the doors, the Regan "R" emblem: painted bright red and a third as tall as the six foot behemoths escorting Patch. Small drip lines at the bottom legs of each letter gleamed as if still wet against the sunlight streaming down through the atrium windows above.

Rumor had it the last living folk captured wandering too close to Reganshire were drained of their life essence and used to paint the door emblems. Patch shivers as they reach the grisly black and crimson portal. He wouldn't put it past Rebecca Regan to have done such a thing.

Another pair of monsters stood before the doorway. Wearing

sunglasses to shade their eyes from the sunlight overhead, the two armed men nod at their counterparts as they meet Patch and his escorts.

"What do we have here? A miscreant yearning for audience and judgement by Regan?" the giant on the left said loud and grandly at Lawrence, Chiseled Chin and Patch. The man sported a head of shaved blond hair with a red, raised R-shaped brand above his left ear. One gold hoop earring hung from his right ear. His meaty fists clench a .30-06, holding it at chest level like he will use it to block the trios' advance.

"Blow it out your ass, Reginald," Patch says, irritated by the steroidal gorilla's showboating. "I'm here to provide an update on our Lamont campaign."

Gold Hoop deflates and grimaces like he's been kicked in the balls.

The guardsman on the right tries to hold it in, but bursts, laughing in his partner's face. "He got you there, Reg." A tall Hispanic, corded muscles, bushy black eyebrows; Luiz Martinez, Patch is sure of his name.

Reginald Gold Hoop snarls.

"Miss Regan is expecting us," Lawrence says looking at both door men.

Martinez and Gold Hoop step aside; Martinez opens the door for them. The huge oak aperture squeals on dry hinges as it slowly slides open.

"It's about time."

All the men jump at the female voice.

Then a waft of intense aroma washes over them, crinkling nose, clearing of throat as the smell plunges down nostril and mouth. A mixture of one too many perfumes flows from the interior of the Regan home, along with a faint underlying—but definitely there—scent of rotting… something.

Rebecca Regan stands just beyond the threshold, pale white

arms folded across her emaciated chest. She frowns at the men outside the door, her bright red lipstick, put on by an obvious unsteady hand, appears like a splash of strawberry syrup on vanilla ice cream. Her dark pupils encircled by yellowing corneas draw across each of the five men. Each man tenses. Her brow furrows deeper as she casts her gaze upon Patch half-hidden behind the Redwood-tall guardsmen. Patch feels her piercing cold stare, and it seems to poke a tiny hole in his bladder. He lets loose a little squirt.

"Mr. Hanson, father and I look forward to your report," Rebecca says to Patch, using his formal name. Her complexion changes to lukewarm and one side of her mouth curls in a smile.

Patch looks at the guardsmen who return his gaze, knowing full well who he's really reporting to.

"Good news from LaFleur's convoy," Patch responds. He surprises himself by not stuttering with fear before the demented woman. "They're three miles short of Lamont."

He fights to keep his eye from dropping to her near-translucent blouse and viewing that mottled skin, her shriveled chest, and her arms wrapped in gauze from wrist to elbow. Stained with dried blood and yellowing puss, little wriggling bits of… fat white rice drop from the decaying appendages.

"Come in, come in," Rebecca wags a finger at Patch. "Father's napping, but you can… fill me in on the details."

Chiseled Chin gives Patch a shove through the door. "Have fun," he sinisterly grins.

Two more bruisers stand just within the doorway. They wear bandanas over their nose and mouth like a pair of hulking banditos.

"You can come along, too," Rebecca says, eyes running up and down Chiseled Chin like he's a side of prime beef.

"Shit," Chiseled Chin hisses in a small voice. "I'm gonna kick your ass hard when we get out of here." He says just loud enough for Patch to catch.

"Come along, gentlemen. We can relax on the western terrace

as Mr. Hanson fills me in on the Lamont affair," Rebecca says as she turns down a corridor adorned with large carpet remnants hanging from the cold concrete walls. "Father will so love to hear the update."

The heavy perfume smell and the underlying scent of decay make the hairs on Patch's neck stand erect, or it's the gnawing feeling in his gut that this whole place isn't right. The statement outside in the commons area, from his gaunt faced friend, "biggest kiss ass." Yeah, he reflects, maybe that isn't the best moniker to have.

The two men follow the willowy figure of Rebecca Regan past locked doors and expansive, empty rooms. The place could house half the people staying in tents and shanties outside.

They approach a new set of double doors, regular sized household doors.

The rotten meat odor beneath the eye-watering perfume smell threatens to make Patch gag. He balls his hands into fists, fists so tight his dirty fingernails dig into flesh. It is the only thing to do to keep his hands from visibly shaking.

"Daddy's not feeling well today. Let's stop in and tell him your updates," Rebecca stops before the closed doors. Ornate glass doorknobs smudged with dried red smears beckon to be turned.

"Shit shit shit," Chiseled Chin says under his breath.

Correct, Patch thinks, trying to keep from doing that as his nerves threaten to loosen his bowels.

Perhaps his head on a pike, waving in the hot breeze, is in his immediate future.

Chapter Fifteen

The front Humvee somersaults in the air, boosted by an explosion of roadbed and flame. It comes down on its side, a raging inferno of black smoke and tortured metal. Ragdoll occupants burn. The grunts too close to the vehicle when the RPG kissed it, down; some not to rise, others: slim chance as bullets from the Lamont Outpost cut through the roiling smoke.

"Those aren't our guys," Stokes yells as the entire convoy takes evasive.

The Huron stays facing forward. Her back ramp drops with a clang. A platoon of soldiers spill from the big transport.

"No shit, Sherlock," Phelps replies from the Huron's cab. "But we had guys in there. What happened to them?"

Ahead, though brought to a slightly angled position, Forrester and the Ontario discharge its own group of soldiers. Both groups of thirty men apiece rush out onto the grounds before the small enclosed village. Decayed or demolished home fronts become cover as do the beginning of the steep river valley off the southern edge of the roadway.

"I did this," Largo smiles, sitting on the edge of the Huron's roofline beside Billet's hatch. He wears a three piece suit, a small American flag pin on his lapel. He seems unfazed by the intense summer heat boiling around him.

Jake knows the man isn't real. Still, the knowledge Largo is, in fact, responsible makes him white-knuckle the hatch coaming lest he lunge at the apparition.

A bullet pangs off the armor. Jake shudders. Largo disappears. "Eddie, take out the RPG…" he starts to say over the comm.

A rocket-propelled explosive charge hisses dangerously low. Jake instinctively ducks. "Incoming!" he yells.

The Grizzly stands two vehicles before them; Breckenridge and his gunner upright in their turret hatches. The turret disappears in a billow of smoke and flame.

"Geezuzz," Billet says as the flash dissipates.

Breckenridge still stands torso high in his hatch. Raymonds, his gunner, lies curled over, smoking, black, with wisps of small flame coming off him.

"Need medics on Breckenridge!" Forrester yells, discontinuing his own firing upon the outpost to turn and look back at their commander.

The M3 Bradley in front of the Grizzly spits death from its 25mm cannon into the north guard tower.

Another man toting an RPG rises from the south tower.

"Eddie, take out that…" Jake begins to say.

Already with rifle in hand, Mulholland leans in his rear hatch, lifts weapon, hardly placing eye to scope. Pulls trigger. The tango with the RPG drops with a perforated cranium.

"Done," Mulholland says, placing rifle back into his basket and resuming his mounted .30-Cal machine gun.

Jake keeps his head low as he looks back at the Grizzly. Fighting men and women line up around the M60, laying down cover fire as a group of Red Cross helmets claw their way up the tank's side. The hull hatchways under the turret pop open, hands wave, thumbs up; loader and driver okay. Breckenridge waves off the first medic who approaches him, hand nothing but blood red. A section of the TC's helmet appears mangled and melted to his head. A black splotch paints one side of the 105mm cannon base where the RPG had hit. A foot higher and more than the TC's helmet would've been pulped. As Breckenridge tries to wave the medic away from him, he speaks into his helmet microphone hanging by a loose wire. Obvious in shock, he doesn't know he's off-air.

"Their chewin' us up out in the open here," Forrester calls in Billet's head set.

Jake glances over to the parked-at-an-angle Ontario. Forrester stands in his commander's hatch, hatch lid protecting him as bullets ring off the thick steel body of the Heavy Transport Vehicle. His front gunner, a Native American gent named Chip Raintree, hammers away at the outpost with his a .30-Cal.

Three grunts hug the Ontario's roofline using one of the big topside cargo doors as a shield to fire behind. Two men stand in the rear roof gunner ports; one firing the mounted .30, the other a M4. Jake doesn't recognize them behind their sweat darkened skull-print bandanas.

Years ago, the houses and trees had been leveled and used within Lamont Proper. It also created an open expanse with the road leading into the small fortified village and the gradual sweep to the river valley to the south. Little had anyone figured the wide open space would be used against them.

Lamont had always been around. When the pandemic hit over a decade ago, the bigger cities and surrounding suburbs were hit the hardest. A small community, miles to the northwest of Grand Rapids, and even north of Allendale, hadn't been ravaged by any onslaught of the living or unliving; able to wall itself in and survive with the assistance of the Coopersville-Eastmanville Communal. The only reason the big city had taken a liking to it was because of the rail line cutting along its northern edge.

A few years back, Lamont residents, with free pass and homes provided, moved into Grand Rapids or Coopersville. A company of GRCC took the residents' place to guard the center link rail junction between Muskegon and Grand Rapids.

Over the sound of gunfire, in the distance, a shrill train whistle blew.

Jake clears his throat and hopes his cords to work. "We're gonna pile up before we get inside," he says to Forrester across the way. The other man nods. "We're going in. Now."

Forrester stops nodding. "Wait a minute, Captain. We don't know what they got in there, other than the armament and weaponry we stationed. They smoke you, and we're down men *and* a transport."

"Lou, rev'er up," Jake says. He waves in two score soldiers hunkered around the Huron. "Load up. We're going to knock their front teeth in," he points towards the Lamont gate.

Fighting men and women scurry inside the Huron. The men grouped up on the Ontario's roofline behind the half open roof bay doors gave him an idea.

"Open the cargo doors halfway, ramp three-quarters up." Billet watches the soldiers file in, listens as the rooftop cargo doors hydraulics hum. "I want a fire team six per side, target straight in front of you. Two additional shooters cover our backside. Rear gunners, arc of fire only around your respective corners. Overlap only if clear."

Jake looks at Stokes who chews a stump of cigar and waits for *his* orders anxiously. "Sergeant, no rubber bullets for the shit inside Lamont."

"Ay, sir," Stokes replies, flexing his fingers before wrapping them back about the grips of his quad .30's.

M16's, M60 machine guns—and one musket—and pistols throw hot lead, the nuns of the West Side Apostolate roll up beside the Huron on quads and Dodge Ram trucks.

"We're going with you, Captain," Sister Mirose says, standing in the bed of the pickup truck closest to the Huron just below Jake's station.

A crudely welded machine gun mount stands just behind

the armored rear cab window, a .50-Cal machine gun. The barrel smokes. Shell casings litter the bedliner. The big machine gun is in the grip of Mirose's black gloved fists. Painted in white letters on the body of the weapon: Holy Ghost. Her postulant sits in the rear corner of the truck bed, combat helmet over cloth veil, dirty dusty face, pistols in each hand raised with hammers poking her shoulders, eyes hard, ready.

Jake opens his mouth to tell her to stand down, back off.

He knows the big battle-hardened nun would never listen to him. He nods his acceptance and turns his eyes forward only to have Lettner kneeling before his mounted .50-Cal.

"Bring the holy sister along. Keep her close," Lettner says, dressed in a black suit like he was heading to a funeral. The late NSC Commissioner casts his eyes at the nun and back to Jake. "You might need her." He leans forward, pressing the barrel of the big machine gun against his head.

Jake snarls, grabs at the gun grips and fires. The bullets throw up huge clots of dirt a few yards in front of some GRCC soldiers behind a piling of old tree stumps.

"Damn, what ya shootin' at? The enemy's in front of us," Stokes says as he fires towards the gates ahead.

Billet growls.

Lettner laughs in his head.

"We got another RPG mounting the south tower," Mulholland says.

"Lou, get us in there," Jake commands as the Huron lurches forward.

More bullets pang off the transport's hide. A soldier groans behind Billet and sags. Helped by his team mates, the wounded grunt is brought down into the bowels of the vehicle and another soldier takes his place.

The GRCC men and women who lay down suppressing fire near the front of the line hold up as the big M213 growls by. Some pump their fist in support. Some pour on the bullet swarm to direct enemy fire on them.

"Could use that 25mm cannon right about now," Stokes said as the Huron increases speed, front dualies spit dirt, weeds and cobbled roadbed. Rear tracks roll over and mash all back into the earth.

The retrofit 25mm cannon turret sits lifeless behind them.

"Wasn't it your decision to not take on extra munitions?" Loutonia says from below.

"Real reason is he lost the r/c helmet," Eddie cuts in.

"Shut up," Stokes blusters.

"I hope flattening the gate doesn't come out of our pay," Loutonia adds. "I'll be paying enough to fix my baby's paint job," referring to the Huron.

A tall, two layers thick double-doored chain link gate spans the west and eastbound rutted lanes of Leonard Street leading into the Lamont compound. On both sides, fifty yards in either direction, more fencing wove with steel bands and small "murder hole" apertures. Jake has been in the place before what seems eons ago. He knows the lay of the land within the outpost, the entire "downtown" village area re-fitted into a small but efficient military compound. Homes and old businesses along the main street were converted into barracks. The old post office, fortified, and made into the command HQ.

The images of a candle shop where Jake's parents brought him and his siblings during Sunday jaunts to Spring Lake and Grand Haven enter his mind. And the Quonset hut store: a vehicle repair shop, used to be a button factory building. The home next door: a mess hall that looks over the river valley below.

The east gates draw closer. A pair of insurgents rise up in the south guard tower near the gate, one hefts a rocket-propelled grenade launcher to shoulder.

The Lamont compound fades, replaced by a small vibrant

community. Trees caught in the warm summer breeze clap their green leafed bows. Trimmed emerald lawns run to curb. Colorful flowers dot landscaped yards and window boxes on clean, bright, white painted homes.

Jake's dead parents, his sister and younger brother, Jenna and Joey, stand in the center of the road looking up at him, smiling, waving.

"Hard left!" Billet shouts.

72 tons of wheeled and tracked vehicle snap sideways. Twin Cummins engines growl in protest as do the soldiers who lose their perch and fall into one another.

"Dragon's teeth. How'd you see them…?" Stokes starts to say, eyes cast on the low concrete pyramids resting behind brush just inside the east gate. He cuts his statement short with the sudden presence of the fence and the south tower practically on top of him.

The Huron brakes. Wheels turned toward Lamont. The left rear track stops as the right speeds up, tearing earth and shooting a rooster of grass and dirt into the air.

"Knock knock, motherfuckers," Loutonia says over the comm as the Huron crashes broadside into the looming fence.

The small guard tower, a reinforced tree stand with sheet metal "blind," snaps backwards. The RPG shooter and his comrade flail in the air, wrapped within the wood and steel lattice work. Their surprised and agonized screams are silenced as the fence comes down atop them, followed by a twin diesel growl and the American-built Heavy Transport Vehicle, the Huron.

"Put us near center of town," Billet says as he and every gun jutting from the transport open fire. Mirose and her fighting congregation rush to defensive positions, gunning down any opposition in their way.

"If they're shooting at you, they ain't our guys," Stokes reminds everyone.

A lot of unfamiliars in GRCC uniform, Jake thinks as bullets rain around him while he and his crew return the lead storm.

"We're coming in behind you," Forrester says in Jake's helmet headset.

In the distance, the steam engine whistle bellows sharply.

"I'm going to the depot," Billet replies. "Has anyone been able to contact Honeywell's train?"

"Negative," came the voice of Lance Breckenridge, weak, sounding miles away and hurting bad.

"He ordered no long rang communication," Forrester cut in, "in the event of this exact thing."

Jake's vision blurs. A sudden wave of rage to tear Breckenridge and the Ontario commander limb from limb drowns his senses. *No one fucking clued me in to this gawddamn piece of information.*

He wags his head. The insane anger must be subdued. He flexes his fingers. Joints pop. He hopes Stokes, nor any of the troopers behind him, sees his hands tremble.

Static: someone fudging with a headset. Gun fire comes through everyone's receiver. Shouts of men: "Cover the Ontario!" "For our men on the inside!" "For Lamont!"

"Sergeant Mecon here. Breckenridge, Raymonds need medical attention stat," the new voice, a well-known field surgeon, over Breckenridge's commlink.

Mirose's truck pulls alongside the Huron escorted by four nun-laden quads. The quad drivers have corrugated sheet metal siding draped from their shoulders to protect their flanks, riders hold one such shield while firing pistol, rifle or small single-hand machine gun with deadly accuracy.

"I have medically-trained Mount Mercy Sisters with us. The Candle Shop is the outpost's med center, yes?" Mirose asks, firing the .50 and glancing up at Billet.

Jake looks down at the big nun and her postulant in the rear of the truck. They both flicker in his eyesight. Flesh, internal organs, strong beating hearts, rich red blood pumping through vein and arteries, then nothing but skeletal figures, then back to flesh, back to reality.

"If…" he tries to speak. Back to taut, grindy vocal cords. He clears his throat. "Affirmative. If it hasn't… been overrun."

The Ontario grinds through the collapsed fence line following the Huron's path. GRCC troopers come in behind Forrester's rig. The opposition dodges between buildings and houses, dropping wounded or dead, or retreating deeper into the village outpost.

"Push them to the west end of town," Forrester says. "We'll sweep and secure the buildings as we go."

The M3 Bradley *TOW Nailed* tracks into the compound, its brother, *Skullbanger*, remains on Overwatch beside Breckenridge's rig. The IFV inside the enclosure stops just within the fence line. Jake sees the Grizzly lurch forward a hair but isn't sure who is driving as the crew inside surely still reels from getting their bell rung.

"Love the smell of rotting meat on a hot summer's day," Lettner chuckles sitting between Jake and Stokes.

"Why don't you fuck off," Billet growls low through clenched teeth.

"What?" Stokes says, glancing at Jake.

Jake coughs, made sure throat's clear. "We're rolling to the med center. We'll secure…" Vocal cords tightening. "…it. Then we'll hit the train depot."

"Roger that." Forrester replies.

"We'll bring in Breckenridge when you clear the MC," the voice of medic Mecon says. "Raymonds got some superficial burns and lacerations. Got the wind knocked out of him. The TC…"

Gun fire from up the road blots out the medic's words. Passing 42nd Avenue, still rolling down center of Leonard, an olive-green GRCC MRAP starts up and disappears down the street behind the corner house. Billet tries to recall the ordinance and vehicles stationed at the Lamont Outpost. No tanks, thankfully, but a small and fully equipped fleet of MRAP's, Mine-Resistant Ambush

Protected armored vehicles—lovingly referred to as "bulldogs"—and Light Tactical Vehicles like in their convoy. A M213 would've been stationed here if there'd been any to spare.

"Guy wants to play cat and mouse," Stokes says as Loutonia brings the Huron to a stop at the intersection of Leonard and 42nd.

"Orders, Captain?" Loutonia asks.

"Such pressure, Jacob," Lettner says standing on the street in front of the Huron. He slowly shakes his head with index finger to chin. "Secure the med center, save Breckenridge. Chase Largo's hired guns all over the compound, waste time. Check the train depot and usher your beloved mayor back into this shooting gallery." The late NSC Commissioner snorts with mirth: "Such choices for a good soldier on his way down."

Billet puts his hands to his helmet. He pinches his eyes shut. "Get out of my head dammit."

"Captain?" Loutonia says again in his headset.

"Earth to Jacob Ethan Billet. Are you still with us?" Lettner laughs, also sounding in the headset, or at least Jake's ears.

Poom-poom-poom, the firing of the *TOW Nailer's* 25mm cannon snaps Jake back to reality.

Behind them, the M3 rushes up, firing down Leonard at the west end of the outpost. The Ontario rolls along on the opposite side of the Huron, not on the street but along sidewalk and manicured lawn just outside one of the three barracks on the south side of the street. The roadbed erupts where the Bradley's shells hit. Men in GRCC fatigues run, shooting over their shoulder, not aiming, hitting nothing.

"Okay, I'm pushing for the med center instead. Fire Team One," Forrester calls to the M3, "push them to Eastmanville if you have to."

"Copy that, Ontario," the commander of the Bradley replies as it moves between the two M213's and heads westward down the street, still firing.

Two of the BRV-O's form up just behind the Ontario and on the right side of the HTV. The old Candle Shop building stands not far down the street between 44th Avenue and Mill Street. Directly behind the converted retail shop-to-field hospital off the main street, the defunct Lamont school building; used as the outpost HQ. If there is a battle to be had, it would probably be within it.

The MRAP backs up, comes back into view, taunting the Huron.

Lettner stands down near that vehicle now, waving both his hands like he's scooping water into his face, smiling. "Come on. You can do it," he says in Jake's head like Jake's his dog ready to do a trick. A trick that would surely get him beat.

TOW Nailer stops down the street at Leonard and 44th Avenue. Turret turning northward, it flings lead and cannon fire at something or many somethings up the side street. The train depot is another block west off Mill Street. Billet can only assume Largo's mercenaries amass there.

"We'll get that devil," Mirose calls up from the pickup truck beside the Huron.

Jake shakes as if he's grabbed a live light socket with a wet hand. He looks down at the big nun who unrolls the white sleeve of her vestment, takes a crumpled cigarette pack in hand and fingers out a smoke. Their eyes meet, and for a moment he is afraid she knows he is losing it and seeing things.

Lettner flips him the bird and disappears as the MRAP rolls onto the spot he'd just been standing.

Another whistle blast from the mayor's train: miles away still, but closing. *And no way to warn them what they're walking into,* Jake thinks.

"Get to the train station," Mirose yells as her postulant jumps to her feet and lights her cigarette. "We'll meet you there."

Jake watches Sister Mary Mirose and her young nun-in-training flicker like a strobe light, reality to a bleeding upright corpse, to reality again. He only nods.

With her cigarette hanging out the corner of her mouth, Mirose pumps her fist in the air, drawing the other fighting Sisters attention, and points towards the MRAP. The holy women whoop and holler, following Mirose's big RAM truck as she heads up 42nd towards the enemy.

"Move out," Jake says, his voice like gravel rolling in a tin can. "Depot."

"Roger," Loutonia answers, and the Huron lurches forward.

"See you on the other side," Forrester says as they begin to move forward also.

Maybe, Jake watches the Ontario commander—his friend—pull away. *Lord forbid, maybe.*

***

Lucius LaFleur sits in the back of the black stripped down Humvee. The leather seats are shot, literally with a few bullet holes, figuratively with wear revealed-ripped cushions, cloth and foam fuzzing out. He dabs at his sweaty bald head with the back of his gloved hand, flicking a good dollop of moisture from his brow.

"We lost Burlap and Baxter's transmission, but they reported being about half a klick away when the firefight started at Lamont," LaFleur's driver says with a map of the area folded in hand, making marks with a pencil. "Seems we lost them when they stopped at Linden to use the Angel Whistle."

LaFleur shudders at the thought. It wasn't his idea to bring the damn device into battle, not when they'd be in the thick of things along with the GRCC. "Call in whatever Ferals are in the vicinity to harry the Grand Rapids forces." Rebecca Regan suggested. *Fuck that*, he thinks. *You ain't here to hang with your own kind. I really hope the damn thing didn't work.*

Gun fire continues in the distance, Lamont way.

"What's the order, Mr. LaFleur?" Jeremy Pike says over the

comm. He stands turned around in the turret of his big M1 Abrams, staring over the tops of the smaller Reganshire "military" vehicles behind his lead position. He looks mean, anxious.

Lucius sits four vehicles back from the massive tank, and he can see the ex-GRCC TC giving him the stink eye. He can hear the gun fire coming from Lamont. Largo hasn't been kidding about having guys on the inside, taking the fight to Grand Rapids, intentions on taking the big city's mayor out of commission permanently, so the treasurer can slip into his seat and have things his way.

The Regans had it their way, and over the last year or so, considering Reganshire's expansion, the ruling parties had gotten a little bit… wacky. Lucius can't remember the last time he'd seen the old man, maybe seven or eight months now, though he sent his proclamations through his bat shit crazy daughter.

And now they're going to go in, bust the big city's military balls while they're in the heat of battle, and assist in the assassination of Grand Rapids' top dog. To further the cause of Reganshire. And assist the schemings of a power hungry city official. All for what? So they all could skip through flowery fields hand in hand with the undead? Kumbaya and that shit?

Lucius LaFleur shakes his head, causing a rain fall of sweat to wash down his forehead, into his eyes, dribble off the tip of his sun-darkened nose.

And if his friends from the GRCC militia are in that party fighting in Lamont, specifically his friend, Eddie?

"Kill them all, or you're nothing to me and will pay a high price for insubordination," Rebecca Regan had promised him and his hodgepodge army of Reganites. The heads waving on pikes along the Reganshire fence line, and the ground up rank piles of "meat" to feed their "wild dog" Ferals reveal itself plainly in his mind.

The woman is a tyrannical, murderous bitch.

"Commander?"

LaFleur's navigator sits before him, pulls him from his dire thoughts.

"Orders, *Commander?*" Pike says drawing out the last word. Devastator revs its engines and jerks forward. LaFleur wonders if the guy will take matters into his own hands.

Lucius rises in his seat, looks back at the line of men and vehicles. A slew of armored-up pickup trucks, a half dozen stolen Light Tactical Vehicles, a rickety Sherman tank pulled and re-stored from the VFW down Wilson. Men and fighting women with pistols, rifles, machine guns, and hand grenades; all things that had cost Reganshire a fortune and time to acquire, perhaps all for this grand and glorious hot fucking day.

He waves his fist in the air then snaps his arm straight out, index finger pointing westward.

"To Lamont! Move out!" he bellows.

He knows what he has to do…

His job.

***

"Are we gonna have to pay for any damage done to the outpost?" Stokes asks as shell casings spiral into the air in an almost solid arch of smoking brass. Insurgents in a single level house he fired upon, appear, then disappear. Shattered glass; a cloud of splintering wood the only things left as he rakes the small abode one way and then another…for good measure.

No one returns fire.

Jake doesn't respond but takes potshots at the dancing ghouls of Lettner and Largo as the Huron traverses west along Leverette.

"Captain," Mulholland says from his rear gunner's position. "I was thinking. Long range radioes might not work, but what about short range. If we could get a message to Honeywell as they get closer to us…"

Jake goes to speak. Again, vocal cords tight, dry, raw. He rubs at his throat with a gloved hand. He cannot feel the sensation of the touch upon his skin.

"It's beginning, and this time there's no way back," Lettner says, sitting on a lawn chair in the next yard they draw upon.

Jake fires the .50-Cal at the apparition, blows away a white picket fence, half-choked with thorny vines, into kindling.

"They'd have to be almost upon the west rail gate to receive anything," Stokes says.

Jake nods his agreement at his sergeant's statement.

"You're going to need a little bigger signal than our personal handsets," Loutonia chimes in, swerving to avoid a motorcycle lying on its side near the curb. The right rear track catches it and crushes flat the back wheel, seat and gas tank.

A half dozen men in GRCC uniforms pop up from a tall concrete wall within the yard of the compound's mess hall. They assume they're dealing with a single vehicle, perhaps with only its crew. The soldiers standing in the Huron's open cargo hold hammer them with bullets.

The train whistle blows again. Maybe a mile away. Everyone can faintly hear the big engine hissing and growling as it nears Lamont.

"I know they have MUTT's here with enough boost to get a communique through if their listening," the rear gunner across from Mulholland comments. "I just don't know where they're storing them. I haven't seen any OP vehicle here 'cept that MRAP. Where're they hiding?"

The Lamont Depot, part of the Grand Rapids, Grand Haven and Muskegon Railway, lay situated off Mill Street South, at the end of a horseshoe drive. In the years before the pandemic and the undead incursion, the rail service between Muskegon and Grand Rapids brought big city visitors to enjoy the small town feel, rolling green meadows and the sparkling flow of the Grand River a stone's throw south. The railway which originally ran from the Lake Michigan lakeshore, both Muskegon and Grand Haven/ Spring Lake, to Grand Rapids, had only recently been re-secured for use in greater trade opportunity.

And now it could be the memorial trail for Grand Rapids's reigning mayor, Billet thinks as they draw up to a green field before the small train station. He can just see the red shingled one-story roof line of the structure rising behind a dense line of trees and overgrown shrubbery.

"Shit! Look at that!" one of the men in the cargo hold shouts, pointing back behind them.

The MRAP comes swinging around the corner of 44th Avenue and Leverette with the two big Dodge Ram pickups and a score of quads in hot pursuit. The Huron jerks to a halt and everyone swings their weapons rearward. Loutonia drops the rear ramp, lets the soldiers swarm out and take position. The pesky vehicle isn't getting away this time.

Funny, Jake thought, *pursuing nuns aren't firing at it.*

"Hold your fire," Mulholland calls out, noticing the oddity also. "Somethings not right."

The MRAP screeches to a halt a few feet behind the transport, turning sideways as it does so. One of the Apostolate trucks and several of nun and gun-toting quads break off and speed up the drive towards the depot building.

Jake slips down from his stand, legs almost buckling as he hits the inside grid work of the Huron's interior. His lower body feels numb, as if his upper and lower section are no longer connected. He pushes through it, walking somewhat sluggishly behind the rest of the men who exit the vehicle. The dimness of the Huron's bowels soothes him and, considering he'd just been topside, makes his eyeballs burn when he steps back out into the sunlight.

He pulls off his helmet but unslings the tinted goggles, slipping them over his eyes. He leaves the helmet on the rear ramp as he watches three figures step down from the back of the MRAP.

The hulking Sister Mirose moves from the vehicle, a pair of AA12 assault shotguns strapped across her back, along with a grunt in GRCC fatigues, mouth bloodied, and the little Betty White Nun with a fist full of the soldier's shirtsleeve and a .44 Mag handgun in her liver-spotted free hand.

"We got this rascal, but there is a big problem this fine gentleman informed us of," Mirose says, taking the man by the back of his neck. She jerks him forward, wincing as she moves. She wears a nasty gash on her right arm, just below her GOD tattoo.

Jake opens his mouth to speak, emits only a garbled mishmash of unintelligible syllables. He quickly closes his mouth, tasting the acidic tang of blood rising in his tortured throat. He swallows.

"There aren't any of your men around," Betty White Nun says, wiping a line of sweat from the side of her wrinkly face, "Because they're all at the depot, trussed up, and waiting for the mayor's train."

Jake notices the side of her big pistol, stained with blood. He looks at the side of their captives face, notices a bleeding imprint roughly the thickness of the Magnum's barrel.

"They've put all the vehicles on the tracks, along with the outpost men and women," Mirose adds.

"We stop the train or knock it off the tracks. We kill the mayor of Grand Rapids. All is right as rain," the mercenary says, grinning.

Betty White Nun smashes him in the side of the face with her gun. He staggers, does not fall. The grin disappears only to be replaced by an angry sneer. Blood runs freely from his cheek and side of his mouth.

"You aren't going to do shit," Stokes says stepping up beside Billet. "We got the rest of your friends on the run, shot dead or soon to be. We'll stop that train, and you aren't going to be able to do shit."

The man starts to smile again, mischievously.

He knows something else, Jake thinks, not able to take his

eyes off the blood running down Mirose's arm, and the free flow from their captive's face. Mirose's heart beats strong in her chest. Their smirking prisoner; his heart races, pumping his life stuff through his system at highway speeds. Betty White Nun has a heart murmur.

Jake clears his throat. "Let me… talk to him," he says reaching out and grabbing the man by his shirt collar.

"What about the train?" Mulholland asks, another whistle blast sounds almost on cue after his statement.

A two stall garage stands across the street. Jake starts to jerk the mercenary along. "Try your short range… radio idea. If you get… in contact with them…" He gulps, having a hard time drawing breath. He thinks, if the train stops and there are still insurgents squirreling around in the compound, a well-placed shot, or a lot of shots, or another RPG could do the mayor in, and more of GRCC's finest.

"If you make… contact," Jake rasps, "Tell them to… keep going. Don't slow down… until safely within the city."

The mercenary continues to grin, drooling blood. Sweet smelling blood.

"Get going," Jake says. "Get our men out… of harm's way and get… those vehicles off the tracks."

The mercenary starts to laugh.

Jake snarls and drags him roughly across the street as Mulholland, Stokes, and the soldiers they'd been hauling rush in the direction the other nuns have gone. Only Mirose and a dozen of her compatriots remain.

"What're you gonna do, boss?" the laughing man says as Jake stops at a side door leading into the old residential garage structure.

Jake tries the door. It's open.

He tries to speak. *Wait.* But only a gurgled grunt emits.

He shoves Largo's hired gun through the door, steps in and closes the door behind him. Via a hole in the roof, the interior is illuminated. The place smells of dust and oil. Bikes, garden utensils, and an old lawnmower sit covered in cobwebs and red with rust.

"Pretty slaphappy," Billet says, twisting the man around so they are face to face, "for a man… about to die."

The mercenary clears his throat and spits a glob of blood and spit in Jake's face. "Fuck you. There's gonna be a lot of dying when your guys try to pull your other friends from the cars and trigger the C4 we've stashed in some of the vehicles. We figured if we couldn't stop and shoot Dennis Honeywell, he could take the train and your guys into hell if the train tries to smash through the vehicle barricade."

Jake doesn't loosen his grip on the man, simply shakes his head. A dollop of blood drips from the tip of his nose, filling his nostrils with the tangy scent.

"What're you gonna do now, Jakey?" Largo says appearing behind the mercenary. "You're screwed whatever you do."

Jake breathes in, throat and lungs rattling like dry twigs with the intake.

"No," Jake answers, looks straight at the mercenary. "If there's a will, there's a way."

"What?" the man says. He starts to clear his throat, cough up another wet glob of bloody spit.

Jake's left hand shoots up and grabs the left side the mercenary's head, just over the ear. His right hand claws into the man's shoulder, digging in. With a sudden violent jerk, Jake bends the man's head and neck until, with a gruesome pop, it rests horizontally on the man's own shoulder. Jake snarls and slams his face into the exposed neckline, bites down until skin is punctured. He takes a deep bloody, satisfying bite out of the man's neck. He tilts his head back, chews as the man's blood geysers from the severed jugular, giving the rusting objects behind them a fresh coat of bright red paint.

Jake chews and swallows. He lets the man loose to crumple to the floor, the mercanry's body shakes as his life flees.

"Glad I could help you clear your throat," Jake says, wiping his sleeve across his mouth.

He steps out of the garage, looks across the street at Loutonia, Mirose, and a small group of soldiers and nuns…

…and falls to the ground on hands and knees, and throws up.

Chapter Sixteen

"Hey, are you all right?" Lettner runs up to Billet and puts a hand on his shoulder. "Man, you look like shit." He laughs.

"Everyone needs to submit at some time in their life," Largo says, joining the late NSC Commissioner, taking a knee before Jake, trying to prop his head up. "What happened in there?"

Jake climbs to his feet and snarls, fingers curl, tensing, untensing. In his eyes: red and blood and meat and death. He swats at Largo, connects, solid, like hitting a wall.

Lettner stumbles away. "Captain? Jake?" But the voice: Loutonia's.

Knocked down, Largo sits on his ass. "May the Lord have mercy," he says, though it wasn't him anymore but Sister Mirose.

Jake's chest heaves with intakes of ragged breath. It hurts. God does it hurt; his entire body. Heart squeezed. Brain shriveled and cooked in his skull. Eyes burn. Black blood crawling through his arteries and veins slow as tree sap.

Something nudges against the side of his temple. He glances sidelong.

Betty White Nun stands, just a shriveled bag of flesh and bones in a Pith helmet in his eyesight, holding a .44 Magnum to his head.

"Don't make me, Captain," Betty White Nun says as she flickers back into substance. A gnarled old finger rests firmly on the trigger.

"Jacob," Loutonia says, moving closer again, but not within reach.

Mirose gets to her feet, dusts herself off, stands head to head, straight at him, muscular arms spread. She assumes a wrestler's pose.

"Okay," Jake says, the drying blood about his mouth makes his lips tingle. *That's being alive, isn't it?* He doesn't worry on it long.

Raising his hands slowly, he gently, very slowly and carefully, backhands the .44 Mag barrel from his head, looking at the little old nun. "It's… okay, Sister."

Eyeliner penciled-on brow rising, Betty White Nun doesn't appear convinced but lowers her sidearm.

He sees his helmet on Huron's rear ramp and runs for it.

"Jake," Loutonia says, her voice cracking, as he ignores her and pushes by.

"Captain?" Mirose says, voice low, with a threat of violence.

Jake scoops up his helmet, mashes it on his head making the goggles dig painfully into the bridge of his nose and cheeks. He turns back to the women. Mirose stands with the automatic shotguns unslung, one in each hand.

He ignores what promises to be instant death from the big nun.

"Captain… Billet here," he says, surprised at the sudden clarity of his stunted voice. "The vehicles are wired with explosives, don't…"

"We discovered that, sir." Mulholland. "We're carefully extracting our outpost men." His voice suddenly cracks, and, with broken words like Billet's: "Killed…They killed them all, Captain."

"Left 'em to rot in this heat," Stokes breaks in. "Gawddammit, Captain, those bastards butchered 'em."

Largo stands beside Jake. "Your visions wasn't far off, just a little misplaced," the City Treasurer chuckles.

All around Jake, bodies of his fighting men and women, shot, knived, torn to ribbons. Ferals kneel in the carnage, supping like vultures on the carcasses. Reganshire soldiers stand behind them, guns at the ready, but all of them dead and rotting in their boots.

Jake fights back another chunk of... something trying to claw up his throat. He blinks back tears that dry, empty ducts will not emit.

The scene returns to normal.

The train whistle blows. Closer. The engine hisses. The bell clangs. The iron beast is slowing down.

"Get the bodies out. Carefully. Call the damn train," Jake says, fights tightening vocal cords which want to return to grit. "Tell them... Largo's has hired guns... attacking. Tell them Reganshire... is on the war path. Tell them... full throttle, no stopping, until they hit Grand Rapids." He swallows, nearly chokes. "Do it, Eddie. I'm... counting on you, kid."

"We're already looking at the ones we can move, but you have about a half dozen, they have enough bricks to blow the track."

"We've gotta stop the train," Stokes chimes in.

Largo appears between Loutonia and Mirose. He looks at both women, nods his head, winks his one good eye. "I know why you like these ladies," he says. "But stop that train, and I have more than enough men to mop up you and Honeywell.

"Stop. Stop the train. Please have the good mayor do so," Largo grins.

"Negative, Sergeant," Jake says.

He ignores the leering apparition and looks to Loutonia, Mirose and the few grunts and nuns who stayed behind. "Load up," he nods towards the Huron. "We... have a job to do."

He sees the wide-eyed, fearful stares of the soldiers who'd ridden with him. They look upon his bloodied complexion suspiciously. They know. They know he is Turning, on his way out.

"We'll join the others," one man answers, and the rest follow him.

Loutonia, Sister Mirose, and her handful of Holy Sisters, including Betty White Nun, stay.

The dull pop of a 25mm cannon surrounded by machine gun fire comes from a block over, on Leonard Street where Forrester seems to have the undivided attention of the insurgents.

The train whistle blows again, echoes through the tree-lined rail throughway. A half mile away.

Jake stiffly walks to the left side of the transport. He growls as he does so, fighting his body to move. His brain yells *move it, soldier*. His muscles, nerves, driving organs flip his brain the bird saying *no, we're tapping out*.

Corded, steel fiber tow straps hang secured to Huron's hull.

Jake can tell Loutonia fights to hold her emotions in check, but, shows her best poker face, as she says, "What're the orders, Captain?"

"Everyone saddle up… who wants to," he replies, nods towards the HTV, lifting the steel cables from their hook straps. They weigh roughly 75 pounds apiece. He detaches both tow straps without issue. He can't feel his muscles tearing if they even did so. "We're going to go extract some C4 teeth from the rail line."

***

"Cripes, that son of a bitch wasn't lying," Pike says recalling Rupert Largo's boasting of having hired guns to push his plans forward.

As they come over Leonard Streets curving rise, Pike and the Devastator are the first to see the carnage Largo's mercenaries have spread. A GRCC M60 Patton tank stands in the center of the road just before the closed east gate of the Lamont Outpost— Breckenridge's Grizzly, Pike's certain. A Humvee lays not far away, on its side, a boil of black smoke rising from the vehicle. Two BRV-Os and a M3 Bradley stand Overwatch around the tank and not far from a large section of crumpled outpost fencing: an opening big enough for two Devastator's to drive through side by side.

"The Ontario and Huron made that hole," Pike says to himself.

"What do you have up there, Major?" LaFleur speaks in Pike's helmet headset.

Pike turns in his turret hatch and looks back four vehicles to Lucius LaFleur's command car. "Looks like our guys..." He quickly bites his tongue, clears his throat loudly and re-states, "Looks like the GRCC got up close and personal with Largo's guys. Not much opposition at the front gate any longer. I'm suspecting the rest of the city forces are inside as there is still gun fire coming from within."

"Slow us down a bit," Pike says to Dawson in the loaders hatch beside him, killing the communications line for a moment.

Dawson nods, switches to an internal channel. "Quarter speed, Simmons."

The Devastator slows.

"What do we have directly ahead?" LaFleur asks Pike as Jeremy is sure the big Reganite commander can start to see the gate house.

"Maybe two score grunts on the ground, a couple light vehicles and one of their Bradley's." Pike replies. The Grizzly still doesn't move but men swarm about the tank, taking up defensive positions as they see the Reganshire convoy come into view. He wonders why Breckenridge isn't turning his gun on the approaching army.

"They got a tank up there," LaFleur exclaims as they draw closer. His voice: wary.

"Not moving, though the rest are prepping for us," Pike answers as the M3 spins on track, angling itself for soldiers to find cover behind. Its 25mm gun turret rotates to face the oncoming convoy. The BRV-Os don't move, but their mounted roof top .50-Cals point directly at the Reganshire forces.

Dawson lifts a pair of field glasses to his eyes. "Largo's goons must've thrown some fire power in our guy's face. See a lot of soldiers being patched up," he says scanning the grounds.

"We're ready. Give us the green light, and we'll break formation, roll around you and start the attack," LaFleur says, though again, he speaks carefully, a slight tone of uncertainty.

"Major Pike, I presume."

"Full stop," Pike says to the Reganshire force. "Captain... Vatallis?" He says faintly recalling the voice of the GRCC man who speaks to him on the comm from across the battlefield.

"This is Vatallis. What're your intentions, Major?"

"What's the Sitrep over there, Captain? You guys need assistance?"

Hesitation. "Not from the likes of you or the party behind you," Vatallis replies bluntly.

Dawson bites his lip, cheeks puff, loses the battle and blasts a short chuckle before clamping his hand over his mouth. He shrinks under the angry glare his TC heaps upon him.

"Touché, Captain." Pike says, turning his attention back to the scene forty yards before him. He keeps calm. Vatallis doesn't know what he knows. "Your comment is understandable." He watches the GRCC soldiers tense, weapons trained on the Devastator and the Reganites. "But it looks like you took a pounding from the POS's who've overrun the outpost. If you need assist..."

The shrill blare of a train whistle echoes across the area. Honeywell's train. *Not taken out*, Pike thinks, one burden on his brain relieved momentarily. But the Reganshire forces are there to mop up what is left of the fighting and take out the train themselves.

"Breckenridge's dead," a fresh voice over the open channel announces.

Pike sees a GRCC trooper step around the back side of the Grizzly. He can just make out the battlefield surgeon's medical patch on the man's arm. The doc's fatigues are wet with blood and sweat.

"What're we waiting for?" LaFleur asks.

Pike doesn't turn to acknowledge the Reganshire commander, instead he squints forward, tries to see near or around the immobile Grizzly.

"Say again?" he responds, not sure he heard things right, a side of him knowing what he heard, the other saying he hadn't gotten it straight. A flame starts to grow within him as his brain wraps around the words he'd just heard.

"Breckenridge is dead. AT round from insurgents. Raymonds' out of commission but holding his own," the medic answers, nonchalantly, talking as if Pike knew exactly who he was speaking about… because he did. "Whatever you're here for, Major, do what you've came to do. And damn you to Hell for doing it."

Pike's neck muscles tense as does his jaw line.

He white-knuckles his hatch coaming, tries to keep himself from quaking with rage.

"What're we waiting for, Major?" LaFleur calls again, his driver revving the engine of their vehicle. As if that signals the order to move out, the other Reganshire vehicles do the same. Engines rev. A few of the armored cars and trucks roll forward though the Devastator blocks their path.

Pike had known Lance Breckenridge well. They were both old tank commanders, moved up through rank and file almost at the same time. Breckenridge did things by the book, Pike used his own playbook. But the Grizzly's TC is a good man, *had been* a good man. "Until you brought him down," Pike snarls under his breath, Rupert Largo's grinning visage in his mind's eye.

On the Devastator's internal channel: "The jig's up, boys. Swing us around. Lock on anything with the letter R painted on it."

"Pike, what the hell are you…?" LaFleur, agitated. His words fall short as the Devastator's 120mm cannon swings round, points at the Reganshire procession standing in a nice little straight line along Leonard Street.

The train whistle blares again, closer.

"What side do you want to be on, Mr. LaFleur?" Pike asks ominously. He looks from under his furrowed brow at the line of Reganshire vehicles and their commander standing in the back of his vehicle three cars down. "McGraw, that AP round loaded?"

"Roger that, sir. Ready to fire." Devastator's loader calls from below.

***

Confused and angry voices rise up in Lucius LaFleur's general vicinity.

"What the fuck's going on?"

"Are we attacking or not?"

"Has Pike been playin' us? I told ya he seemed to waltz in too easy when he did."

"What's going on here, Major?" LaFleur asks again as he stretches one muscle-corded arm out and with palm down hushes the others. "Are you trading sides again? Were you ever on our side?"

Lucius knows Pike and his crew had come into Reganshire under strange pretenses, supposedly to deliver a large vial of black market Datropoline to the Regans to get in their good graces. He was there when Pike surrendered himself, tank and crew, stating he'd had enough of the shenanigans of the big city and offered his vehicle and services to the Regans. Many people, including Lucius, raised a doubtful brow at the big TC's offer. The Regans, mainly Rebecca, was all too eager—greedy—to get her hands on the powerful vehicle. It had taken a few months but Pike and crew showed their merit, integrating into the Reganshire militia, even taking the shit job of off-property patrols and Feral hunting-gathering expeditions which no one was really game for after what happened to Butkus's venture near the VSU communal almost a year ago.

"You're a good man, and a good commander," Pike says from atop the big Abram's tank. "I really would hate to see another good man laid low today." The last few words come out between clenched teeth. "It's been good working with you. Not so much the Regan's, if the old man even runs the show any more. But there's another good man on that train..." The train whistle blows again as if to accentuate his statement. "...and there's a true two-faced Grand

Rapids bastard council member in your village who'd hobble his own mother before a Feral onslaught to have a better chance at saving his own skin to survive.

"If anyone wants to work with Reganshire, it's the guy on *that* train." Pike finishes.

"I'm screwed if I go back to Miss Regan empty handed," Lucius says, eyeing the surrounding men. They look at him with a mixture of anger and worry. "Doubly screwed when I come back without you or your vehicle."

"You don't have to go back," Pike answers. "People switch sides every day. I know the GRCC is looking for a few good fighting men and women."

"Ask him if their compensation and health benefits are better than ours," a man in a sweat-stained denim shirt and camo pants says standing beside Lucius's vehicle, gun hanging loosely at his side as if he'd already made up his mind to give up.

The train whistle blows again.

"Heard that," Pike says, then says something into his throat mike off channel.

The Devastator's 120mm cannon purrs and angles a little lower.

Replying to the Reganite's comment and staring directly at them all, the TC says on open channel for the entire Reganshire formation to hear, "Better than me blasting through the whole front line of ya, and you visiting Saint Peter."

Everyone jumps and looks towards the outpost when the train whistle bawls again, followed by the screech and crash of tortured metal, and the pop and crackle of weapons fire, followed by explosions that shake the ground beneath them.

***

"Get the next hooked up," Jake rasps, ears still ringing as Loutonia spins the Huron in a semi-circle. Tow cables drag and bounce along the ground behind them. A smoking front bumper and twisted grill of one of the two Humvees they'd yanked off the tracks grinds, somersaults and falls away as they go.

Jake jerks, something punching him hard in his forearm. Gripping his hatch coaming with two hands, trying not to be thrown sidelong as the Huron swings around, he looks down. Bullet holes in his shirt sleeve. Small splotches of black blood, some torn flesh revealed.

He doesn't feel it.

"Tangos just outside the fence line," he radios to Mulholland, Stokes and the rest of the GRCC troops lining the train station platform and points around it. "They've broke out and circled around, trying to take the train as it enters."

"Copy that, Captain," a familiar voice says in Billet's headset. Honeywell. "We're pushing through."

A stand of tall pines and some stumpy poplar trees line the north side of the track just before the rail fence line. On the opposite side, just before the closed gate stands an old metal maintenance shed. Already Largo's men hunker behind it, use it for cover as they fire both at the oncoming locomotive and the GRCC forces.

"Heavy resistance at the west gates," Forrester says over the comm. "They want to keep us from coming around and flanking them."

"We got this," Jake starts to say. Something slaps him in the side of the head, just above the crown of his helmeted head, canting the head gear.

Jake teeters. His hands fumble for purchase, one on the hatch coaming, one on the grip of his mounted .50-Cal. His head pounds like his brain wants out. His vision grows dark. The Huron swings around, comes in line with the next three, the last three explosive laden vehicles on the tracks. Jake fights to clear his head, his eyesight.

"They got..." he stammers, "...snipers in the trees."

He opens his eyes not realizing he'd shut them. The area takes on an annoying crystalline sheen. So bright. He snarls and rakes at the sun and the sparkling images as a sheer curtain of red rage descends upon him.

"Everything must die. Kill," he growls though the words are an unintelligible garble. "Kill it all."

The Huron turns. Men run out snatching another set of tow cables from the transport's side while others detach the still smoking ones from the eyelets on the rear of the 72 ton rig. Fresh cables are wound about the front end of the remaining three vehicles, the men sweat from the heat and from nervousness, expecting the slightest vibration to set off the charges inside the vehicles.

"Jake?"

A female voice; Loutonia? Jenna? They sound the same in Jake's ears against what sounds like a tidal roar in his skull.

He looks across to the train station. The platform stands devoid of troops though he can still hear their shouting, guns firing, the pounding of strong hearts, the rush of blood through veins and arteries, the smell of sweet, raw living meat.

"Jake."

Jenna stands on the train platform. Young Joey stands by her side. They stand hand in hand.

"Abandon this. Come home." She pleads. A fully formed vision, just like he remembers her. No gore. No melting, tortured flesh, just those soft, pleading blue eyes, her long straight blond hair gently waving in the breeze. "Come home before it's too late."

Something hits him in the back, embeds in his vest, thrums him solidly, brings him back to reality.

"Jake? Captain?" Loutonia says as he rights his askew helmet. "Get down before you get shot or you take a face full of shrapnel."

"Too… late… for that." He rasps back into the mike. "Get these… vehicles off the tracks, Lou."

The Huron swings out, facing north, facing a stand of trees and fence line. Jake grips the mounted .50-Cal, fighting an increasingly sluggish brain to fire nerves to fire down to his limbs and tell his fingers to depress the triggers. His big mg roars, spitting lead death into the tree line before them. He sees his foe drop, the hired henchmen of Largo.

"Lines secure! Go go go!" someone yells to him and Loutonia.

With no one to open the western rail gate, the big locomotive, chugs in at quarter speed, rams the chain link fence.

The massive 2-8-4 Berkshire, the re-furbished Pere Marquette locomotive 1223, pushes into the outpost. Outfitted for the times, extra steel plates, black as night, run the length of her from steam box to cab. Its cowcatcher, affectionately re-titled "The Eviserator," is a slope of welded pipe and pieces of rough-sawn steel, angled this way and that, ends sharpened to wicked points. A section of gate rattles against the heavy iron face of the engine, caught in the deadly frame along with remnants of unfortunate Ferals hanging in rotted tatters.

A fresh barrage of gun fire throws itself at the train from outside the compound. The nuns and GRC troops return fire. The hot summer air grows thick with racing bullets.

The Huron lurches. Engines whine loudly. 72 tons of heavy armor pull against three 6 ton vehicles to clear the path for 400 tons of steam locomotive, a 160 pound man the real prize within the loco. The assumed weight of the explosives in the booby-trapped outpost vehicles, several hundred pounds in each, amazingly could blow a hole in the track line and possibly the train.

Jake turns and snarls at the vehicles behind them as the train grows closer.

Largo and Lettner sit on the hood of the lead vehicle directly behind them, smiling.

Lettner flips Jake the bird, and then waves at him.

"Say good-bye to our beloved mayor," Largo says as clear as if he spoke right next to Jake's ear. The City Treasurer smiles broadly, a grin which literally curls from ear to ear.

The late NSC Commissioner and City Treasurer's car explodes in a roar of smoke and flame. The concussive blast snaps Jake backwards against his hatch coaming and gun. His helmet tears from head as he bucks. The blast sets off the other two vehicles in tow, and again Jake is violently thrown into the coaming and machine gun. His unprotected head cracks into the grips of the .50-Cal, tearing a long gash across his already scar-striped forehead. A fist-sized chunk of searing shrapnel slaps him in the side of the head, driving deep into scalp and skull.

Jake howls. No pain, all rage as flames and smoke and wreckage boil all around him.

The Huron howls along with him, engines racing then dying. The entire heavy transport shudders then grinds slightly sidelong before coming to an abrupt halt.

A train whistle blares over the fading explosive din. A long black shape cuts through the smoke and flame. Bullet-scarred, an armored passenger car reveals itself as it goes by. Jake blinks back black blood and thinks he sees a face in one of the barred windows: Mayor Dennis Honeywell. The man salutes him as the train pushes by, picking up speed, it will not go so slowly through the exit gate that will let it out to home.

"Threw a track," Loutonia says, her voice small within the Huron below him. "We're out of commission."

Jake groans, claws his way out of his hatch onto the Huron's hot roof. Bullets still pang off the armor hide. Lead bees painlessly punch into his arms and legs but he does not fall. He goes to hands and knees on the top of the transport, pounds with steely fist upon the cargo doors.

"Ho-mmm," he rages in thick gravel-drown voice. "Ho-mmm!"

Loutonia rises from Stoke's usual emplacement. "Oh my God. Jake!" she cries.

GRCC troops rush to the Huron; Stokes, Mulholland and the

towering Sister Mirose lead the charge.

"Give him to me. Lower him. Gently, gently," Mirose says as she points and waves at a group of nuns still firing at the destroyed west rail gate. They stop and lower weapons as some actual soldiers take their place. They rush to one of the huge pickup trucks revealing its nose just around the train station platform.

Jake feels hands all around him, grasping him. He smells blood. He smells fear. He smells meat.

A soldier screams and falls away as Jake rakes at him, connecting, tearing four great red streaks down the soldiers face with his nails. Jake bites at him as the man drops from his crimson-tinged view.

Hungry. Hungry. Kill. Torture the living souls. Torture the fortunate. Maim. Tear. Kill, the thoughts convulse in Jake's head as hands and arms wrap about him, pulling him down.

"Over here. Quickly. First aid kit," Mirose yells as they bring him to the ground.

Jake looks up. Two female forms—he can smell their sex— loom over him. Their skinless faces peer down upon him. All he sees is meat, muscle, veins and organs.

"Jake? Oh gawd. Oh gawd." A fading recollection in Jake's mind: Loutonia.

Wet, salty drops fall from her face and upon his, burning.

"Captain?" A new voice. Male. Young. Familiar. Eddie Mulholland. "Hang in there, sir, we'll get you patched up."

"N-n-no," Jake responds, teeth gnashing, trying to fight back the rage he shouldn't have at the young soldier.

A new presence; short, thick, stinking of bad breath and cigar tobacco.

"Captain, hang in there, buddy." Stokes. "I'm ready to take command if you need."

"You asshole," someone says. Mulholland.

"No, I mean… Well, I meant it, but only if he's gonna need…" Stokes, stuttering, backing away.

"Shut up. You're only making it worse." Loutonia, wetly, sniffing.

Cool, rough hands take and touch the sides of Jake's face. "Be at peace, Captain." Another female. Hard to recall. Mirose?

The hands press firmer against his skin. He hasn't realized how hot his skin is until the cool hands send a chill shot across his tortured flesh. The wave of coolness seems to pull his mind from the red quagmire of anger and murderous thought.

He opens his eyes fully, a hazy image, dark short-shorn hair, square face, breath of tobacco and wine. Something slips from neck line, cool metal, cross-shaped.

"Be at Peace, Jacob, child of God." *Mirose*, he thinks, he knows. "We will see you home. The Lord will see you home."

Chapter Seventeen

"We're going."

"No, you're not. Too much going on here. Pike's back, along with LaFleur and a bunch of Reganites. Forrester needs help mopping up here. We can take him out there. It's what he wanted."

"We got our own field doc. And what about the Huron? You going to leave your *baby* in my hands?"

Silence. Hesitation.

"It was his desire to see his old homestead. God is my witness, I have vowed to do this for my friend and your captain."

Click of a gun safety.

"Are you stepping up on me, sister? We don't have to go that far."

"And as far as stepping up on you, Mr. Stokes, I could simply step on you."

Chuckles. Some uneasy.

"What the fuck? Are you kidding me? You're one mouthy holier than thou bit…"

"Stokes, drop it. Let them go before it's too late for the Cap."

"You gonna fix our rig, Eddie?"

"As a matter of fact, I can."

"My baby is in good hands, Sergeant. James. Please, we need to be going before…" Heavy swallow, and then words hard to expel. "…before he changes any further."

243

"But someone might be able to help him. They're making all sorts of head-way at the BTF. Well, if it hadn't been overrun and wrecked by… its own… experiments…"

"Get going, Lou. Stokes and I will grab some guys and get the Huron fixed up and then be right behind you as soon as we can."

"Thanks Eddie. Thanks James. I'm sure the captain, Jake, is grateful."

Closer. Pressure on arm, needle-like.

"That was nearly my last double diazepam dose, Corporal. If he starts to shake that…"

Low, sad voice. "I know. I know."

Hot sun on his face, Jake tries to open his eyes. Hurts.

"He's waking up a little," a young girl says, nervous. Racing heart. Strong heart. Sweet smell.

"Keep him shaded. I'm sure he's very sensitive to the sun." Loutonia, it is Loutonia now that speaks.

Nylon sheet ruffles in the wind. Yellow-white hot light dissipates to a small pinpoint glare. Still annoying. Keep eyes shut tight.

He is moving. Not the Huron. Big truck engine; gasoline and motor oil. Thick treaded tires hum along pavement.

Jake tries to move. Strap across chest. Strap across abdomen. Strap across waist. Strap across legs.

"He's fidgeting," the young girl's voice again.

"That dose didn't last long." Smell of tobacco. In front of him, to the right. Coarse female voice. Mirose. "Terese, prep the last diazepam epi. Don't use it unless he starts to really come around."

"Looks like we might have a storm front moving in from the big lake." Another woman, sweating, to the left of Mirose. Driver?

Jake tries to open his eyes. The tiny pinprick glare of sunlight still too much. He feels to rage. He feels to tear apart everyone in the vehicle with him.

"Oh Jake." Voice soft. Loutonia.

Cool hand and cool wet cloth touches his face. He smells blood, thick, drying and dying. His own.

He wants to bite the hand. Tear it. Mangle it. Chew the life from it. Hate life. Life is a tease, a torture.

He wants to cry. No tears. Tear ducts dry.

He wants to tell Lou…

"It's okay, Jacob. You'll be home soon." Jenna. Sweet Jenna. He can't smell her, can't hear her heartbeat.

It's Loutonia. It's Jenna.

"We'll be waiting for you, daddy." Young Joey. Joey who lived to nineteen before he and his mother melted away out of his life. His son. His little boy. How he misses him.

Jake wants to scream. He bucks against his restraints.

Kill. Kill. Kill. The living are a joke. Need to die, horribly. If he can't have life neither can anyone else. Kill. Kill. Kill.

"Um, he's acting really irritated." Young girl. Terese. Mirose's postulant.

"Shoot him up." Mirose. "Lord willing, this keeps him until we get him to the place."

Terese again. "And then what?"

Silence except the hum of the big tires on the asphalt, wind howling, nylon tarp flapping.

Loutonia's cool hand.

A whimper beside Jake's ear.

A salt tear on his cheek, burning.

Pressure. Needle prick, driven like a nail into his arm.

No pain. No fear. No anxiety.

But voices. Small. Far away.

"I told you I'd see you home, Captain." Lettner. No Largo, only Lettner. Laughter in his voice. "To watch you die."

Jake waits for Largo to cut in.

Nothing.

***

"Water! Would someone give me some goddamn water? So much for negotiations, or *anything*, with Grand Rapids if this is how you're gonna play!" Frustrated, clothes sopping with sweat, no longer spring time fresh as he hasn't bathed since he'd been picked up by the sonofabitch traitor tank commander Pike, Rupert Largo jerks on his chains and roars like a rabid dog.

"Shut up in there," someone yells back, punching the tent flap, offering the City Treasurer a small waft of air circulation. Smells like rain.

The dirty one-eyed mechanic has not returned from earlier in the day. Rupert has no idea what the actual temperature is outside but inside, it is sweltering. The bucket they'd given him to piss in stinks to high heaven. Captured Ferals are treated better.

"Fucked with the wrong guy," he fumes, quieter.

And he'd make sure Old Man Regan, his insane daughter, and all of Reganshire will pay dearly when he returns to Grand Rapids to take his seat of control in place of Dennis Honeywell.

He hears commotion outside, the sound of excited, anxious voices and the growl of engines and movement of vehicles. They had taken his watch, but another tent across from his, when his tent flap is agitated just right, reveals a clock mounted on a wood post just outside the other tent.

It is well past the time Honeywell's train would've gone through Lamont. With his hired men and Reganshire forces, he can almost see Honeywell's body in the twisted wreckage and himself behind the mayor's desk back in the big city.

"Hello? Could I have some assistance… please?" He decides to change his tone though he feels as ferocious as an unfed Feral.

A grease-stained hand slips through the tent and parts the flap. An unshaven, sweaty face pokes inside the folds. A dirt-stained index finger draws up and scratches a spot just under the eye patch covering the individual's right eye.

"What's all the yelling about? I told you I'd be right back," Patch says, irritated, adjusting the tent flaps, tying them back.

Largo blinks until his one good eye adjusts to the glare from outside. Air blasts in, hot like a furnace, and he thinks for a moment maybe it's better the tent be closed. Luckily, the sun isn't as bright as it had been in the morning.

"It took you long enough," Largo snarls, patience gone again. "What's the hold up? Is there word on your troops and Lamont?"

Patch steps to the bucket of piss, blanches, and picks it up, careful not to jostle it too much. A swarm of flies erupts from the container. He puts it outside the tent. He turns back to meet Largo's angry gaze.

"What happened?" Largo commands, seeing the other man's downcast expression.

Patch starts shaking his head, mumbles under his breath as he goes about the tent straightening up. "Doomed. Doomed. We're all doomed," he curses almost in a whisper. His hands start quivering, and he clasps them together to keep them from convulsing.

"Gawddamn, tell me, you idiot. What the fuck is going on?" Rupert barks.

Patch snaps to a stop; his turn to glare. "You might reconsider wanting counsel with the… Regans… right now."

"What? What's going on? Is something wrong?"

"Everything's wrong," Patch says under his breath, starts to roll his dirty hands together again. His one good eye looks to the open tent flap and beyond, like looking for escape. "Me coming here so long ago. Wrong. Could've had a nice job at a quiet service station in Saranac, away from the crazies."

"Hey!" Largo shouts, snapping Patch back to reality.

Anger consumes the Reganite again. He thrusts a dirty finger at the City Treasurer. "It's your fault. You, your city, damnable mayor, and army, and greed," Patch snarls, gnashes the few teeth he still has in his mouth. "You could've shared the wealth, but, no, you make us smaller towns pay until we have no choice but to look for other options to survive.

"You made us greedy by your own greed. And greed, in this day and age, breeds some insane ass survivalists," the Reganite finishes.

"What in the hell are you talking about?" Largo says, straining in his chains to reach the man. Throttling him might get his head back in the game. "Grand Rapids always had an Open Door policy and shared its wealth, but it's not like we need the barter system anymore. Even-up trading went out the window in 2020 when everyone started getting back on their feet." He wants to add, *but the Regans were just slow on the upswing so you got what you got.* He decides better.

"I guess it depends on how one wanted to get back on their feet then," Patch counters. "I came here in 2021 from middle of the state, only because there was more here in the West. There was… because people were still fighting over it."

"It's Old Man Regan who wanted to keep fighting about things," Largo responds. A wisp of warm air blows into the tent. He wants out. "You guys wanted to do things your own way, be fully independent from Grand Rapids. We just had to keep an eye on the old man to make sure you weren't sneaking up and taking too much of what wasn't yours."

Patch shook and moaned every time Largo mentioned *Regan*.

"I need to see him. Hell, both of them, even his crazy daughter. Now that Honeywell…"

"…is alive and well and probably almost to the city by now," Patch interrupts, still shaking.

"What?" Largo's jaw drops. "Bullshit. There's no way with my men *and* your forces…"

Two huge shadows block the wane daylight coming into the humid tent.

Patch looks over his shoulder and trembles anew, backing into the corner away from the opening.

"Your men failed. Half our forces have returned already without firing a shot," Patch says in a small voice at Largo, his lone eye so wide and white it almost glows in the shadowed corner.

"Shit," Rupert snarls through clenched teeth. "Half? What happened to the other half?"

A huge and solidly muscled black man, dressed in military garb, with a brand in the shape of a crude R, steps through the tent folds. Behind him, another behemoth of a Reganite guard stands with a short-barreled riot shotgun in hands.

"Our leader wants to see you," the tall black man says with as much enthusiasm as a UCRA zombie; *Lawrence* scrolled across the name tape of his sweat drenched shirt. The other man steps in and roughly unshackles the City Treasurer's hands and feet.

Largo looks at Patch as the two Reganite men start to haul him out of the tent. Peering at his shoes, trembling, Patch makes the sign of the cross with his grubby hands and drops to his haunches. His face seems to be sweating profusely…

…or he is sobbing.

***

Still hot, but no blinding sun. No hum of tires on pavement. No movement beneath. No straps to hold him down, Jake rises, slowly. His fingers feel the makeshift gurney below him.

"Where am I?" the words in his head, the actual verbalization comes out in a broken tongue-tied mess.

Far off, the rumble of a summer storm. The air smells heavy with moisture and other things: living flesh, hot dry paint, green meadow grass, wild flowers, warm tar scent wafting with the warm breeze.

Jake slides from the gurney. Legs shaky, he crawls.

"In a truck," more thoughts, but he can't remember how he got in it, or on it, who was driving, or what the purpose was for the ride. He can see all; black truck liner, empty shell casings, boxes of ammo. Can smell the gunpowder and brass within the boxes when he focuses.

Staring at the ammunition boxes, he misses the lip of the open tailgate and rolls off the back end of the truck. Hits the dirt, gravel and weeds; an overgrown two track road.

Teetering like his body isn't quite in sync with his brain, he rises. Joints pop and crackle. A dull pain throbs through his limbs and his face as he stands. If fluids flow within, they run like molasses. He can't feel his heartbeat. *It must be*, he thinks, but really doesn't care. All thoughts of him flee as he turns and sees *it*.

"Home," he says, just a low growl.

Before him, a white, two-story home. Gabled roof of tar and asphalt tiles. The wrap-around porch, white pillars support the roof over the white railed and gray-painted wood porch. Overgrown arborvitae hem in the front of the house. An old plastic hanging flower basket swings in the breeze to the left of the porch steps. The dead, dried withered things within the basket spring to life magically as he looks upon it, and the basket is again brimming with mixed flowers of every color.

"Home. I'm home." He shuffles around the truck, his left leg seems not to be in time with his right. Nevertheless, *home*.

The birds sing loudly in his ears, as do yellowjackets and the buzz of honeybees. Amped up. Though he knows he has taken many wounds, he can't feel them, no pain, but auditory sense and sense of smell, jacked up beyond belief.

As fast as he can, Jake hurries up the old driveway. The tall weeds melt away in his vision, replaced with fresh mown lawn. He sees a heat haze image of his old Toro rider parked across the yard, a can of Centennial IPA in the cup holder.

Drawing closer to the house, the arborvitae shrink to a size he last recalls. How many years ago? The rotting porch steps with weather-crackled paint breathe and reform themselves. Fresh, clean paint. Smaller flower baskets perch on the sides of each step. The concrete walkway leading to the porch; weeds melt away into the cracks, busted cobble repairs itself.

It is like his old West Olive homestead is rolling the red carpet out for his return.

Jake feels happy. He smiles. It hurts, and his facial muscles seem slow to react, but he smiles.

"Honey? Jenna?" he calls. "Jenna? Joey?"

The tips of his worn combat boots, now pristine in his eyes, hit the flat of the first lower porch step.

The front door opens, its outer screen door creaking—a grand, comforting, warm sound to Jake—and a figure steps from the dark insides of his house.

Jake snarls at the beast, the abominable creature, the man who steps to the edge of the porch.

"Your wife and son are out back, Captain," William Lettner says, grinning, "You gotta deal with me first."

***

"You don't have to drag me, I can walk on my own." Largo struggles between the two Reganite gorillas as they literally lift him so his toes barely touch the ground.

The big black man, Lawrence, glances down at Largo, frowns as if bored to death, and focuses forward without a word.

Passing up the intersecting lane of the compound, Largo spies the returned Reganshire troops and vehicles. Soldiers sit outside Humvees, modified civilian trucks and cars—a 1973 vintage Chevy Impala sits in the mix, body of primer gray and a .30-Cal machine gun mounted where the sunroof would be. The men and women, looking like they'd been dowsed head to toe by a fire hose, drink heavily from water bottles and coolers while talking with much hand waving and expression about the mission they'd just returned from; the conversations are lost with Largo's distance from them.

A few Bradley Fighting Vehicles parked in the mix; one Reganshire black with a large sloppily painted red R drooling down its side; the other partially painted but also showing a Grandville-Wyoming boat wheel-and-wave militia emblem. Many of Regan's military vehicles had been acquired illegally.

Rupert sees no sign of the towering Reganshire commander amongst the returned—*LaFlower or whatever his name is*—and wonders if the big man is already inside getting his ass reamed by the old man and his daughter.

"So your men weren't successful in bringing the GRCC or the Grand Rapids city mayor down?" Largo asks, trying to glean any type of information from his handlers.

The giant Reganite grasping Largo's right arm gives it a painful squeeze and a violent shake, nearly popping the City Treasurer's arm from its socket. "For all this bullshit I'm getting my measly pay docked and half provisions. Probably be thrown back outside into the RCF. For all *your* bullshit," the chiseled chin man growls at Largo.

"Quit crying, jackass, we're all in the same boat," Lawrence responds at his companion. "Rebecca's just pissed and intent on making us suffer for our military's failure and for LaFleur and his group."

Largo perks up as the tips of his shoes skip over the entry threshold of Regan's massive building and living quarters. The pneumatic doors open and shut with a heavy airy shush behind them. He feels a sudden chill as the much cooler air indoors washes over his hot, sweat-moist skin. He immediately knows why Chiseled Chin doesn't want to have to be back outside with the hot and sweaty Reganshire Command Force.

"Commander… LaFleur," Rupert makes sure he pronounces it right, "is back? He's with the Regan's right now? Briefing them on things?"

A young woman sweeps her astro-turf lawn while garments

hang on a clothes line, a small child swings on a swing set nearby, looks up at Largo and the two guardsmen as they go by. Largo smiles at the woman. She stops sweeping, scowls at him, flips him the bird.

"LaFleur defected with half our troops and some vehicles to Grand Rapids with that tank commander who tricked us into believing he was on our side," Chiseled Chin says. "Rebecca Regan asked for you, for you to brief her on what happened and why."

A glass atrium overhead lets dim daylight pour upon the massive double oak doors of the Regan's estate. The exterior walls and doors are painted black; the Regan "R" emblem carved into the wood doors, painted bright red. The two giants slow as they near the entrance to the indoor manse.

"Shit," Rupert Largo says under his breath as the huge doors loudly creak open.

***

Lettner steps down from the porch, smug grin on his face. He runs a hand over his bald head, flicks it though no perspiration is drawn. He wears a black suit over a white shirt and black tie. "Hot one today. Enough to boil flesh from the body."

"Get off my property," Billet growls.

"I don't think this is anyone's property anymore." Lettner laughs. "No one's farmed or habituated out here since, well, you know, my little unauthorized event."

"Get out of my head." Jake mashes his fists to his head.

"What? You gonna get mad and beat me up?"

Billet walks towards him, ignoring his own jerky strides. "Done it before."

Lettner turns, walks around the left side of the house as leisurely as if he were going for a Sunday stroll.

Jake follows, stumbles, goes down to the ground on his side, then his back. He tries to rise, cannot due to, suddenly, Lettner sits on his midsection. "Can't beat me this time. You've lost, and you're lost."

Jake feels the muscles in his face tighten even before the blow. The late NSC Commissioner strikes. Jake's head snaps to the right, then to the left as Lettner punches him again and again.

"You've lost, Captain," Lettner says leaning down into Jake's face nose to nose. "Honeywell is, perhaps, back in the city by now, but you failed to bring down Rupert Largo. He's like me, and unlike my old lakeshore populace, there's a whole lot of people who want change, want their lives back, want to be able to go where they want, back into their old neighborhoods and homes, without sharing it with the dead and rotting."

"He won't win. Everyone knows now he's behind the attacks on the city, the failed chemical dusting of the West Side. If the city doesn't do it, the GRCC will take revenge for the murder of our troops in Lamont," Jake snarls, tries to buck Lettner off, fails.

"Keep telling yourself that," Lettner says. "Tell yourself both sides of the story. Believe what you will, there'll be a day the undead will be cleansed from this land. It might not be me, or Largo, but there'll be someone like us, fervent to return the land to the Living."

"And my crew and I will be there to stop them," Jake growls.

"You aren't going to do anything, Captain, but be a target for people like me," Lettner says, swings again, connecting. "Don't you get it?"

Jake flinches as fist descends, boot heels digging into the ground. He closes his eyes as if that might shut out the oncoming blow.

No blow comes.

He finds no one atop him.

He climbs unsteadily to his feet. The world slants, wants to throw him back down.

Lettner stands at the corner of the house before the backyard. The NSC Commissioner crooks his index finger at Jake, smiling, coaxing him forward.

"Come on, Captain. Come to me."

Tall grasses and weeds rise along the side of the house. Where white paint had been, now weather-rotted warped bare wood. The frill of an old lace curtain flutters through a broken window as if the house breathed.

"Stop," Lettner suddenly says.

Jake stops.

"Do you feel that?"

"I feel nothing."

Lettner laughs, nearly doubling over backwards. He bends forward, hands on his knees, and looks at Billet. Pupil-less eyes, full blood red orbs.

"You're dead, fool," Lettner crows. "That mighty vaccine you service men were given…used up. Gone. All the years being amongst the afflicted, their filthy touch, their spitting and coughing, biting, scratches, wounds has finally burned the Datropoline out of your system.

"You're like your old friend, Renald Nielsen," Lettner continues. Something brushes against the broken window but inside the house. "You didn't even bat an eyelash when you heard he turned. Sometimes, you know, that happens to good soldiers.

"Your crew thought you were having a heart attack a few months back. No, I think you had an inkling of what was happening to you. Did you enjoy the coma? They should've let you die when you had the chance. But then…" Lettner smiles, mouth wide, wider, too many teeth. He glances under his brow at Jake, blood red eyes boiling. "…we couldn't have had our fun now."

Movement at the window. Jake throws his hands against it, into it and then is forced back as the sheer white drapery blasts out the window, slicing his hands and arms. He rakes at his face to brush the sharp shards away. The white mass hits him, tackles him to the ground upon his back again.

"You cheated me," Rebecca Regan shrieks at Jake, straddling him like Lettner had a bit ago. Nothing but skin on a skeleton, flesh red, creamy white, crawling with maggots. A emaciated face, wisps of colorless hair shrouded in a white veil. "You were supposed to give me your secrets, that drug. I was to be immortal." She hisses, serpentine tongue, goat eyes, fangs like a snake.

Jake recoils at the putrid young woman, thrashing upon the ground to unseat her.

"Now I will eat your dead heart, Jacob, my love, my meat, my captain," Regan screams.

She punches downward with talons for fingers, drives her slender hand into Jake's chest. He howls and gnashes and fights against the heaviness about his chest. She yanks her hand back; a syrupy dark lump drips in her claws.

It is too much. Too much for him. He roars, thrashing, tearing up clumps of dirt and grass.

Rebecca, gone. Only Lettner stands there, grinning, fingering him to follow him.

"Come. See what I have done," the NSC Commissioner titters.

Rising, jerking to his feet again. No thought, just kill him, kill Lettner, again and again and again; Jake shambles forward, combat uniform ripped, hanging in shreds, skin raw and raked, glass in palms, hands bleeding. He moves without further words towards the visage of William Lettner.

Coming around the corner of the house, Jake stops, eyes wide, mouth agape.

"Look what I've done," Lettner smiles as screams fill Jake's dwindling senses. "I've taken your family from you. You missed them then, you'll miss them now."

Before him, though he hasn't moved, he stands before his pristine white farmhouse on a summer's day. Blue skies. Tall grass blowing in the breeze. His wife and son outside, little Joey playing.

A dark cross slides across them from above. A yellow mist rains down. Jenna runs to Joey, clutches him close, curls over him to protect the boy.

"Nothing you could do," Lettner's voice in his ear. "Nothing you could ever do."

Flesh, muscle, organs melt away in the yellow mist raining from the sky. Grass shrivels. Flowers droop.

The yellow downpour subsides. Before the house, on a scorched earth yellow and red, the skeleton of his wife hunches over his boy. Gone. Gone. Gone.

"Nothing you could ever do," Lettner says again.

"Go away," Jake snarls, vertebrae popping as he thrashes his head from side to side. No, no, no, no. He staggers, back before the corner of the house again. He grasps the corner of the house, rotted wood falls away in his angry grip.

"Nothing you can do." Lettner's voice, but fading.

"Nothing you could do," a new voice, sweet, soft, soothing: Jenna's. "But come to me."

In a glass shed, sparkling as a ray of sunlight breaks the encroaching storm clouds and glances off the thick panes, Jenna stands, beckoning Jake forward. Her hair like gold. Her eyes as blue as the sky. A smile warm and welcoming.

"Come home to me, Jacob," Jenna smiles as Jake slowly teeters to the glass burial shed, "Now, my husband, before it's too late."

Somewhere behind him—he does not care—a vaguely familiar voice, female, says: "It's time. It's what we agreed on."

***

"You cheated me," Rebecca Regan snarls, slapping Rupert Largo across the face. Her nails catch flesh. He grimaces, winces, as a burning sensation and trickle of blood runs from his slashed cheek. "You said your men would open the gateway and help our forces exterminate Mayor Honeywell."

Held by the two gargantuan Reganshire guardsmen, Rupert tries to lean away as she rakes at him again. He can't and spits blood as her fist completes a rock-hard blow to the side of his mouth. The blow dislodges his eye patch. The eye cover falls to the floor, revealing a puckered and pale pink, ruined socket.

"Oh, baby," her tone suddenly changes, sugar sweet, concerned. "How'd that grievous wound happen."

The two guardsmen stiffen as the young woman moves closer, bony white delicate hands to the City Treasurer's bleeding face. Largo tries to turn his head as she looms in, her face nose to nose with his. Her breath reeks. He can see the blue veins beneath the near-translucent skin of her face. Her dull gray eyes, maybe blue at one time, appear fogged over, a yellow tinge to her eyeballs. Something wriggles from her sparse hairline, drops—plump, white, like a living grain of rice—wetly down his cheek, and falls to the floor.

"Baby, baby, baby," she coos, sniffing all about his face like a dog. "You have a fight with a Feral, or your abused wife finally got the best of you?"

She's obviously read up on him.

"Enough games," Largo snarls. "I want to talk to the old man, your father, the real leader that runs this place." He shakes her hands away.

Rebecca snaps upright as do the guards at Largo's side, roughly yanking him to his feet.

She brushes his face upon standing. Her hand shows a smear of his blood. She notices it, sniffs it, licks it and smiles. "The real leader? Yes, let's go see daddy. He hasn't been feeling well but says he so wants to discuss things with you."

"It's about time," Largo says. "It's not my fault things went south at Lamont, or the mayor got through. Even so, there are still opportunities."

Rebecca saunters down a long dimly lit hall before them. Her gossamer gown, sheer, reveals nothing underneath. Largo tries not to look, has seen zombie women before, but there is something awful and different about her. He'd heard rumors of her shooting herself up with chemicals, with even black market Datropoline. He'd never given it much thought as he never entertained her, only her father, back in the day when Old Man Regan came to city meetings. The old man never would bring her along, and peering upon her in close quarters now, Rupert knew why.

They stop before a set of double doors, ornate door handles, maybe brass, smeared with dried blood.

"There are always opportunities," Rebecca says quaintly, reaches down and pulls the doors open.

"I can't go in there again," the guard to Largo's right, Chiseled Chin, says, instantly releasing him. The big man turns and runs down the hall.

As the doors swing open such a stink of rotting meat and garbage assail the City Treasurer, he coughs and struggles to swallow the wad of bile trying to escape his throat.

Largo's remaining guard, the big black man, Lawrence, loosens his iron grip and shoves his captive forward, through the open portal. He mumbles: "Father, son and Holy Ghost. May the Lord have mercy on my soul." And backs away.

Largo stumbles upon a roll of carpet, falls, slides forward on hands and knees. Nose clogged with the great stink, eyes burning, his mouth fights to keep his stomach from erupting from it. He rises to his feet.

Rebecca closes the doors and saunters by him, humming happily then skips the rest of the way, like a small child, to a raised platform in the center of the room. Chains rattle. A single skylight beams the dull daylight down upon the great oaken throne-like seat before him.

Largo wipes his burning, runny eye, clearing it. He looks upon what Rebecca now hugs and cuddles with on the chair. His belly surges, and he falls back to the carpeted floor and vomits until he can only dry heave.

"Daddy really doesn't like you throwing up on his floor," Rebecca titters as Largo regains his faculties and shakily rises again.

With her slender, sickly arms draped over his shoulder, her father—Old Man Regan, Silas Regan—what had been the man anyway, sits half curled over in the huge chair. A rope wrapped about the old man's broad chest keeps him from falling out of the chair all together as he has nothing below his naked waistline. Nothing but raw, torn flesh, shattered pelvic bone sticking through the gristle and gore, crotch gone, gnawed to the upper abdomen.

"What... horror... is this," Largo pants, unable to believe his eye, the sight and stink making his stomach want to surge again.

"Daddy doesn't understand what you're talking about. All is fine," Rebecca coos, circling her fingers around her dead father's collarbone, the pulped flesh, head, upper body, armless torso looking like a massive holiday ham that's been ravaged by a pack of hungry hounds. "He's just feeling..." She smiles wickedly, "A little under the weather."

"W-what do you want?" Largo demands, looking at the girl, not wanting to look at the gnawed carcass of the old man.

"It's not I want," Rebecca hisses. "It's what *we* want. We can't have bad decisions making us lose men, lose vehicles, lose face." She runs her finger around the top of her father's chewed skull like she's teasing a tossle of his hair. "We need strong, young leadership to make the right decisions for our community."

Leaning in, Rebecca kisses the side of her dead father's head, where his ear should have been. Kisses it, licks it, nibbles it tenderly. "Father has given me full reign over Reganshire, full control to bring us into the future.

"You know," she continues, "I've been thinking, you have touched on something, made sense. I think we should still work with Grand Rapids to bring our two communities closer."

Largo gags. "What?"

"My father grew so suspicious of the city, he started drawing us away from them," she explains. "Mind you, we've made great progress on our own. New farms. Small, new industries to trade with other communities.

"But we pulled away from the big city, that has so, so much to offer," she says licking her dry, cracked lips hungrily. "I think daddy made the wrong decision distancing us from the city. I tried to talk to him before he became deathly ill this last winter. Such a hard winter. Poor daddy." She kisses the dead man's torn flesh again, smiling mischievously.

"The city will never want to discuss anything with a sick, demented bitch like you," Largo hisses, standing straight, standing firm. "I can guarantee you that, whoever runs the show. Honeywell. Myself."

Rebecca gives her father's torn husk one last kiss then skips away. Largo tenses, waiting for her to pounce on him as she goes by. She goes to the closed double doors, humming sweetly. With a twist, she draws the dead bolts into place, securing the room from outside intrusion.

"I have emissaries to do my bidding if I don't feel up to it," she says, returning to her father's side.

She struggles with something behind his back.

The bloody carcass quakes slightly.

The ropes fall away, and the chunk of meat that had been Old Man Regan thumps heavily to the floor at the City Treasurer's feet.

"I'll figure out how to deal with Honeywell later," she says. "But for you, my handsome, virile Mister Largo…" She wags her thin finger his way then points at the gruesome, empty seat.

Rupert Largo opens his mouth to scream.

Rebecca Regan, a flitting phantom in white, descends upon him, mouth open—black gums, sharp teeth—hands out, fingers curled like claws.

Outside the room, the big black guard shudders, holds hands to ears and runs down the hall, his thoughts to head outside, to the nearest gate, head out of it, and never turn back.

***

Billet stands at the glass mausoleum. Inside, vacant urns of dark dirt stand, not yet watered or planted with flowers like he did every Spring season. He looks on them with vision flitting between crimson, and brightness, and normalcy. His bleeding hands rake at the thick glass. Tears do not come but great sobs shake him, steal his already ragged breath.

"I was supposed to be here for you," he says though the words drift in the spiraling thoughts within his head. "I was supposed to be here for you and Joey. I'm sorry."

Jenna, dressed in a floral print blouse and jean overalls, how she probably was dressed in the day they'd died, tends a garden that now is no more than a barren patch of overgrown weeds.

Blond hair drapes about her neck, over her slender shoulders. Red full lips, mouth and brilliant blue eyes smile. "But you're here now, Jacob," she answers, standing within the thick glass enclosure, the back of her heels touch the heavy concrete burial slab with her name upon it, etched in moss that has formed there.

"I have changed," Jake growls but not out of anger. "I may not be here for long. May not remember you or Joey at all, in my next phase of… life. I am alone here, Jenna. I am lost."

"You are never lost, or ever alone, my husband," she says, placing her hands, palm up against the glass in line with his. The glass shimmers, ripples, and suddenly her flesh presses against his. "Someone has always been there for you. It has made me happy."

Fingers entwined, Jake looks deep into his wife's eyes. "She promised to take care of you when the time came," Jenna says, smiling. "Come home to us now. Go home to be with your loved ones. Be at peace, Jacob Ethan Billet." The last words from her mouth sound of a different voice.

Jenna's image fades as Jake focuses on the glass. His hands press against the warm pane, no longer entwined with hers. His eyes see his reflection, torn, bloody, flesh gray-blue.

He sees Loutonia in the reflection, standing behind him. Sister Mirose behind her, stern.

Loutonia's face, dark cheeks wet.

She lifts her arm straight up, level with the back of his head, one of her .45's in her fisted hand.

He smiles though only in his tortured mind, the last realization…

"I love you," Loutonia says, then pulls the trigger.

Epilogue

"You keeping my baby safe out there? She's been through a lot. I need her back in one piece, no scratches or dings."

"Roger that, Sergeant Phelps," Mulholland says, in his rear gunner's cubby atop the Huron, parked at Bridge Street and Indiana Avenue.

The day, warm, but pleasant versus the scorching summer they'd had. The patrol has been, so far, uneventful, normal, considering they stand upon an area that had been a dangerous spot a few months ago. Plane crash. Flesh-eating chemical fog all around meant to eradicate the city's undead. There'd been two planes which had flown unhindered into the air space above the enclosure, paid for by corrupt City Treasurer Rupert Largo. The west side, back to normal—though some citizens still disagree on that—except for the burned splotch of ground across the street from the old Marathon gas station and a now neutralized, yellowish residue on the street and some of the buildings.

"Captain Stokes?" Loutonia's voice rings in Stokes earbud.

Stokes stands before Bob the gas station attendant zomb. An important "satellite Zee" for the city, medics had patched the old guy up good: a steel plate cranial implant to cover where his head

265

had been partially blown off, a glass eye and some grafted flesh. Bob stands as a patchwork man, a little new, a lot old, but all Bob, including the new vintage service station clothing he'd been fitted in post-op before they released him back out to the "wilds" of the UCRA.

"Yes, Miss Phelps," Captain Stokes says like a corrected school child. "We'll keep your baby nice and pristine for you. How long before you pull yourself from desk duty and come back to us? Bob's slobbering all over my new duds." The little gorilla of a man says, rubbing the shiny silver bars on the flap of his combat uniform. Combat uniform the same but silver Captain's bars new, and he liked them shiny.

"Not coming back 'til Spring. Shrink's orders. Jackson feels better that way," Loutonia replies. "You'll have to just keep letting me translate Bob's ramblings from here.

"Speaking of which, Bob says we still have a few BTF troopers hold up over near Fulton and Marion. I'll send Campau the coordinates," Loutonia finishes.

"Copy, Sergeant. Glad to be part of the team again. No matter what Stokes does, I'll keep your rig sparkly."

"Enough of the chitchat. Get us ready to roll, Campau," Stokes says, turning, still looking down, buffing his silver bars.

The Huron diesel engines growl to a start.

"Uh, Captain, better get onboard quick, got some locals heading our way. Should we drop cargo, they look a little…hungry."

"Shit, shit, shit," Stokes says running to the right side of the massive transport, routine, instinctively, forgetting his station is now their late captain's.

Hungry civilians, used to the area being a food drop point, stagger from houses and alleyways, moaning, clawing at the air.

"Sheee-it!" Stokes swears again as he touches the first rung to take him up to the top of the carrier. He can see the barrels of his familiar quad .30-Cals just above his head.

The locals amass around him. If they are truly hungry, he'd never make it.

"Ed-deee, some cover fire here." Stokes sings nervously as two rotting citizens draw closer, their blank eyes focused on him.

"Hold on, boss. Hold on," Mulholland says, his own .30-Cal still tarped tight. He starts fidgeting with the bungie cords wrapped about the weapon.

"I got it. Jeezuz, Stokes, takes a rookie to pull your fat from the fryer?" A new voice.

Lucius LaFleur draws himself up and out of Stoke's old station, his GRCC uniform, sleeves rolled up tight to his bulging biceps, Corporal rank insignia upon his beret, grabs the grips of the quad .30. He taps the trigger, once, twice, three times, sending a precision hail of rubber bullets at the feet of the oncoming civilians, not touching a single person. Only a dozen spent shell casings bounce off the Huron's roof.

The civilians stop approaching. The two on Stokes turn and shamble out of immediate range of the gun-toting vehicle.

LaFleur leans over the edge of the roof, offers Stokes a hand.

"Watch the smart-assisms, rookie, or I'll write you up for insubordination. Wouldn't look good on a fresh record," Stokes warns as he takes the offered hand.

"Hey, at least we'll be saving on expended ammo. Dang, Luce, I didn't know you were such a good shot," Mulholland says as Stokes clears the roofline and slips into his commander's hatch.

"I went through the same training as you, buddy," LaFleur smiles as the Huron jerks to a start, slowly crawling west.

"Hillbillies," Stokes says under his breath but still on the comm.

Bob waves from the street corner though he faces in the opposite direction of the armored vehicle.

"Take us to the Apostolate. We'll let Mirose and crew feed the locals today," Stokes says, settling in. He rubs again at his silver bars, thinking he sees a small speck of dirt on them.

"Copy that," Campau says from below. "Got the coordinates on the ZT's we can roll to afterwards."

"Hey, Lucius," Mulholland calls out. "I ever tell you the story of when Stokes almost clipped down a bunch of newly planted trees downtown and nearly got us all written up?"

"Sergeant!" Stokes growls at the rear gunner.

"Love to hear it. I heard some other stories, too. The exploding porta-john is one of my favorites," LaFleur laughs.

Stokes pounds his fist on the Huron, winces as pain shoots up his arm, fueling his anger.

"You nasty Alabama-bred sons a bitches!"

"Just sayin'," Mulholland chuckles.

The Huron rumbles onward.

Don't miss Sergeant Loutonia Phelps "Litany from a Lost Linguist" commentary about post-Uncivil War events, and further series-related insights, character info, artwork and book-related author updates at:

grandrapidsaltered.blogspot.com

Roll out!

GLOSSARY

HTV – Heavy Transport Vehicle

APC – Armored Personnel Carrier

AAV – Amphibious Assault Vehicle

BRV-O – Blast Resistant Vehicle-Off Road, a LTV to replace the Humvee

LTV – Light Tactical Vehicle

OP – Outpost, e.g. Bridge Street OP

GRCC – Grand Rapids Central Command

UCRA – Urban Civilian Retention Area, also Undead Civilian Retention Area (derogatory)

NSC – North Shore Coalition

BTF – Butterworth Test Facility

FZ – Feral Zombie

Datropoline – the vaccine given to military service men and women at the onset of the zombie affliction, later discontinued and banned due to its after-effects upon mortally wounded soldiers

RCF – Reganshire Command Force

HEAT round – High Explosive, Anti-Tank round

ZT or ZiT – Zombie Trooper

ROT – Rate of Fire

A-O, Alpha Oscar – Area of Operation, "What's your A-O?" "What's your position?"

H7N9 – the 2013 Bird Flu virus pandemic which initiated the current zombie apocalypse

West Side Horde – a derogatory term for the UCRA citizens

SOWT – Special Operations Weather Technician

WOUNDED WARRIOR PROJECT

Zombie Troopers are fictional. Our wounded armed service men and women are not.

This author supports the Wounded Warrior Project. Will you?

http://www.woundedwarriorproject.org/

About the Author

Peter Welmerink was born and raised on the west side of pre-apocalyptic Grand Rapids, Michigan. He writes Fantasy, Military SciFi, and other wanderings into action-adventure. His work has been published in ye olde wood pulp print and electronic-online publications. He is the co-author of the Viking berserker novel, *BEDLAM UNLEASHED*, written with Steven Shrewsbury. *TRANSPORT* was his first solo novel venture. He is married with a small barbarian tribe of three boys.

Find out more about his works and upcoming projects at:
www.peterwelmerink.com

Transcend reality with Seventh Star Press!

On the following pages we would like to introduce you to some of our titles featuring Sword and Sorcery, Post-Apocalyptic Fantasy, Epic Fantasy, YA Fantasy, and more!

To get more information on Seventh Star Press and our titles, please visit:

www.seventhstarpress.com

or connect with us at:
www.twitter.com/7thstarpress
www.facebook.com/seventhstarpress

Hellscapes, Volume 1
Venture through the infernal, where angels fear to tread!

From Stephen Zimmer, a new horror series set in realms where the inhabitants experience the ultimate nightmare!
softcover ISBN: 978-1-937929-36-7
eBook ISBN: 978-1-937929-37-4

Now Available from Seventh Star Press,
the horror stylings of
Michael West!

Trade Paperback ISBN: 9780983740209
eBook ISBN: 9780983740216

Trade Paperback ISBN: 9781937929718
eBook ISBN: 9781937929725

Trade Paperback ISBN: 9781937929954
eBook ISBN:9781937929831

Trade Paperback ISBN: 978-1-937929-18-3
eBook ISBN: 978-1-937929-19-0

Now available!   A Seventh Star Press Anthology
from editor Michael West!

eBook ISBN: 978-1-937929-69-5
Softcover ISBN: 978-1-937929-60-2

Vampires Don't Sparkle! poses the question: What would
you do if you had unlimited power and eternal life?

Would you...go back to high school? Attend the same classes
year after year, going through the pomp and circumstance
of one graduation after another, until you found the perfect
date to take to prom? Would you...spend your days moping
and brooding, finding your only joy in a game of baseball
on a stormy day? Or would you...do something else?

The authors of this collection have a few ideas; some fanciful,
some humorous, and some as dark as an endless night.

Join us, and discover what it truly means to be "vampyre."

From Bram Stoker Award-winning Editor Michael Knost!

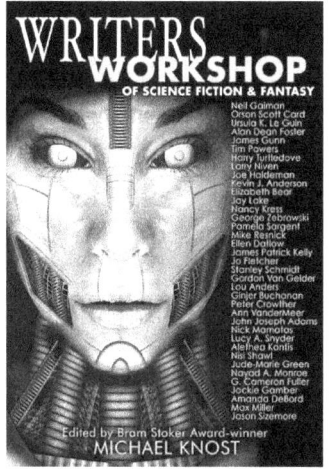

Softcover ISBN:
978-1-937929-61-9
eBook ISBN:
978-1-937929-62-6

Writers Workshop of Science Fiction and Fantasy is a collection of essays and interviews by and with many of the movers-and-shakers in the industry. Each contributor covers the specific element of craft he or she excels in. Expect to find varying perspectives and viewpoints, which is why you many find differing opinions on any particular subject.

This is, after all, a collection of advice from professional storytellers. And no two writers have made it to the stage via the same journey-each has made his or her own path to success. And that's one of the strengths of this book. The reader is afforded the luxury of discovering various approaches and then is allowed to choose what works best for him or her.

Featuring essays and interviews with:
Neil Gaiman, Orson Scott Card, Ursula K. Le Guin,Alan Dean Foster,James Gunn, Tim Powers, Harry Turtledove, Larry Niven, Joe Haldeman, Kevin J. Anderson, Elizabeth Bear, Jay Lake, Nancy Kress, George Zebrowski, Pamela Sargent, Mike Resnick, Ellen Datlow, James Patrick Kelly, Jo Fletcher, Stanley Schmidt, Gordon Van Gelder, Lou Anders, Peter Crowther, Ann VanderMeer, Joh Joseph Adams, Nick Mamatas, Lucy A. Snyder, Alethea Kontis, Nisi Shawl, Jude-Marie Green, Nayad A. Monroe, G. Cameron Fuller, Jackie Gamber, Amanda DeBord, Max Miller, Jason Sizemore.

Shadows Over Somerset from Bob Freeman!

Softcover: 978-1-941706-11-4
eBook: 978-1-941706-12-1

Michael Somers is brought to Cairnwood, an isolated manor in rural Indiana, to sit at the deathbed of a grandfather he never knew existed. He soon finds himself drawn into a strange and esoteric world filled with werewolves, vampires, witches... and a family curse that dates back to fourteenth century Scotland. In the sleepy little town of Somerset, an ancient evil awakens, hungering for blood and vengeance... and if Michael is to survive he must face his inner demons and embrace his family's dark past. Shadows Over Somerset is the first Cairnwood Manor Novel.

Appalachian Gothic! Jason Sizemore's Irredeemable!
18 Tales of dark fantasy, science fiction, and horror

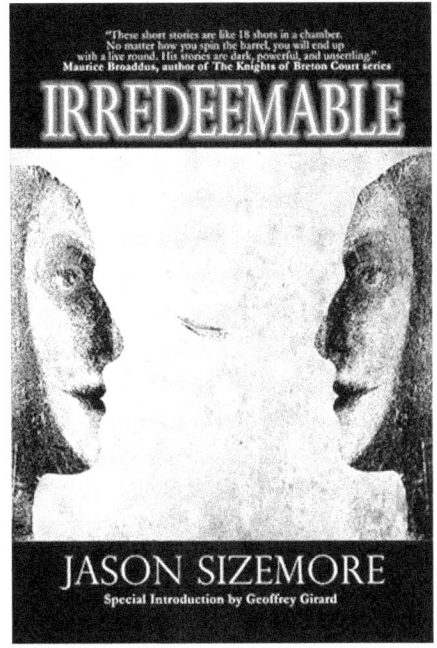

Softcover: 978-1-937929-59-6
eBook: 978-1-937929-68-8

Flowing like mists and shadows through the Appalachian Mountains come 18 tales from the mind of Jason Sizemore. Weaving together elements of southern gothic, science fiction, fantasy, horror, the supernatural, and much more, this diverse collection of short stories brings you an array of characters who must face accountability, responsibility, and, more ominously, retribution.

Whether it is Jack Taylor readying for a macabre, terrifying night in "The Sleeping Quartet," the Wayne brothers and mischief gone badly awry in "Pranks," the title character in "The Dead and Metty Crawford," or the church congregation and their welcoming of a special visitor in "Yellow Warblers," Irredeemable introduces you to a range of ordinary people who come face to face with extraordinary situations.

Whether the undead, aliens, ghosts, or killers of the yakuza, dangers of all kinds lurk within the darkness for those who dare tread upon its ground. Hop aboard and settle in, Irredeemable will take you on an unforgettable ride along a dark speculative fiction road.

A Horror Anthology from
Editors Alexander S. Brown and Louise Myers!

Softcover: 978-1-937929-54-1
eBook: 978-1-937929-64-0

From the fiery abyss of the underworld comes 20 hellish tales from the south and southwest. Within these charred pages are stories that will introduce you to the many demons that stay hidden but are always nearby...

20 authors provide stories of possessed people, objects, houses, highways, and the devil's favorite playground - the forest.

Dare to meet Deidless, a demon who is a buyer of souls. Discover what kind of demons men can summon. Read of battles between good and evil. Learn of ancient artifacts and stones that crave sacrifice. Finally, become acquainted with legions of evil.

Again, we invite you, sit back, dim the lights, and prepare yourself to meet the devils in the darkness.

Southern Haunts: Devils in the Darkness is the next in the exciting anthology series that began with Southern Haunts: Spirits That Walk Among Us.

www.ingramcontent.com/pod-product-compliance
Lightning Source LLC
Chambersburg PA
CBHW060518260626
47161CB00003B/701